WRITERS REPUBLIC

CRUSHED WINGS

An Unearthly Novel

MAY HOWELL

WRITERS REPUBLIC L.L.C.
515 Summit Ave. Unit R1
Union City, NJ 07087, USA

Website: *www.writersrepublic.com*
Hotline: *1-877-656-6838*
Email: *info@writersrepublic.com*

Ordering Information:
Quantity sales. Special discounts are available on quantity purchases by corporations, associations, and others. For details, contact the publisher at the address above.

Library of Congress Control Number:	2021931564
ISBN-13:	978-1-63728-188-8	[Paperback Edition]
	978-1-63728-189-5	[Digital Edition]

Rev. date: 01/12/2021

This book is dedicated to Carol: thank you for being you, always keep it groovy, silly lady.

1.

BOOM!!! BOOM!!! BOOM!!!

Mark scattered mini explosions onto the mountain that was looming in front of him as a horde of disgusting looking creatures continued to pour out of the mountain face. Today's mission had landed them in Spain to clear up a mutt hive that was causing trouble in the nearby town. Mark had been hacking away at the creatures for hours and could feel the slow burn of his muscles as he lifted his hand and started to fire off another round of magical blasts. Mark's skin was tight from the repetitive strain his body was put through as he bunched his muscles to brace from each molting hot blast he was firing from his palm; no matter what these creatures weren't giving up in their futile attempts of escaping the mountain. Blood and gory soaked his clothes as Mark prepared for the next counter attack the creatures would try to use to escape; only moments earlier one of the creatures had latched onto his arms in an attempt to kill him to let the others escape. It had managed to get a few rakes in before Mark summoned the white-hot magical energy inside himself, and, focusing on a thin protective coating he self-destructed. It hurt like hell, but it did the trick and he was free to keep holding off the next wave of creatures.

The creatures looked like a mixture of different animals and humans. They were once witches but they ate their familiar counter parts to gain more power and were now a disgrace to the witch blood line. The creatures were such an abomination their entire race was given the name mutt; with their mutated bodies and feral appearance they looked disgusting and atrocious. They came in all sizes and colors, some had fur in places while others had scales or skin making each one more atrocious than the next. As the laws of the ancients decreed those creatures were an abomination and extremely lethal to their world, if they were allowed to wander the Earth they would expose the Magicae Vitae to the normals and that wasn't allowed to any of their kind.

Snarling and growling the newest pack of mutts tried dashing in all directions not realizing they were on his radar as he lifted his palm to fire another explosive blast. Did they really think his coven was stupid enough to leave an exit open for them to escape? Not hardly. Laughing he fired off a few mini blasts herding them into a tight cluster as adrenaline pumped in his system.

BOOM!!!

Another day another battle field this time it's a Mutt Hive next time it could be anything, Mark Monroe thought as he was clearing up the fleeing mutts that were running franticly away from the rest of his coven as they were running rampant in mutt territory exterminating any creature they found.

Born as the eldest child to a higher-ranking witch coven, the Flemings, he was blessed with strength like no other; Mark's element was explosives and that made him a walking powder-keg, so when the rest of the coven went inside clearing out the rest of the mutts, he was left outside the mountain waiting for the stragglers to flee. He couldn't really blame his coven: his magic was disastrous in small spaces, let alone a small place covered in over ninety thousand pounds of dirt and rubble; he wouldn't want to have to fight with the constant fear of being buried alive, should he miss fire.

They were just off the coast of Spain in one of its smaller mountain ranges; the coven was close enough to the coast that they could hear the waves colliding with the rocks. Usually, areas like this one would be covered with signs of wildlife, not this one though. There weren't any deer tracks in the surrounding area but given the size of this mutt hive it wasn't much of a surprise. It was one of the first things that Mark had noticed when he and his brothers arrived and it had set the pace for the mission. They would go in hit them hard and leave to report everything to the king.

Boom!!! Boom!!!

"Come on, bitches, line it up for me, it'll make bombing you all the easier!" Mark tossed up his hand and prepared to do another blast at the oncoming creatures as they continued to pour out of the mountain side. He couldn't help but grin as it was just too damn funny that they seemed to believe there was a way to escape his coven when they were in sync and at full strength. They were making this too easy the way with they were lining themselves up; he wasn't even breaking a sweat and he had been at it for several hours. It was almost disappointing how easy this was; Mark had been revved up for a more serious fight but as luck would have it more mutts came pouring out of the mountain.

"Shit."

Looking up at the new wave of mutts coming out of the hive he could see them start to trickle off; he could even catch glimpses of his brothers as they followed the enemy out of the hive shooting and slicing their way to him. From Mark's point of view, they looked like they were all unharmed for the most part, just covered in dirt, sweat, and blood. The bodies of the fallen mutts made it difficult to maintain a firm footing as he was swarmed by an oncoming wave of creatures. Mark's shadow began to move around and expand upwards as his youngest brother stepped out of his element revealing his disheveled and rather pitiful appearance. At six-four he was rather small in comparison to the rest of the Monroes, but he had the same blonde hair and deep blue eyes that the rest of his coven had; he had toned muscles and a broad chest, but he was clearly weaker than the others due to some poor health as a child. He was the baby of the family at twenty-three years old, but he was just as lethal with his use of shadows as Mark was with his explosives. He and his familiar could wreak havoc from above and below with their aerial assaults: both had a high prey drive and, as familiars go, seeing the coven and their hawks was intimidating to most who stumbled in their path.

The two fought in sync with one another ducking, blasting, and slicing their way through the enemy. A knife came flying out at him as he braced himself to flip over the assailant; throwing out his knife he sent a tiny explosive to the end of it that exploded on impact sending body parts flying in all directions and causing blood to splatter on the ground, making it slippery. Mark landed quickly on his feet sending tiny tremors through the surrounding earth; the tremors gave Danny the boost he needed to take to the air and throw his opponents balance.

Danny landed after dispatching three mutts slipping in the pools of blood below his feet. He managed to stabilize his hold as a mutt came at him with claws; with a quick movement he took off the mutt's claws and drove them deep in the creatures' jugular effectively dispatching the beast. A massive creature appeared behind Danny before he could arm himself and tackled him to the ground. The pair wrestled as flesh, blood, and sweat pooled on the surrounding ground. The bulk of the mutt cut off Mark's line of sight to his sibling and the cries of battle muted any hope of hearing his brother. Suddenly, the mutt let out a cry of pain and sagged. Danny had the audacity to pop up from under the dead mutt with a dumbass grin plastered on his face.

"Thought you could use some help over here Jon and Jase told me to bugger off and let them handle the rear, said I would dick around too much."

"That's because you would be the one to dick around in the middle of nowhere with mutts on your heels, Danny-boy. Don't bother saying you wouldn't, we have been out here for hours and we still need to go get a break in before our next mission."

"Hey I don't mess around that much and besides I'll stop goofing off when angels come falling out of the sky" Danny said, as he created shadow bullets and began firing at will into the onslaught of mutts heading their way. "I think I have better aim than you, Mark, come on catch up."

Across the battle field Jase was kneeling as he stared creating an ice wall to encompass the whole battle field; he was taking no chance of a survivor. Jon was covering for him as lightning danced at his fingertips; electricity rained down on any mutt that tried to leave the area and those too close to the pair were fried on the spot. Jon's eyes glowed with the current as he released a massive lightning bolt from the sky and angled it into the large crowd of creatures. Jase rose from the ground and as he did so massive walls formed on all sides. Panic set in to the remaining mutts as they saw they were trapped with nowhere to run. If a mutt had the chance they always chose flight over fighting and this time was no different as the panic-stricken mutts began their attempts to scale the icy walls.

Mark began to fire off blasts when he got an alert from his familiar, Akand, that had taken to the air hours before: there was a creature of some kind hurtling towards the battle field below. A large shadow blanketed most of the area around him, making it harder to see than it already was with all the dirt flying around. The size of the shadow made him wonder how big the wings were on this aerial mutt that was coming at them. The shadow covered a quarter of the battle field. He glanced up to confirm the location of the creature before he lifted his hand at blinding speed and fired off two large blasts effectively knocking the massive mutt out of the sky.

The body hit the earth hard, much harder than it should have, throwing up dust and rubble. The impact of the body created a wide crater in the Earth that swallowed up part of the mountain side. He looked over at Danny and indicated they surround the fallen creature; it was hard to see from the angle that they were at, but the wings were massive (they had to be nearly six feet long), but they were bent at odd angles: clearly, he broke them. As they began to converge on the wreckage, Jon and Jase fell into place behind them and they circled the damage. Feathers and blood littered the ground surrounding the crater that was made upon impact. The group froze in shock when they looked inside the crater.

Danny whistled and pat Mark's shoulder, "Bro, you're going to hell for sure now...in a handbasket. You killed an angel."

He began to panic as he looked over the wreckage there was just so much red, he began cursing in his mother language, *"Dracu 'ma inapoi."* He slipped into the crater to, hopefully, gently retrieve her and see if there were any signs of life and, if there was, she would be coming with them.

It was bad luck to kill an angel; they always traveled in groups and were known to be fiercely protective of their females.

Danny snickered, "You kissed our mother with that mouth?" Mark threw him an icy glare that could have frozen hell over. "Ouch, if only looks could kill."

"Shut the fuck up Danny now is not the time," Jon stepped forward to look into the crater, "Mark how is she looking? Do we need a medic?"

The first thing that caught his eye was her long, thick crimson hair that was tussled all over her face and fanned out around her as she lay on her side, one of her midnight black wings was tucked under her while the other was bent at an odd angle poking out of the crater. She was wearing odd red robes that clung to her curves and split up all the way to her small waist, exposing her soft cream-colored skin. Along her wrists and thigh were strange symbols one inked blue the other green, they crept around both areas of her skin to meet at the other side forming an intricate bracelet and garter belt. Her face was small like a pixie, with high cheek bones and a small button nose, making her face almost feline. A soft moan drew his attention to the cupids bow that was her mouth and a plump full lower lip that made it look lick-able. She had open gashes and bruises that looked to be fading clearly not all the damage that was done to her was from his blast and it looked as if she had been flung from somewhere forcefully. She would be needing a medic to look over her and hopefully repair the damage to her wings. She shifted slightly and another gentle moan left her lips he looked up to examine some of her other wounds near her face only to stop and lock eyes with the most startling jade green eyes he had ever saw. Her eyes were at half mask and he could clearly see pain there, "Hang on, this is going to hurt, but I'm taking you with us and getting you medical attention." She gave a slight nod before her eyes drifted close and she fell back into unknowingness.

"She is still alive I'm going to bring her up. Jon can you call that medic you know? She needs medical attention and it looks like this isn't the first battle she has been in today." Jon had been elected the leader of the Fleming coven and had a huge network of people he could contact in a tight situation such as this. Gently, he rolled her off of her wing and hoisted her up into his arms; careful not to jostle her wings he levitated them out of the crater and into the protective circle of his coven. "I don't think she is an angel; she doesn't have the right wings and they are too big to be a tengu. Not sure what she is, but it looks like she is coming with us." Jon let out an audible sigh of relief, clearly, he was worried about an angel retaliation; glancing over he sees Jon hanging up his phone and looking over.

"Maverick says he will meet us back at the coven house in ten minutes, he needs to get his bag together. Is she going to hold up when we materialize out or do we have to take her on Avis?" Jon was almost as tall as he was with the same blonde hair and blue eyes, he was a strong fighter and thrived with electricity. He had bronzed skin and often honed and trained his muscles alongside him on their training field.

"She should be fine to jump she was strong enough to remain in one piece after two blasts so she should be able to handle the trip. Besides if she was going to have to be carried on one of the hawks, she would be riding on Akand. Let's head out boys." Mark could blow a sign of relief. Maverick could come immediately that hardly ever happened. Medical witches were a popular demand.

Summoning the energy needed to materialize, he envisioned the coven house nestled deep in the mountains of Romania far enough away from human civilization. Praying to whatever god or goddess was watching them today for this to be as painless for the woman as possible he let go of the energy and immediately, he was engulfed in the portal; he was surrounded by the familiar feel of his bones and muscles being pulled at an extremely fast and harsh rate as he was teleported from one end of the planet to another. The whole process felt like days but had only been seconds as he arrives at the coven house in northern Romania with the woman sheltered snuggly in his arms. He rushes inside to lay her on his bed and make sure she wasn't hurt in the transition to the house.

The air around the house pulled and rippled signaling the arrival of his brothers as they filed into the house, each coming to check on him and make sure all was well before Maverick arrived and ushered every member of the coven outside the room so he could have the room to work on her wings and the privacy to tend to the other wounds as well. What he didn't realize, as he tended to her wounds, was that her eyelids began to flutter as she was processing information.

****

Oh God what the fuck happened, Lilith thought as she began to regain conscience; she felt like she had gotten rolled over by a bolder. No, worse, by her brother, Taurtis, she mentally corrected herself. Rolling her muscles around slightly as she began to assess the damage, she realized she should have remained still as a grunt of pain left her lips; as she relaxed back into the soft bed, memories of what happened came flooding back.

Lilith sat with her siblings in their makeshift hut out in the fields of their home world Domus Meus. Night had fallen as they silently waited for news from the council of elders. it had been two days since the announcement of Lord Moteo's murder, he was a Custos high lord that had a few lesser-known habits. The man was a bastard that liked to hurt woman and children and then sell them off when he was done playing with them. The triplets had made sure he suffered long and hard for what he did and that his crimes were finally exposed to the council of elders. Moteo hadn't died quickly, they had made sure of it; Lilith had made sure that the man had experienced every horror he had forced upon his victims that had unwillingly entered his estate. It wasn't too big of a shock to Lilith when she saw that the council concealed Moteo's crimes from the public, such news would have caused an uproar. What did shock her was that even after Taurtis had left their calling card no one had come to collect them yet.

There had been signs throughout the day that she had noticed that alerted her suspicions, as time ticked by, they sat in silence. Soon they were sure the council would send someone to collect them for punishment. This time was different than the other times they were brought before the council. Taurtis and Lilith were well known for their many thefts and fights they had done all around the city and Daina was a well-known prostitute that had many highly respected clients That's how they had gotten into Moteo's estate: the man couldn't pass up a night with her. The three of them had been in bad positions before, granted they had never murdered anyone that high up before. Taurtis and Lilith were the warrior class members of the family, both highly developed senses and quick reflexes they were sought after often to do assignments others deemed too hard or tedious. The pair were once members of the military that fought for the council, but not now. Now they were branded as criminals.

A creek sounded from outside as Lilith held a finger to her lips. They are here...

How many? Daina sounded worried as she stood up and went to the door.

Two dozen I believe. She wasn't certain as she listened to the sound of fabric as moved in the field. Wait, it's just under two dozen. Will you be okay to open the door D?

Daina took a deep breath and with shaky hands she threw open the door. Daina was a healer not a fighter and she knew that the soldiers outside wouldn't see her as a threat when they caught sight of her. It would be much different if Taurtis answered the door. It'll be fine Lil; we are giving ourselves up anyway so just don't fight them and everything will be fine.

I don't like this. Taurtis finally spoke up, we did them a fucking service and yet here we are about to get punished for it. It's bullshit.

Hopefully not too harshly if we just go with them and get this over with. Daina added hopefully as the first of the warriors entered their line of sight.

D, something tells me that this isn't going to go over as easily as you think.

The warriors filed out of the field and surrounded the hut. One by one they lined up as the captain stepped forward and looked them over;

Taurtis had trained the man when he had first joined the warriors corp. Looked like he had made a name of himself in their absence. "Taurtis the Impenetrable, Daina of the Hearth, and Lilith of Tragedy; we are here to bring you before the council for the crime of treason and will be subject to flogging before your trail. Come silently and without fighting or we will be forced to use lethal means."

Flogging before a trail? What the fuck? She couldn't believe what she had just heard as she led Daina and Taurtis forward. They never flogged before trial not in the history of their kind. There was usually debate before hand with the council then sentencing. It was almost worth fighting back. Almost...

Irrumabo! Where are Daina and Taurtis? The triplets were, as a rule, never totally closed off from one another, but the High Council decided to go and do something foolish. There would be a calamity on this plane like it had never seen. We need to *regroup first then discuss a plan...wait... Where the hell am I?*

Slowly she relaxed and let her mind reach out to the strongest presence she felt nearby...*Who is that?*

2.

It had been a few hours since Maverick ushered Mark and the others from his room; the group grew tired of standing outside the bedroom door after a while and each went to their rooms for a well needed shower and change of clothes.

Mark had used the guest bathroom since his room was otherwise turned into a make shift sick bay. He turned the water up as high as it would go while he rinsed the grime and blood off, finally there was time to reflect from the mission. They had scouted the area from above for hours before they saw where the hive was located, protocol had them contact the king's right-hand for further orders. The bastard had taken his time getting back to them. They had waited half an hour before finally receiving the go ahead from Iblis to wipe out the hive. His words had been to level the place to the ground if needed. Mark grinned at how much he would have enjoyed that but unfortunately just blowing the hive up would have risked a few survivors and they couldn't have that. Jon had given them their orders before they had arrived and they group was set to go, like a plague of death the coven had descended over the unsuspecting mutts.

Closing his eyes as he rinsed his hair Mark saw the faces of the fallen mutts then flashes of crimson and green had his eyes flash open. Green? Like the purist jade stones...The mangled woman's face burned into his memory...her eyes were the most enchanting green he had ever seen and her lips though slick with blood looked plump and kissable....

*No! The woman doesn't matter...*He tried to reason with himself but Mark knew he was lying to himself. For whatever reason, that woman mattered to him. She hadn't even spoke and yet she had stolen something from him with just that pained look he was lost. A knock sounded on the door snapping him out of his thoughts. The room had grown steamy he noted as he turned off the water and stepped out of the shower. Mark had apparently lost track of time while he was in there. The knock sounded again against the heavy door.

"I'm coming."

"Good we need to talk before she wakes up." Jase sounded cautious as ever.

Shit! Did I project that to everyone?

"Heard!" He quickly threw on the clothes he had grabbed from the dryer and was toweling off his hair as he opened the door to find the spare room already had everyone there. The room was filled with mostly stone cold and emotionless faces, a family trait they had adopted from their wayward father when something serious needed discussing. "Sorry I'm late to the party lost track of time."

Jon looked him over with a guarded expression as he pulled out a chair and sank into it. *I hate it when you do that.* Mark projected to his younger brother. He knew that Mark hated it when he guarded his expressions from him and hated it more when Jon grinned about the annoyance he caused.

Ah but you have something on your mind and this is the fastest way to get to the root of your problems...the angel was consuming your thoughts in there. You were projecting loud enough; don't worry I blocked it from everyone else but did you have fun jacking off in there?

*Prick...You know damn well I wasn't doing that in there...*The fucker was amused...Just because Jon was elected the coven head didn't mean he had the right to go into his thoughts whenever he wants.

Hey I don't want to know what's in your head just as much as if not more than you don't wanna know what is in mine. Don't project so loud and it wouldn't have happened.

"What are we going to do with her?" *Ah there it is.* Jase hated new people.

"Why don't we keep her around for a while?" Danny as usual was more than happy to welcome strange people into their lives for the sake of feeding his curiosity.

"No! What if she is dangerous?"

Her haunting eyes appeared in his head once more, like a soft protest from a distance he felt a presence touch his mental walls. Jase had a good point but Mark wasn't ready for her to leave yet, even if it did go against his better judgement and risking his coven. The soft plea and the sound of internal whimpering softened his better judgement.

"She is a fuckin' angel Jase, how bad could it be?"

"Her wings are much bigger if you haven't noticed and solid black! That is no angel dumbass, it could be a tengu for all you know and those fucks aren't friendly."

"She is neither you two," Jon's voice silenced the two's bickering and drew all eyes to him. "Can't you tell? Her wings are too big and dark to be either one of those creatures and she isn't wearing the tengu uniform they are required to wear. I can't speak for all of us but I have never seen anything like her before. She is small and her wings could easily cocoon her, the main point is she may be a strong ally. What is she is a rare form of archangel?"

He hadn't thought of that. Her wings were indeed massive but they didn't have the slight point at the top joint of the wing like a tengu did either, and the size and color were off for angels as well. From what Mark could tell they had a rounded top and pointed ends; it was the coloring of the wings was throwing him off. Mark had seen archangels' wings before and they were different colors from not only the rest of the angels but from each other's as well. Unfortunately, there wasn't a female archangel so that was out.

Jon glanced at Mark and smirked, "What is your input brother?"

With a sigh Mark dropped the towel he was holding into an empty chair and paced the room as he spoke, "Honestly, I agree with Danny we should keep her with us if only to keep her from the human population and monitor her. We don't know what she is or what she can do so she stays." Mark hoped that he didn't sound too eager to keep the woman around for a while longer. "Also, I disagree with you Jon she is no archangel I have seen them on a few occasions and Vex says there are no female archangels."

Jase looked shocked that Mark would want to keep her around and usually he would be right to look concerned. The coven was his family and no harm would come anywhere near them if it could be helped; Mark's most important job was to guard the coven and all its secrets and right now he was blurring the line between safe and not. "Don't look at me like that Jase you are all old enough to protect yourselves and I do not feel this woman is a threat."

"Can we trust Vexrial's word? He is the archangel of greed after all, who is to say that he gave false information since nothing was exchanged." Danny sounded like he was in deep thought as he recalled how Vex operated. "After all the things I have heard about him his staple statement is, 'Nothing is given if nothing is taken,' so how did you get the information from him?"

"I called in a favor he owed me to get some information I needed for a mission. Just so happened I needed intel on angels." Mark shrugged as he passed by Danny to check the hall for signs of Maverick.

He could hear the others continue with discussing what the woman could possibly be but Mark could care less. All he wanted was to make sure she was well taken care of and he knew he looked a little worried for the woman as he paced back to the group.

"You have a bone for her! It's all over your face! Fuckin' finally you show interest in somebody." Danny had a wide smile on his face and the snot nosed git had the audacity to look proud of that little deduction he made.

"I don't have a bone for..." It was too late. Mark could feel the heat rising in his cheeks.

Jon doubled over laughing at Jase's shocked face. "Don't lie you have a different look in your eye then normal and you are turning pink."

Even Jase looked amused at his dismay. "I walk away for one minute and this is what you were discussing?"

"Of course, what else, with you being in lala land over there." Danny picked up the discarded towel and threw it over his head while he rushed over to Jon. "Oh dear, whatever will I do? I do not dare think the worst for the poor dearie."

Danny pitched his voice high as he pretended to swoon and speak like a lady. Jon joined in wrapping his arm around the others waist wiggling his eye brows he added with a bad performance, "Fear not for she has the best medic we could find, your darling will be fine."

"Fuck...Can't you guys leave me alone just this once." Mark knew he sounded like he was pouting and he felt like he was as well but he didn't want to look weak or soft as his color continues to redden.

"All you had to say was that you fancy the woman and I wouldn't have protested as much," Ah Fuck...Jase held up his hands in surrender as a slow cocky grin formed.

"All of you are dicks you know that?" Mark began to grin when suddenly....

CRASH!!!

"The fuck?"

With practiced speed the men filed out of the room and rushed towards Mark's room.

****

Lilith felt someone's hands on her as she lay assessing the damage that had been inflicted; she didn't recognize the touch or the power that flowed from it as it slowly relieved some of the ache. Moments before she touched someone's consciousness but was too weak to break through to see what was going on. Jetting up in the bed she comes face to face with a strange man with brown hair and dark eyes; ignoring the blinding pain that racks through her body, Lilith grabs his throat turns and slams him on the bed effectively pinning him so he couldn't move. "Who the fuck are you and where the hell am I?"

CRASH!!!!

Lilith's wing hit something cold and hard as her wings flexed to add weight to her roll and pin. She didn't dare spare a backwards glance just yet to see what had fallen.

Coughing and wheezing the man scowls up at her at the sudden assault, "My name is Maverick I'm a medical witch that was called in to assess and repair any damage that you sustained by the order of the Fleming coven. You need to lay down and let me finish tending to your wounds before a bone sets wrong." he practically growls at the strange female. "What the hell are you? Your no angel or Tengu nor are you any other creature that I've ever seen."

She was what her people called a Custos, neither Tengu nor angel, she was a Guardian each one different from the next. With her massive black wings, she was often mistaken for a Tengu and occasionally fallen angel; Lilith took great pride in her wings for there wasn't a pair that looked like them anywhere. They were unique in size and color. When she would walk, they would drag behind her on the ground like a cloak; they were the color of midnight and often seen as dark and bland until the rain dripped off of them then they looked like the starry sky.

The man she now knew as Maverick continued to struggle but with the custos superior strength he couldn't budge her hand as she took in her surroundings and scents that were lingering in the air. They were in a large room on a very spacious bed that had a canopy with pale yellow drapes cascading down the sides to create privacy blinds. The room was a muted cream color with a high ceiling and few pictures adorning the walls.

On the floor was a shattered vase of some kind, that must have been what she had knocked into with her roll. *Oops*...There was a large wooden dresser along the wall that matched the solid oak bed and two doors that lead out of the room, where they went, she wasn't quite sure but she was absolutely sure that this room belonged to a male. Her kind had a superior sense of smell and Maverick was not the owner of this room, the room smelled clean like summer rain but sharp like spice she liked the scent but at the moment it did nothing to disarm her as the medic struggled to get loose without further hurting her.

Annoyed she glared down at the man as he tried to wiggle free, "Would you stop it I'm trying to focus?"

"Would you let me up I'm getting paid to......"

The two froze as the sound of more than one set of heavy footsteps echoed throughout the house getting closer to the room that they were occupying. Lilith tensed, her hand tightening on reflex, as the door was thrust open and four figures stepped into the room weapons in hand ready to strike at an unknown enemy.

They were hot, like, honest to god hot, she would be lying if she had said that this wasn't the first time she saw this kind of raw masculine beauty. With their pale blonde hair and deep blue eyes that she could just drown in. One of them, he looked to be the oldest, took a step forward and put away his weapon, his hands up as a sign of surrender. He reminded her of books her mother had read her as a child, he was what she had envisioned the Greek hero of old.

Now was not the time to be star struck, Maverick had just been about to say he was being paid to do something... *Gwenevere Silver...This was her fault!!* The woman had crossed her for the last time. She could feel the anger begin to overtake her as the man stepped forward it looked as if he could see her mood change from confusion to rage.

"My name is Mar...."

Cutting him off, Lilith let her rage and speculation apparent as she all but shouted. "Look here Hercules you may be hot but you will not be holding me here against my will I don't care what that bitch Gwenevere Silver told you or how much she is paying you."

There she said it now with that out of the way he would most likely torture her or something. After all most men didn't think much of her size but she sure as hell could handle herself and Gwen held a bitch of a grudge so death wouldn't come fast.

"My name is Marcus Rolan Monroe of the Fleming coven; most people call me Mark. I know that this must be disorienting but..."

"Disorienting? You try being separated from your siblings and thrown to a place you've never seen before and tell me how you feel." Cutting him off once more, Lilith knew she sounded snippy but damn it all she was tired and hurt so she had the right to be royally pissed off, no matter what Sir-Hots-A lot said. She had just been banished and separated from her siblings; they had been picked up from their hideout, chained to the floor and whipped before the sentence was even passed on them. To make matters worse she woke up in a house full of strange men so damn right she was disoriented but she would always hold her head proud no matter the outcome.

"Miss if you keep interrupting me, I will have to put tape over your mouth to shut you up!" He looked furious and fully capable of doing just that he had a very imposing aura about him and obviously he didn't take talking back well.

She decided to keep her mouth shut and listen and look for her escape routes, a girl always needed her escape route as she recalled the two doors that looked like ways out, though she noted that they had all come in through the door on the far left of the room which left her to believe it was the only way out. Her eyes kept drifting back to the man that was silently waiting her response.

This man, Mark he called himself, was huge he looked to be six foot seven or eight and was a giant of a man. His eyes, oh god his eyes, they were a deep-sea blue that showed so much about the man; he has a face that could have been carved from stone there was a scar on his right cheek that went downwards towards his chin but stopped just short of it. Mark's voice sounded deep and gravely that had a strange accent to it that she couldn't quite place. His scent was the same rain and spice scent that was flooding the room making him the rightful owner of this space. She could almost laugh at the sight of the scowl that she placed on his perfect lips. He wore a black shirt that clung to his well-muscled chest; you could tell this man was made out of rope after rope of muscle as the shirt highlighted the perfection that was his abs, he was wearing jeans that hugged his hips and his perfectly firm rounded bottom. This man was made for battle and he had been in many if she was interpreting the many scars that littered this man's otherwise flawless body, his bronzed skin proved he was outside a lot and she could bet he spent most of his free time training. Surely this was what the fabled Hercules looked like she smirked to herself.

Movement below her hand reminded her that she still had ahold of Maverick, she glanced down, he seemed to be trying to heal wounds from the angle that he was at which was admirable especially since she was being less than pleasant to the man. Lilith gave the man one last squeeze to the throat, a warning, then released him. "We can talk while this one fixes me up, if you don't mind, I feel like my brother used me as a punching bag."

"Miss I am truly sorry that you were hurt when you fell," all frustration drained out of his features as he looked her over, maybe he wasn't but so angry at her interruptions? With a quick glance, he glanced over at one of the men as they made a choking sound, " Ahm...as I was saying we

19

brought you back to our coven house to give you medical aid and a place to stay. Who are you? Where are your siblings? Where are you from? I have never seen anyone like you before." She watched as his eyes traveled from her face down her body but his face never gave anything away to her disappointment, she knew she had good curves and a decent enough face, but he could have shown just a little interest.

Pouting ever so slightly she debated what was safe to tell these men. It wasn't like she could say, "Hey guys I'm from a different world plane where we have titles that rule our society oh and by the way I was banished with my siblings by the High Council." That is just not what you say when you are going to try to use someone's house as a home location. *Come on think... guess we can go with mostly the truth.*

****

She was beyond beautiful and she had a fully trained witch, medical or not, pinned to the bed, looking as if she was a fierce warrior goddess with her crimson locks flowing around her. They had wanted to remove her torn robe but without a proper change of clothes they had voted to keep her in what she was wearing to accommodate her wings, something he was grateful for at the moment as her garments were clinging to her curvaceous form and fluttering around her legs showing off her pale silky skin that he had only glimpsed at earlier. He surprised himself when he was able to keep his voice somewhat normal. Her jade green eyes were mesmerizing, enchanting even, and seemed to be trying to command him to do her will, thankfully he had already had that happen to him before so he knew the signs; though none of the signs were there.

Hercules? Did she really call him that? Damn she was a brave woman but he probably wouldn't hear the end of that new nickname for a while. Mark couldn't help but get a surge of satisfaction at the thought of her liking what she saw; make no mistake he couldn't not see the appreciation in her eyes as she looked him over eating his appearance hungrily.

"My name is Lilith, Herold of Tragedy; I do not know you so I will not tell you where I am from or how I got here but I am now the unwilling

Guardian of Lost Souls. As for my siblings, I do not know for when we left our home plane, we lost the ability to communicate but I will find them." The fiercely determined look that she had on her face made his body stir and demand her attention. She had the deep accent of the olden times; it rolled off her tongue in a thick sexy way, he had never heard a voice so enchanting. Underneath the determination worry was in her eyes as she warred within herself. She took a deep steadying breath she looked to have come to a decision on something. "My brother Taurtis can handle his own, really its Daina that I am worried about. She isn't a fighter at all, as in she couldn't hurt a fly if you held a weapon to her head. When I'm all patched up, I will head out to look for them."

Maverick looked over at him, "Don't count on leaving anytime soon; she has five cracked ribs, her wing is broken in three places, she was whipped, has lacerations on her wrists, ankles, thigh, and a slight laceration on her neck. Not to mention the bruises and burns that are littering her skin. I can only heal but so much of this."

"*La Dracu!*" Mark's voice sounded like a whip of pure fury as he began spewing profanities and curses in his mother language. Who had whipped her in such a way? Why was he feeling such a connection from a woman he never met before? It didn't make since. The look of pure murder must have been on his face because Maverick flinched, "Fuckin' ballpark recovery time."

The coven was born and raised in Romania. The language could sound beautiful one minute and harsh another. Mark was pissed and his accent always sounded rougher than intended, like the crackle of a whip making Maverick flinch.

"Estimation around four to five weeks...if she was able to put her wings away and not keep them out it would help keep them immobile, then I would lean to four weeks; but I will do what I can to speed up the recovery time." The slightly older man was clearly under distress and worried that something may happen to him which made Mark force himself under control and to focus on anything but her recovery time.

"You said you are from a different plane? How do you plan on finding them?" Jase offered as he put away his brass knuckles and sat lazily in a chair with his legs sprawled outwards. Jase was his second youngest brother that had his brawn but didn't quite have his height, he was around six foot five so still a fairly intimidating man when he wished to be and right now, he appeared to be relaxed but Mark knew he was ready to pounce at any moment if need be. Aside from his abilities with ice. Jase was the resident torture expert. He excelled at gathering information and would use any means necessary. To be honest his younger brother worried him.

Jase had a painted on a lazy smile that didn't meet his eyes as he tried to get Lilith to let her guard down and give out more information; clearly the small female was not going to be tricked by his act as she remained tense on the bed.

"Yes."

"Have you ever been to this plane before?"

"Well...No not really but it can't be that hard to find those two they are bound to stick out." Lilith said it with so much confidence that he was worried that the three of them would reveal the existence of the Magicae Vitae to the humans in their search for one another and that would bring everything they fought for to an end. "My brother was sent to this plane before on an assignment; I had stayed behind to take care of my sister at the time. Taurtis knows how it works here better than the rest of us."

"You do realize there are over seven billion people on Earth and you are looking for two? Its' impossible without help and you could be looking forever since you don't know your way around." As Jase delivered the blow, the worry and determination increase in her eyes.

Something about this woman called out to him. He couldn't take the worried look in her eyes and wanted to fix it as soon as he could. *Why does she affect me so?* Awake she was small but her eyes shown so much pain as she tried to mask it, not trying to show any weakness in front of an unknown presence; something he had done many times when captured by witch hunters. At first glance entering the room he could tell she was a seasoned warrior by the type of hold she had on Maverick, not quite a suffocating hold but it was enough to pin the man while she got her barring. Maverick wasn't tall but he was bulky. With Lilith's small frame it should have been near impossible for her to keep him pinned in that position. She had to have some serious force to behind her. Noted. He was equally impressed she was able to hold herself upright with all of the damage that was inflicted to her during the fall and his blasts.

"Lilith, sweetheart, we can help you find them. We have allies that can keep a lookout for them and we can even go out when we are on missions and search as well." He tried to keep his voice even and calm as he tried to word his next question, "Maverick said if you could put your wings away it would help a great deal with healing is there a way you can put them away or hide them so they are immobile? You won't be able to leave the coven house with them out anyway since it is against *Magicae Vitae* law to show or prove the existence of anything... not normal... to the humans."

****

"You want me to hide my wings...my beautiful, one-of-a-kind wings? Just so the humans can remain ignorant?" she asked in utter bafflement and slight discontent. Her wings may have been a mangled-up mess but they were still magnificent in their unique way. Besides, it was possible for her to do it but she believed that they were her one redeeming quality, even when they were molting, they were breathtaking.

"Yes?"

"How about go fuck yourself." she said with a smirk.

The men that came in with him (they were obviously related) doubled over laughing, which made her laugh as well at the sheer stupidity of the situation. One of the men (he was nearly as tall as Mark) was making a strangled sound as he tried to contain his laughter; "Only if you join him, honey."

That was all he was able to get out before another wave of laughter erupted from the group, one even dropped to the floor as she watched blush steal up Mark's neck. The look of embarrassment crossed over his face as she witnessed him reach out and strike at the man that made the comment. By the way he reacted, they had to be brothers. She has many fond memories of tormenting her siblings like this. It had been a while since she smiled like this so freely, but she couldn't help it watching the men in front of her.

Watching them it brought up the last week she was in *Domus Meus*. The triplets recently found peace and laughter in the meadows. They would set up a small table in the soft grass watching the animals while drinking different hot teas and laughing with one another. Daina always made sure she had food and a nice hot tea ready for them when they got from a haul no matter how hard she herself had worked that day.

Clearing his throat and looking uncomfortable Maverick stepped away from her giving her a look over, "Miss Lilith...if it is at all possible, that is I think it is beneficial in the long run if you can put them away, I would be able to bind your ribs better and the wings would heal faster."

Unfortunately, Maverick was right and she knew it. Begrudgingly, she gingerly lifted her heavy wings from where they drooped around her as she moved them upwards pain shot up her spine and she let out a cry closing her eyes as the pain seemed to absorb her every thought, her skin was suddenly moist from the thin sheen of sweat that formed from the effort it took to remain sitting up. She barely registered the firm hands that encased her shoulders, as they seemed to be trying to ground her threw the pain, she drew the power from inside her and forced her wings to dematerialize and reappear on her flesh as nothing more than tattoos. The pain began to lesson and her breath began to even out. *Deus dampnas. How long has it been since I've done this?*

There was a gentle squeeze on her shoulders as she opened her eyes to find the piercing blue that was Mark's eyes. He was looking her over with worry and anger in his eyes, when was the last time someone looked at me with worry other than my siblings? Her hand was caressing his cheek before she realized what she was doing. A light stubble was dusting his jaw and the piercing blue gaze turned liquid as he relaxed into her palm. Mark reached up and grabbed her hand before she could pull it away his face softening as he did, making her stomach tighten in ways it never had before.

"Are you okay?" the deep baritone of his voice cut her out of the fog even as his accent wrapped around her. She was often annoyed by many things but found she could listen to him for hours and not get tired of the sound. Blush stained her cheeks as she realized she was just staring at him with her mouth slightly agape, something she had never done in all her years. She nodded and turned her head away in an attempt to hide the blush but by the commotion she heard coming from the other men she didn't do such a good job.

"I'm going to leave some medicine for you to take over the next few days, after that I will be back to do another checkup but until then you need lots of rest and no strenuous exercise. I mean it, you will need to follow the instructions to the letter if you wish to get better."

"I understand and thank you for your help Maverick...sorry about the whole throat grabbing thing." She gave him an apologetic smile, "If you see someone that has my eyes please tell them where to find me." Lilith never was one to so much as tilt her head down but she was overcome with the erg to bow her head ever so slightly at the man in thanks as the man disappeared before her eyes leaving her with the strange group of men.

"So... You hungry, Angel?" her head shot up at the close proximity of one of the men as he grinned down at her; her attention had been mostly focused on Mark she had all but forgotten the others position in the room. Lilith hadn't heard or smelled this young man approach her; he was smaller than the others not as bulky but no less handsome. He had long well-kept blond hair that he had pulled back with a band and his eyes were very playful and full of youth. The only scent on him was sex and adrenaline.

"Angel?" Erupting into a fit of laughter at the absurd thought of her being called one of those boring creatures. He was something else for sure. Clearly, he was young and naïve if he thought that. "If you think I'm an angel I'm sorry to disappoint, but I am starving, Eros."

"Eros?" the young man's eyes were bright with mischief and curiosity.

"You are handsome but I'm sure that you don't have much other than sex on your mind." She couldn't get out the rest of what she wanted to say do to the giggles that were building up.

"Damn right!" he bellowed out as he laughed.

3.

Lilith had barely reached Mark's armpit when they were next to each other. The woman was small, couldn't be taller than five-three, but the two looked very compatible together. The woman was very striking and no doubt would draw unwanted attention whenever Mark wanted to take her out. Getting her out of the bedroom had been a fun experience; Danny was pretty sure they would have had to drag her out kicking and screaming. It was nice that she graciously agreed to let him show her around; the two of them had been walking around the house for a few minutes and in that time, he had quickly realized she had no idea what anything was.

Danny couldn't help the mischievous streak that ran in his veins; out of all of his siblings he was the one that would cause the most problems due to his natural urge to mess with people. Now was one of those times as he showed Lilith the outside of the house. He had already taken her into the massive bird atrium, as well as all of the bed rooms so she could maneuver around the house and find everyone easier. Though by the fire he had seen in Mark's eyes he could bet where she would be often. Danny had gone ahead and introduced Lilith to most of the familiars, he hadn't been able to find Mouse but he remembered Jase saying he had gone out to fly for a bit.

Figuring what the hell he might as well be casual at this point, "So, Lil, can I call you Lil? What do you think of everything so far?"

"Go ahead and call me that if you want too, that's what my brother calls me anyway. Honestly, I think your home is wonderful, there is so much to see and so much I need to learn if I'm going to be here a while." Lilith was giggling, that's a good sign, she looked like she was enjoying his company at least.

"You speak of your brother often but not your sister, did you know?" It was strange he felt more relaxed than normal around Lilith; it was like she was lifting a long-forgotten weight from his shoulders.

"I know Eros, I spared with him often at home. The three of us are close but the two of us are partners; we cover each other's back in battle. My sister, Daina, often took care of our injuries and got mad at all of our fights with the locals. She is soft and good. If that at all makes since." She had walked further ahead of him closer to the garden but she tossed her head over her shoulder to look back at him. *Eros? Looks like I have a new nickname.* He didn't mind that she called him that opposed to everyone else calling him Danny or Danny-boy; those had become bothersome but he allowed it for his family's sake. "What's wrong? Did I say something?"

"No, but I believe you said the right thing Lil."

"Wanna talk about it?" The wind tussled her hair gently around her face as their eyes connected Danny found himself bewitched. Lilith looked the very definition of what people in the fifteenth hundreds believed witches to look like. With her wealth of crimson hair and her shining jade green eyes; her robes blew in the soft breeze exposing the beautiful tattoo that was wrapped around her thigh. She was breathtaking. Mark was a lucky man. The general concern he could see in her eyes was refreshing; Danny couldn't help but use the situation for the best. He was sure he could win Lilith over and learn more about her family, where she was from.

"I'll tell you about my problems if you tell me about yours."

"It's not a problem so much as a worry; Daina is weak and she is all alone, she can't defend herself at all and is quick to use her body to get anything she needs." The worry was genuine, she really must love her sister but that worry he could tell wasn't just for Daina. He could tell by the sound of her voice.

"When I was young, I lost my mother and older sister to witch hunters; they used to call me Danny. Now everyone calls me either Danny or Danny-boy and it always reminds me of them. So, when you called me

Eros it felt nice to not...I don't know...feel like I was still a kid always crying for my mother from my sick bed.

I was sick as a kid, had a disease they call cancer, it was in my blood you know; very painful, many people didn't believe I would ever complete the training required to be a soldier for my kind. To be honest I myself had started to give up when my sister had found a medical witch that could help. The guys specialty was blood magic; his treatments hurt like a son of a gun but I pulled through. I went with my brothers the night of the incident; we had tracked the hunters down to a warehouse in the Bronx someone had left a door open so we slipped in side and found our good friend Ms. Stephine Greene chatting up the hunters while she had her traitorous hands around my mother's throat. Lindsey was strung up in the raptors by her throat, she wasn't moving; Stephine was giving orders for my mother to be next. The worst part about everything was that you could hear my mother crying out for Lindsey, it was the most heart wrenching sobs I have ever heard. They weren't soldiers, the two of them were doulas; so, they weren't ready for any combat. Stephine must have heard us because she alerted the hunters and they struck at us before we could even register where she had gone with our mother...but we did find her with her throat cut a few blocks away. Mom died broken and worried about all of us. Dad hasn't been around much since either. He left and gave up the position as coven head. We voted and gave the title to Jon."

"Why would the witch hunters listen to a witch?"

"She can use a form of mind control we think; anyone she talks too has the potential to be controlled. Not sure what the actual requirements she needs but there you have it; my very depressing story of my boring life."

"You fought hard warrior," Lilith looked at him with a strange glimmer in her eye as she took his hand and ran a strange symbol along his middle finger. The symbol looked like an axe with strange ruins engraved into the sides, at first it glowed pink but slowly it faded into a light gray mark. His face must have revealed just how confused he was because Lilith sounded amused as she continued, "this is a form of communication devise, it will give you a direct link to speak telepathically with me. I don't like being alone with my own thoughts so please feel free to speak freely with me. Being sent here...it made me lose the link with my siblings...we always have been in each other's heads so I guess I'm just a little lonely"

A wave of victory ran through him as he absorbed the information. He was grinning so hard his cheeks were sore as he began feeling around his mind; he always thought of his inner thoughts as a bright yellow light, warm and peaceful, Danny searched to the edge of his consciousness and found the swirling black tendrils that was Lilith's thoughts. She felt uncertain and more than a little lonely. *Testing. Testing. Do you read me?*

Loud and clear Eros!

The pair laughed as they entered the empty oversized garage that housed everyone's vehicles the most popular being the massive Harleys that where resting in a line. The garage was littered in beer cans and food wrappers. Tools were hanging from every wall and were thrown around on a well-used work bench. the entry had massive barn doors to easier remove the bikes and windows ran along the walls creating more natural light inside the garage. Danny was surprised to not see Jase in here messing with his beloved bike; the man spent almost every waking minute he could in here with the thing. Swinging around because he heard a gasp; he saw the amazement and wonder creep into Lilith's features as she hurried over to Mark's giant bike.

"What creature is this?"

"Do you have horses where you are from?"

"I think so? We have creatures that carry us around when we need to go long distances, why is this a similar type of beast?"

"Not so much as a creature as it is something, we ride to get from one place to another. We store them in here so they stay taken care of and aren't damaged by the weather, think of them like easily taken care of horses."

"So, who's beauty is this?" She was still pointing and gawking at Mark's bike as a thought popped in his head. Oh, he could have fun with her.

"That's belongs to Mark, he isn't in here taking care of her like he used to but he loves the thing. That one," pointing in the direction of his bike, "is mine I ride her every day. You should come ride with Mark and me sometime."

Lilith flushed slightly and the way he spoke of his brother, "You think he is hot don't you Lil?"

"N... No, I didn't say that!" She was beat red as she stammered her denial. "Stop you jackass I didn't say that."

"You don't have to I saw it on your face when you were caressing his face back in the bedroom."

"Saw what on her face?"

The sudden intrusion had both of them jump and whip around to face the door where Jase stood staring at the two of them in amusement as he began to get out of the pair's way. Danny headed to the door to leave, "That she think's Mark is hot but she doesn't want to admit it."

A gust of wind sent an oily rag flying at his face, *someone must have left the window open*, Danny struggled to get the rag off as he caught a glimpse of Lilith's mischievous smirk. *Did she just do that?*

"Don't pick on the girl or I'll have to bring up the fact that you used to think Justin Beiber was hot until you realized she was a he...oops, did I say too much?"

Color ran up his neck as he turned to find Lilith a few feet behind him still smirking, "You're an asshole Jase, come on Lil let me show you the TV and DVDs."

"What are those?"

31

He headed back towards the house with Lilith in tow. *For the record Lil, he looked like a really cute girl when he was younger.* For good measure he pictured the young singer and hoped she saw him. Lilith began to laugh her bell like laugh causing him to laugh as well as they entered the back door of the house.

****

Mark listened in as Danny was explaining electricity and the purpose of television as he was making dinner, which to be honest was hysterical to hear. Never had he heard someone ask if they each have our own "tiny people" who perform for them. Mark had offered to carry her to the living room so she would be more comfortable but she had threatened to rip his eyes out if he tried. Besides, even with the injuries it didn't look like she was having trouble getting around.

This was one fiercely stubborn female she seemed to know what she wanted and had no problems whatsoever in doing what must be done to just be able to do it herself and to be honest she would fit right in among the Fleming coven. Lifting his head when he heard her bell like laugh, he felt peace and happiness to his very soul it made a man think that this was where that woman belonged. That shocked him to his very core. His brothers would one day find their own women and move on with their lives having children, grandchildren even but not once had he ever thought of such things for himself. This woman fell right into his lap bringing hope to have a family of his own one day if the fates allowed it; one never knew what battles he would have to face the next day. Mark was a warrior who lived for the thrill of battle, he thrived in it; dominant was a word that could be used to describe him but Lilith would be the perfect partner. She was his. *His.* Mark knew that Jon must have seen the realization that he would find a way to keep her with him written on his face.

Jon straddled his chair in the kitchen drinking lukewarm beer and watched him make the families most sacred of holy foods; large meat lovers, cheese, pepperoni, and for Danny Hawaiian pizzas. It was a wonder they all weren't in the kitchen, for a family of hawk witches they acted like vultures over pizza.

"You've got that look in your eye Mark, what's troubling you?" There was a teasing note of amusement on his voice.

Oh yeah. He saw. "She threatened to claw at my eyes. How am I supposed to work with that?"

"Well, she can only claw them out once. Besides, it's not like you want to keep her. Unless if you changed your mind?" There was definitely amusement in his eyes, which made him want to hit his brother for the second time today, leader or not.

"Damn fine idea you have there. Why don't we let her claw your eyes out, and you can tell me how it feels? I know you know what I was just thinking, don't make me beg, just help. She fits here." You couldn't miss the twinge of desperation in his voice as he stated the raw truth.

Locking eyes with his younger brother, Jon stated in a more authoritative tone, "Clearly, the rest of the coven accepts her. Aside from you, Jase is the most defensive when it comes to new people in his space and he seems okay with Lilith being here. We'll help you find a way to make her heel," and adding in a less serious tone, "Either way, we could always ask Danny to tie her up and stick her in front of his personal troupe of 'Tiny People'."

Mark walked to the fridge and snagged a cold beer. He had a great sense of pride for his family. When all hell broke loose it was these men that would always back him. They lived in the mountains a few miles from a small Romanian town that was under their protection. It was peaceful out here and the coven had been living in these mountains for generations. It was just the brothers up here now. Their father had disappeared what felt like so long ago. They had miles of land to train in and fly around without the eyes of normals and it was a pretty sweet setup as far as life as a witch goes. Most witches had to go to one of the secret training fields that were scattered around the world. The higher your covens rank the more money the coven had to their names. The Flemming coven was a very high-ranking coven and was well respected. They often assisted the king with an array of different assignments.

Hearing the back door close, they know Jase must've smelled the pizza and rushed in from his bike. Jase stepped into the kitchen looking murderous and frantic; he was dripping oil and grease onto the floor with a furrowed brow and a scowl firmly in place. The two looked at each other and erupt into roaring laughter at the look on his face as he looked frantically between his older brothers.

"I'm going to kill him." Jase stated in a frantic but no less murderous tone. Jase was covered in grease and oil. His normally blonde hair wasn't up in its usual Viking style in its place was this dark mass of knots and tangles as the oil and grease had penetrated his golden locks. His clothes were ripped and clinging to his broad muscles and his shoes were completely tarnished.

"What are you going to kill him for this time, Jase?"

"I went to get on my bike to de-stress before dinner and the damn thing exploded out from under me. Now either I've upset you in some way, Mark, which I know I haven't, or Danny did something to her." The laughter from the living room spilled into the kitchen increasing his rage. The room grew colder as Jase's rage climbed. Jase balled up his hands into fists as he grew deathly still. By the time Jase exploded Mark could see his breath. "DANNY. KITCHEN. NOW!"

Silence swept over the house as Danny entered the kitchen and Lilith was on his heels, both giving Jase puzzling looks as they were trying to assess the situation. Mark watched as Lilith scanned the room before entering and focusing her gaze on Jase. Danny placed himself defensively in from of his older brother putting distance between them and the rest of the room; Jon, the asshole, smirked and continued to sip his beer seeming content to watch the show.

"What's up Jase? You look like shit."

"What's up!? My bike exploded and I know it had to be you; there were carrots shoved in the tail pipe!" Jase was clearly struggling for calm as his breathing grew heavier. "Fuckin' carrots bro!"

"Why the hell would I take out your bike? She's the only thing that stops your PMSing."

Without a second thought Jase launched himself at Danny punching him in the stomach and face. Danny managed to get in a few good hits into Jase's kidneys before Jase had him locked in a head lock and was forcing him to the ground. Danny tried to tap out but Jase, being the bigger man, was relentless in his hold.

****

Lilith watched the two men wrestle on the floor Jase clearly had the upper hand with his size and muscle mass. His muscles were nearly as large as Mark's were, stretching his shirt over his broad chest. There was no way that Danny with his smaller frame could win in a fair fist fight with a man of Jase's brawn. The room was freezing and Jase looked to have a thin layer of ice forming on his skin. Danny couldn't get a good grip on his brother as the blows continued to rain down on him. Danny blocked and tried to get away but Jase already had him pinned to the ground.

Danny was putting up a hell of a fight as he tried to roll out of Jase's hold. He had managed to score a cheap shot at Jase's groin causing the larger man to slip on his hold; no sooner had it loosened did Danny quickly get free. Jase lunged to grab Danny once more jumped away; throwing an onslaught of punches where ever they could connect his older brother Danny was slowly fighting him off.

Are they talking about the weird silver and black horse that was outside? It wasn't moving but it was being good. Lilith was trying to wrap her mind around why this man was so upset over feeding his horse; did they not need to be fed around here?

Silence stretched the room as four sets of sea blue eyes turned to stare at her some in amusement some in absolute horror. *Had she said that out loud?* She tilted her head in confusion as she watched Mark reach out and pull her closer to him; she barely came to the middle of his chest so she had to tilt her head upwards to meet his eyes. It was the concern in his eyes that made her uneasy.

"What?" *Was that her voice? Oh god he will smell my nerves!* Lilith couldn't look away from Mark as he continued to encroach on her space. He looked both worried and amused. Jon had placed his drink down and stood as he stared at her.

"This is very important, did you feed all of the horses in the barn?" His voice was pitched low and his face was serious as he waited patiently for her response.

"They were being good, even if they are the weirdest horses I have ever seen. They don't move much, do they?" As if her voice was a loaded cannon the men ran out of the room, all but Mark who watched them leave.

"Jon!" Mark called after him.

"On it bro!" Called back to Mark who visibly began to relax.

"Those aren't horses, they are motorcycles, and they don't need carrots for fuel," his eyes were bright with amusement as a chime filled the room, "and that would mean its chow time; grab a plate and load up, we have to go over the game plan to find your siblings."

The hell was a game plan?

4.

Biting into the slice of heaven in her hands, Lilith couldn't help the involuntary shudder as her taste buds sang to the high heavens. She finally understood the meaning of the word enlightenment; *Is pizza a religion? If not, can it be? When was the last time she ate like this?* She was so fully engrossed in her food that Jon clearing his throat made her jump and let out a warning growl.

Jon quirked up an eyebrow at the sound. "So, you are Lilith, Herald of Tragedy, correct?"

"What of it?"

"That's an odd name, I was thinking your siblings would introduce themselves in a similar fashion which would make it easier to locate them and bring them here."

She snorted nearly choking on her pizza, "Lilith is my name and the Herald of Tragedy is my birth title. It's something that my kind is given at birth, we are all born with special gifts."

"What does it mean?"

Shrugging her shoulders, "It means I was born with the gift to find tragedy before it starts to happen and stop it or I can spear head it into motion. If I step into a new relm the ground will be scarred with my foot prints upon my arrival. It's kind of like marking territory." taking a bite of her pizza she watched Jon shift slightly in his seat as he watched her.

"Why aren't your foot prints being left around as you are walking now?" he asked curiously.

"Usually only happens when I'm not around Taurtis, my brother, he has high enough energy and power and it seems to ground mine thankfully. I suspect the reason is because of him" jerking her head to the side in the direction of Mark.

"Me? Why do you think that?" Mark's eyebrow shot up at her.

"Obviously, you must give off the same energy as her brother." Danny chimed in as he ate his fourth slice of pizza. The men could eat. She was still on her first slice and they had already eaten a good portion of their pizzas. The group had moved to the table and added an extra chair for her from the other room.

"Guys I hate to be the one to ask her this, but Lil', are their titles just as bad as yours?" looking uncomfortable, Danny then realized what he had implied and threw his hands up apologetically, "Not that yours is bad, I just want to make sure the world isn't going to end while we search for them; would be nice to know if we were looking for let's just say... the 'bringer of the end'."

She gave another rather un-lady like snort. "Not likely you will be looking for a trail of broken hearts and a stubborn ass mule."

Though she didn't want to think it but if one of them were to have a child before they could meet up again it could get bad. Custos handled pregnancies a little differently than other species given the amount of power the parents have the child could be born anywhere from three to nine months' time. Out of the three of them she worried for Daina, she was the most likely to use her body to get where she wanted to go.

"What are their titles? It could help."

Placing down her pizza she sighed and looked around the table at the men surrounding her. "You must understand what I say in this house for as long as I am here must never leak out." Each gave a nod and she continued, "I'm not even supposed to explain the titles to outsiders as they are private to my people. Giving out this information could expose them to the monsters of this plane, and my first priority will always be to protect my family." Mark reached out and took her hand drawing her attention. His fingers drew lazy circles across her palm putting her at ease and reassured her that she was safe. He had a way of putting her at ease.

"First off, I think you don't fully understand what a title is; each individual that was born on my plane, *Domus Meus*, was born with a blessing and a curse which we call a title. For example, mine being the herald of tragedy usually makes people run away with hopes that just bumping into me wouldn't have caused bad things to happen to them." She sighed recalling the loneliness that always followed in the absence of her siblings, here she was telling secrets to men not of her own world. *Times change, I guess.*

"I can bring more than just misfortune to others; I am aware of horrendous things before they happen and if I choose too, I can prevent them; but given my history I can see why people just ran. It is a common enough rule that we are not to leave Domus Meus without special permission; the High Council likes to monitor the people and titles that are coming and going to prevent secrets from being leaked out to other planes." smirking at the small victory she was having over the council just for talking she continued with a stubborn lift of her chin, "Our titles define us, are a part of us so deeply ingrained that it is the base of our very nature; and that is how we will find Daina and Taurtis. Yes, they may introduce themselves like I did but they will try to camouflage themselves and try to regroup with me like I am them. Being separated is something we do not handle well so keep a look out for natural disasters or escalation in crime; Taurtis is more likely to cause the bigger scene in public to get noticed."

"If your people are so secretive why did they give you three permission to come to Earth just to separate you? Wouldn't they have known how you would react?"

"It wasn't our choice and according to the council we will never be allowed back to Domus Meus. They thought we needed to reflect on some things and were each given something we were to protect and shepherd. Don't think they thought about the consequences of taking out our telepathy; we might have been more inclined to do what they wanted if they had left that connection." She clearly remembered being hauled away into the very familiar Council chambers they had placed chains on them and beaten them into what they thought was submission. They would never get them to submit to them, not ever. Her eyes must have flashed blood red because there was a swift intake of air from somewhere in the room but she was too focused on Jon to look and see.

Silence stretched out in the room as her words sunk in to the men; Mark kept a firm grip on her hand as Lilith tried to extract it from his.

"Banished?" Mark had a curious note in his voice that she couldn't place; worry, anger even?

"Yes." her defiant little chin jetted upwards refusing to cower or show shame in her actions. She had no shame so why should she pretend.

"Why?"

"We're street trash. Retired warriors that wouldn't listen to the corrupt orders any longer. Filth of the streets of our home world."

"That doesn't give them the right to banish people without cause." he sighed and sat back in his chair still maintaining the lazy circles he was drawing on her palm. She liked that but had to say everything, jerking her head to face Mark she continued.

"Oh, they had plenty of reasons; there wasn't a month that went by that we weren't brought before the council with an array of charges against us. Taurtis and I were always fighting people on the street; we were thieves, liars, cheats. Daina was charged many times as a prostitute, she was active in many cases of adultery by men and women I might add, anything to make money so we could get by. We were given the nickname Street

Hellions; we were seen as nothing more than street mongrel." Laughing bitterly to herself over the memories, "I guess the final straw was when we broke into a High Lord's house to kill him."

"Why would you want to kill a High Lord? Don't sound so pleased with yourselves, just listening to this is making me never want to take my eyes off of you to ensure you don't cause trouble." Jon sounded shocked though he tried to keep his face devoid of any emotion as to not spark anything from Mark. To him, they had allowed a monster into their homes and he was right to get defensive but to not even hear the rest of the story....

"I can't help it, he had it coming to him; the man was a sick bastard that abducted women, beat them into submission, and sold them to the highest bidder, but only after he raped them repeatedly. Daina was our way in she seduced him and got him to drop his guard before letting us in." Lilith surprised herself at being able to get it out without growling in anger.

"Still, you were banished for doing a public justice?" She could hear the anger enter Mark's voice as it became gravelly and deeper. His hand had stopped drawing circles and he had become absolutely still. A predator locked on its prey.

"They didn't believe us. That bastard was doing business away from his home and under a false name. The lack of evidence condemned us but we knew that going into this and before you say anything, I would do it again." Lilith shot Jon a quick glare. She didn't appreciate his sudden suspicion no matter how warranted it was. "The council sent their goons into our makeshift house the next night. We went willingly but still they paraded us through the streets. When we got to the council building they chained us to the floor. They beat and whipped us for what felt like forever before even passing a judgement." The men grew still as she finished her story and picked up a slice of pizza. She tried her best to look nonchalant as she bit into it.

Mark was staring at her and it made her want to squirm. He opened his mouth and was about to say something when phones began to buzz around the room and the atmosphere changed. Mark looked fierce as he looked up from his phone capturing her eyes.

"We have to go. We aren't done with this conversation though and will finish it when we get back." Figures he wouldn't let it go....

"Where?" she said with a swallow as she watched the change over the siblings as they began to file out of the room. "You're all leaving?"

"We have a mission, but don't worry we will be back." As he stepped away from her, he turned back and brushed a kiss on her cheek. "For luck." He murmured as he followed his brothers out, not looking back.

Lilith could feel the heat rising up her neck to her cheeks as she watched Mark leave; she was thankful he didn't look back for her hand had risen to the cheek he kissed as if to pull it closer to her. She was beginning to forget what it was like to be without Mark's gentle gestures that she could swear made it look like he actually cared. *For luck* he had said. Never had anyone referred to her as lucky; she watched them walk out the door, battle ready, and, for the first time, sent up a silent hope that tragedy would not befall them and they would return home.

5.

Taurtis sat at the small café table looking up at the server in disbelief; this woman wouldn't know good tea if it hit her in the face. He had ordered tea and in its place was a cold sweet beverage that looked like tea but tasted like shit. *What was wrong with this country? You know what? I don't wanna know.* Only hours earlier, Taurtis had found himself unconscious in a hole in the woods, after a short walk to the nearest town, he quickly realized two things. One: normal people didn't have small horns protruding from their heads now a days; and two: he had landed himself in Houston, Texas, and man did he hate the heat. Last time he was here he was sent by the council to feudal Japan and was thought to be a demon. Those were the good days. Now all he could see was buildings and metal horses. Taurtis could see the heat radiating off the paved streets there was cords and cables connecting to tall poles and the buildings. It was so cluttered and he hated it.

He had managed to sneak into a house on the edge of town and steal money and a few changes of close while the residents weren't there. Taurtis ended up at this café when he ventured further into the town and found himself faced with this annoying woman. The young server had a pretty enough face and a nice body but she wasn't appealing to his tastes. Still, she found the need to flip her hair and jet her breasts in his face all the while unaware of the nuisance she was making of herself. Most men would have jumped at the chance to sample the woman, but he had seen enough tricks like this to know she was after his money and sex. Two things he wasn't planning on giving away.

"Is there anything I can get for you Mr...?" So boldly, the woman devoured him with her eyes looking him up and down, her eyes lingering on his groin. Her voice pitched slow as she attempted a sexy husky sound as she purred the request.

He knew he was a good-looking male; he was tall, well over six foot five, and muscular with tanned flesh, dark hair, and jade green eyes. Faint silvery lines littered his tanned flesh; most woman loved the bad boy feel he threw off. If only she knew who she was dealing with she would probably have pissed herself.

"Actually, sweet pea there is, you could get your filthy body the fuck away from me before I turn you over my knee. You are being nothing more than an eye sore; I don't want to look up and see your god damn face staring down at me like I am candy. I have no need or want to fuck you, so you can put your tits away. Oh, and send someone to get me proper tea before I get pissed." Smiling, he watched as she ran away in tears to the server stand, no doubt telling the person there what had happened. Serves her right, if she wanted to act like a whore, she would be treated like one.

A sound caught his attention to his right as he turned his head to look at a box with people inside. They were talking about a massive crater that had appeared out of nowhere in northern Spain, the lady went on to say that there weren't any meteor showers or fallen satellites reported in the area and that the crater had been discovered earlier in the day. The humans thought it was a sink hole that had formed due to the shifting of fault lines but he could see that the crater had burns and ash surrounding it and the trees had been blown back in a peculiar pattern; peculiar to the humans maybe but he would recognize it anywhere. *Bingo...found you, Lilith, now where did you go?*

It looks like his day would be getting better after all; he had his starting point all that was left was to track down Lilith and get her to help find Daina. Taurtis sent up a silent prayer that they were okay and hadn't been too damaged in the fall. He had failed in his job to be the family shield; he could take a lot more damage than his sisters and still he let them fall and didn't get a chance to grab onto them. Thankfully though he was able to hide his spear beneath the seal on his stomach, he would have to thank Lilith later for showing them how to do that.

If she had hit the ground with that much force Taurtis wondered what kind of damage her wings had sustained. They all had been whipped and beaten and he vividly remembered watching both of his sisters get hurled unconscious onto this plane. Lilith had been tossed into this world with her wings unfurled and was unable to tuck them as she fell. If she hit the earth, he knew, she would have hit hard. The soft clip of heels caught his attention as he heard them get closer and stop suddenly at his table. "Excuse me sir?"

A husky southern voice caught his attention as he turned to face a reproachful looking glare coming from a stunningly beautiful woman. Her clothes didn't quite fit her frame as they were too loose on this slip of a woman. She wore her blonde hair in a messy bun fixed in a knot at the top of her hair and little to no make-up from what he could tell. Her Hazel eyes were fixed on him in a very sexy way.

"Yes ma'am?" Her eyes widened when she heard the way he spoke in an old dialect it was a tale tell sign of his Custos heritage.

"So, you do know manners." She shifted her hands to her small waist as she continued to watch him.

"Of course, I do. I show them to people who deserve it; who might you be miss?" Taurtis knew he was laying on the politeness thick. He liked the confusion she was trying to hide as she studied him. The server probably had told her he was a scoundrel. "Is there something I can help you with?"

Color stole her cheeks, "I am the manager of the girl you ran off in tears. Why did you tell her you would beat her? By all rights, I should be calling the police." Outrage filled her voice as she stared down at him.

"Not necessary miss; and I said I would put her over my knee, not beat her. The waitress was throwing her breasts in my face and staring at me in a way that ground at my nerves. Plus, she was so focused on my dick that she got my order wrong. I didn't realize that I walked into a brothel because she sure as hell wanted to take me out back and fuck me. This is a café and not a brothel and she should learn that before she meets someone who will take her on. Now that we have that covered, what is your name miss manager?" He knew he was sounding like an asshole but he couldn't help the amused grin that formed on his lips.

Color stole up her neck, drawing attention to the faint freckles that dotted her creamy skin. Visibly, she relaxed as she began to grasp what had transpired between the waitress and him. "You don't have to use such vulgar words, buddy. I will talk with her myself about her behavior, that is not acceptable in this family-run kind of place."

"What? Dick? I didn't mean to offend only to defend my actions, miss...?" He needed her name.

"Yes, that word, sir." The woman checked her watch and looked back at him, "My name is Maddison and that waitress has a history of that, so I do apologize and I will bring you your correct order in just a moment."

"Maddison, could you also bring me a piece of whatever pie you have on special today?"

Maddison looked slightly taken back for a moment before nodding and walking away. Taurtis watched her walk away with the swish of her hips; now that is how a woman should be. He returned his attention to the strange box for a few minutes only looking away when she brought him his tea and pie, watching again as she walked off to do her job. He would have to remember to take his sisters here, they would love it.

A woman slid into the chair in front of him; she was average height with a round face and long forehead. Her muddy brown hair was pulled up in a tight ponytail that hung to her shoulders, her brown eyes were round and made her look like a doe while her lips were slim and pulled in a tight thin smile that she was trying to pull off as a polite friendly one. He had been around people long enough to know the ones that were there to help and the ones that where there to use someone. She was here to use him she was sure she lacked the innocence around her to try to help.

46

"Hello sorry for interrupting you sir; my name is Stephanie Green I'm a low-ranking witch and was wondering if you could help me." As she spoke, a pain filled the corners of his mind as he felt her words physically assaulting his mental shields; she was going to try to manipulate him. *Interesting little thing, this must have worked a thousand times for her...pity.*

"If you were truly sorry, you wouldn't be doing it, now would you, canis?" Now, he was getting annoyed with all these bitches popping up and disturbing his peace.

"This is true..." the woman, Stephanie, dipped her head as if ashamed. False sadness was in her voice. This one was quite the actress as the feeling of dread suddenly assaulted his emotions.

"How do you know if I could help? You really shouldn't go around telling others what you are, especially if you're worried over something already it could get you killed."

"I could feel the power coming off you in waves...a high-ranking coven murdered my loved ones and stole a precious family heirloom; I need help getting it back and also to seek revenge against the coven."

"What coven is it and where are they located?"

His skin pricked as it always did when someone told him a lie and this woman just spat out a huge one. Still, it felt like something was trying to compel him to do as she asked. His eyes glazed over and he gave into the sensation that was wrapping its way inside him, *Only for now.*

****

Stephine couldn't help the grin she let slip out as she mesmerized yet another helpless fool; she poured power into her voice to distract them from the electrical signals she was sending to his brain. Men were too easy to manipulate and most felt the need to help a damsel in distress. Just a few tugs on certain areas in their brains and voilà a man puppet.

She needed this fool; it was no lie when she said she could feel the power coming off him, it was downright terrifying, she wasn't too sure she could pull off her ability on him but she did. She tried to put on an innocent enough face as she looked him in the eyes and summoned up tears, "It was the Fleming coven in Romania..."

Word had traveled fast to her ears that those fools had picked up a strange woman and she was living with them. What's more Mark Monroe was moving hell to find her family, that made her a weakness to him. That woman will bring him to his knees and she only wished she was able to get past the barrier to do it herself; the bastards locked her out, but could they lock this man out?

"Show me the way...I don't mind being your spear." Beautiful jade green eyes shone brightly as they had fully glazed over; *Perfect!*

"Grab your belongings, sir, we leave on the next flight," with a smile she left the small café, there was a phone call to make. She passed by a woman that just stared at her suspiciously as she walked by. Looks like she might have to keep an eye on this place...*just in case.*

6.

Please be alright. They had been away from the coven house for three days, far too long to have left an injured female that didn't know about modern things. Sighing to himself as he recalled kissing her cheek before leaving, he had wished he'd done a little more than a peck on her cheek at the time he wouldn't have been able to stop and duty called.

The mission had been to track down a missing member of the royal guard and to bail him out. It had taken too long to find him; the man had been captured by witch hunters and was on the execution list. Cutting and slicing their way out after retrieving him, the coven had to make an official report to the King of the Witches, Ash Wolfpaw. The King ordered them to stay and recover after the individual reports; he had sustained a wound to his arm when a knife grazed him after he had snapped the neck of one of the executioners. He hated being stuck in the same building as the king and Iblis, it tended to make the whole stay very tense. Ash tended to hover around and collect whatever info he could get from the coven. He rarely left the castle grounds and when he did it was for nothing good. Iblis was an asshole which made him insufferable to be around. Nobody really knew where Ash had picked up the odd ghoul but he liked to wander around the grounds at night and sing which made it hard to sleep.

Sniffing the air as he materialized onto family lands, he smelled something divine on the air. Stepping into the kitchen he came to an abrupt halt at the sight of her; she was at the stove cooking up what looked like a breakfast casserole. She was wearing one of his old tee shirts that swallowed her feminine curves. Her hair was pulled up in a messy knot on the top of her head exposing her neck. Mark crossed the room and circled her waist with his arms pulling her into him as he buried his face in her neck. *Three days was too long to be away from her.*

"Welcome back, Hercules," she called to him without looking to make sure.

"I'm back; where did you learn to make this?" Stepping back, taking a seat at the table, so she could have room he watched as she worked with fluid grace and ease. The smile that lit her face could have stopped wars as she held out a sample of the dish.

"Food channel. I've been learning a lot from the television while you were away. Where are my other boys?" Mark could hear the satisfaction in her voice as she finished up with the food. Lilith looked to have become quite acquainted with his kitchen. He noticed she was swishing her hips in a happy dance. The movement was both adorable and alluring as it caught and held his attention.

"Your Boys? Danny or Jase could be the same age as you." chuckling at the thought of this female thinking of them as her boys, "They are still at the king's summer castle in South Ireland, don't worry they are all fine and will be here in a couple hours. You do realize we don't travel around like a pack of dogs, right?"

"I know you're not a pack of dogs, I've just never been alone with you. Oh, and for the record they could be children compared to me." It was the sickly-sweet smile that tipped him off that she wasn't playing around about her age.

"How old are you, *sufletul meu?*"

"You shouldn't ask a woman their age, it's not very gentleman-like, don't you think? What does that mean anyway?"

"*Draga*, humor me, please. What *sufletul meu?* It's a term of endearment here, it means something close to sweetheart." *So, he fibbed a little in the meaning,* truly he was calling her his little soul.

50

She shifted from side to side looking sexy as hell but also uncomfortable. "I'm one hundred and sixty-seven years of age."

You're shitting me?! "You don't look a day over twenty-five."

The answering smile brought his cock to attention as her face flushed a slight rose color; she was stunning walking around the kitchen in his shirt cooking for him. Lilith was clearly pleased with how he handled her age, though he was telling the truth: she was breathtaking. He watched as she plated the food and stored the leftovers in the fridge.

"Do you mind getting me a beer while you're over there?"

"Sure thing."

He couldn't take his eyes off her mouthwatering ass as she bent into the fridge, the shirt she was wearing slid upwards as she bent revealing the round, heart shaped cheeks that were peeking out from the bottom of the shirt ever so slightly. His cock jerked and, if possible, grew harder. Lilith straightened out, effectively making the shirt fall back into place as she made her way to the table with the beer in hand; she walked with a sexy flare of her hips that he doubted she was aware of. She brought him his beer before turning to the counter to retrieve the food and place it on the table in front of him.

"Eat up, I want to know what you think." She was clearly oblivious to what her body was doing to him, but he couldn't deny her as he heard the note of uncertainty in her voice.

He took a bite and the flavors were perfect and savory; smiling back at her, "*Draga,* this is perfect, thank you for preparing it for me. How did you know I was on my way home anyway?"

"This is going to sound strange, but the wind told me you were coming home today, so I felt like cooking you something since you last cooked for me." She had the sexiest accent as the old dialect dripped from every word. It sounded as if it was a mixture of Galic and Russian maybe. He couldn't quite place it but the slurry sound of her voice made the sound fit her perfectly.

"It's not the only thing I plan on doing for you this week." He was grinning at he watched the confusion and skeptical look cross her face. *There is no way in hell I'm letting anyone see her wearing a tee shirt. That's for me.* "I'll try to see if I can find you some sweats to wear, we are going shopping."

"What's wrong with my robe?"

"We don't wear robes here, besides having a few extra outfits would be practical; you also don't own a pair of shoes."

"I don't need them: soon my wings will get better and I could always hover on the air." A gentle breeze swirled around the room lifting her up so she could perch in the air; she smirked as she crossed her legs proving she didn't require solid objects to sit on. Batting her jade eyes as if trying for innocence, "See? Who needs shoes?"

Why am I not surprised she can float?

"Need I remind you that normals don't have wings nor can they do whatever it is you are doing. I'll be right back with the sweat pants for you." He left the room smiling at himself, *really woman you're not even wearing underwear.* Was it possible for a witch to achieve sainthood? Because damn he wanted her. He had to stop his thoughts short. She isn't ready yet, don't want to scare her off.

****

Pants are so restricting!!

They had been to several small stores in the neighboring town but she had yet to find anything she liked. Mark was being nothing but patient with her as she rejected garment after garment that was offered to her; she was about to give up when they walked by an odd-looking shop. Curious she had dragged Mark inside and was amazed by all the different fabrics and styles; this place was perfect; the fabrics were breathable and soft, perfect for her to move around in. She couldn't help but focus on the different fabrics and styles for several minutes, she didn't know when the next time she could do something like this again and everything had to not only look good but also be battle ready at a moment's notice. She wasn't like Daina, she kept reminding herself as she browsed, she was a warrior and had to be ready for any fight coming her way. She wasn't cut out for the soft flowing dresses Daina often wore. She dressed for battle because she was born for it. Daina was soft and needed more protection.

"Oh, look over there Hercules!" Pointing while she ran over to the far side of the store; she couldn't hide the excitement over finding furs and leather!

She found several different sets of clothing and, at Mark's urging, she went to the changing rooms and tried them on. The tops were beautiful. Most of the selected tops had a lace up the side, back or front and were in an array of different earth tone colors. With Lilith's bright crimson hair she always felt that the earth tone colors always suited her well. The tops were loose on her and hung off her making it easier for her to move around in if she needed to move fast. She struggled to lace the front of one of the tops she was wearing, a mischievous glint twinkled in her eye as she thought of asking Mark for help. Poking her head out of the dressing booth, she spotted Mark looking at accessories, "Mark, can I get you over here for a bit?"

As soon as he turned, she was hit with the full impact of his lust filled eyes as he slowly took in her appearance; she hadn't secured the front of the red velvet and lace corset top she was wearing and it exposed the tops of her full breasts, she felt more exposed in that moment than she had ever been before.

Mark was a handsome man and was catching the eyes of every female that had walked into the small shop but he only seemed to have eyes for her; he made her feel like she was worth something more to someone other than her siblings. For the longest time her world was small, it had just been the three of them, and all of a sudden here comes Mark slowly prying open the locked door to her heart. She was scared of the feelings she was beginning to feel for this man, no this witch, he was more than just a man. *He could be your man... Dammit Daina!* Memories of the countless times Daina tried to get her to claim a man ran through her head. *I don't need this right now.* It was bad enough the past three days she had been thinking of the way Mark had touched her hand and kissed her cheek; she wasn't sappy like this but she couldn't help it. Mark was charming.

"You called, *Draga*? Let's get you back into the dressing room."

"I need help with lacing this top and I also would like your opinion on these clothes as well."

She sucked in a breath as his calloused hands brushed the top of her breasts as he expertly laced the shirt. Taking a step back she shimmied into the shorts that clung to her curves like a glove, the shorts were on the shorter side and exposed the intricate tattoo that was around her thigh. The top was a soft red velvet that was laced up the front and exposed her back, all of the tops she had amassed were a similar style they would make it easier for her to use her wings without having to tarnish the shirts. She looked herself over in the mirror and began to adjust her hair; Mark caught her hand and turned her to him.

"Don't. You're absolutely beautiful, *sufletul meu*, don't change a thing." Mark's hands were softly brushed her cheek. Lilith eyes were locked with Marks as the air went electric with sexual tension. She could feel Mark's breath as he slowly bent his head and captured her lips. Fire shot through her bloodstream at the contact, he kissed her gently at first, almost reverently, as he molded his lips to hers. Lilith accepted his kiss and she moved her lips below his, encouraging him and trusting him as she kissed him rather unpracticed back. She had never really had much practice when it came to kissing or sex so she felt unsure as she let Mark take her over. Lilith let go giving into the depths of the kiss.

Mark took her mouth more fiercely as he licked the seam of her lips slowly encouraging her to open for him, his tongue plunged into her mouth and her tongue met his, dueling with him as she circled his neck with her arms pulling him closer; soft moans escaped her as she heard his aroused growl tear from his throat. He was sexy as hell. The unexpected growl had her breath hitch and speed up with excitement as adrenaline pumped into her system. She tunneled her fingers into the wealth of his blonde hair, pulling and tugging, she demanded more. He reached down and cupped her heart shaped ass pulling her closer to him as he lifted her legs to circle his waist, fitting her soft, drenched mound on his hard bulge. A moan escaped her throat as he pressed into her, the only thing separating them were the thin layer of clothes. Mark rubbed into her causing friction and sending another wave of juices to spill between her legs; her clit was throbbing as she arched herself and began to grind on him sending a shudder of pleasure shooting through her. This wasn't like her at all. Lilith knew they could get caught at any moment but the thought was met with pure pleasure and thrill of the moment. Let them see he is mine...for now at least.

Mark peeled his mouth away and Lilith followed him until he placed his forehead on hers. "Your beautiful." He huffed out.

"You mentioned that." Lilith smiled back.

"Did I?" Mark was breathing heavily as he went back for another kiss.

A knock rasped at the door startling them to let go of one another as Mark placed her back on her unsteady legs; they were both breathing heavily as Mark lowered his head to hers once more giving her a gentle kiss. Another knock sounded at the door disturbing her thoughts.

They remained silent as they waited for someone to say something, the store was eerily silent given it was full of people just moments ago, Mark went for the door and paused as vigorous banging shook the changing room door, "Get the fuck out of there! You don't want me to make you get out of there, do ya bitch?"

Years on the streets had her reaching for Mark before he opened the door; she pushed past Mark and gripped the handle. Whoever was on the out there hadn't seen Mark come in the dressing room, which was a good thing. He would be a big surprise for whoever it was that knocked. Mark grew deathly still at her side as the warrior part of him took over. They stood in silence waiting for a response from the other side, the seconds felt like minutes as adrenaline rushed her system. A familiar feeling began to set in. The room went dark as she saw the events that were to happen.

There would be blood splattering the walls and bodies lining the floors; a single man would be the cause of a horrific massacre and this shop would be the first of many. So much unnecessary loss, so much blood; and for what? Lilith was faced with a decision; did she wish to not intervene and leave the humans to face the massacre alone or did she wish to help them? It was the sound of a baby's cry that wrenched her away from the vision that plagued her and, decision made, she slipped out of the dressing room, leaving Mark to trail after her.

The man had moved into another room and was waving around a hand gun, on his belt was a hunter's knife, he easily would tower over her but that didn't matter, he was human. Lilith moved as he lifted his gun to an elderly couple, she slammed into his side and retrieved his knife as he turned and fired his weapon at her.

In a blur Lilith swiftly got out of the direction of the bullet. Lifting her arm in an arch, she sliced open his eye blinding the man. A howl of pain left the man as he cradled his injured eye and began firing madly in her direction. Dodging she stepped into close range and slammed the knife deep in his stomach twisting it around before yanking it out. The man, blinded and in agony, fired off more shots trying to hit her as she dropped to the floor throwing her leg out, she swept his legs out from under him and brought him to the ground. Jumping on him, she pinned him to the ground one knee on his open stomach wound making him curse and yelp, the other knee pinned his gun hand to the floor. Lilith's steady hand had the hunting knife at his exposed throat as the fight left the man, it had only taken mere moments to bring him down. The man had only managed to graze her one time nothing more. Humans were weak plain and simple and this man called to her for some reason.

"Kill me!" the man pleaded.

"You aren't worth the effort to kill, but you will be handed over to someone who will be willing to deal with you." Disgust filled her voice as the sound of sirens filled the shop, the people that were crouching in the corner slowly stood up realizing that the man wasn't getting up. Lilith had been sent here to protect souls according to Gwen, is this what she meant? Looking back at the man she realized he was just another lost soul, bending down so only he could hear her she softened, "May you find peace someday but this isn't the way, trust me in this for I to have been where you are now."

Mark slowly went to the door and let the officers in, the man was sobbing as he was taken away. She sat on the floor of the shop watching as everyone gave their statements to the officers as an older woman crouched down next to her, Mark watching nearby.

"Thank you, child, for saving us, you were splendid. How did you do that?" The older woman searched her eyes appearing to be seeking something.

"I am no child ma'am, and it wasn't your time to go." Lilith focused her energy and made a murage of her wings and projected so only the old woman could see them. The elderly woman clutched her chest and made a small gasping sound as she looked at her.

"My god...you're an angel..." There was reverence in the old women's voice.

"No, I'm not, I am a warrior and guardian of lost souls. I am glad that I was here today for all of you, and, I was glad I was here today for that man." Lilith motioned to the emergency vehicles as it pulled off.

The older woman paused and lifted her hand to her mouth in thought, "Why on Earth were you glad to be here for that man?"

"Is he not just a lost soul in need of virtue? I will continue to hope that he learns from this and does not take this path again. There were too many lives at risk and I'm not ready yet to see anyone to the other side today." The older woman warmed and nodded as a hand dropped on her shoulder and she knew it was Mark. He crouched down beside her and scooped her into his arms; he held her like she weighed nothing and he cradled her to his chest like she mattered to him.

"Mrs. Marsha, I left money for the clothes on the counter under the register. I'm sorry this happened in your store and if there is anything I can do, please let me know; my brothers too, you are like family and we watch our own." He spoke to the older woman with affection in his voice. "I really must take my little warrior home and get her some rest; I'll bring her into town more often."

Wait. His. Warrior. When did I agree to be his warrior? The scowl that she sent up to him was ignored as he flashed a grin at the woman and headed for the door; they didn't speak a word as he walked down the street and turned a corner.

"You're going to feel slightly uncomfortable."

That was the only warning she got before she felt a strong pull; it felt like she was moving at a rapid speed or falling while spiraling. The force made her squeeze her eyes closed and what felt like an eternity later the pulling feeling stopped.

****

Mark sat her down once they had entered the kitchen. He had been terrified when he watched her move in on the gun man; she had moved with fluid grace and clear skill that came from years of practice; she hadn't even noticed that a few of her wounds had opened up. His little warrior had taken down an armed man that was a foot taller than her in mere moments and he couldn't be prouder.

"Be still let me look over some these gashes."

"I'll be fine, Mark, they will heal in a few days between the medicine and my kinds fast healing rate." She sounded sleepy and she didn't fight him when he removed some of the bandages. The gashes were bleeding and draining it seemed; the only wounds that looked at risk for infection was the one thick long gash at her ribs and the deep gash on her thigh, both of which were bleeding and puss filled.

"They don't look too bad, but I do want to disinfect them to prevent an infection, this one by your ribs looks angry." There was a first aid kit in the cabinet: he retrieved it and began patching her up. A shimmer of light, hardly noticeable he would have missed it if he hadn't had been so close, flickered over the tattoos at her wrists and vanished as if it had never been there.

"What do these tattoos mean?" Lilith looked surprised that he asked the question and he could see her soften visibly. He knelt between her legs to better clean and fasten the bandage on her ribs.

"My brother made them as a way to always stay connected no matter what; they haven't really been tested but they glow when each of us are close to the other. It's kind of like the Marco Polo game except no words obviously." She looked comfortable as he poured the disinfectant on her thigh and he was glad for that.

"So, they both glow? Is this how you had planned to find them?" Mark gave her a curious look. He hadn't realized how similar both of their kinds could be, witches often marked each other in similar fashions for different occasions.

"How do you do that?"

"Do what?" She was just too cute he couldn't help but grin at the look of disbelief that was etched on her face.

"Raise your eyebrow like that; Taurtis can do it to but he told me it's a strictly guarded male secret." A sigh escaped her as she pinched her nose clearly trying to look annoyed but he could see the affection she felt toward her brother, and he hoped, for him as well.

"Well, I can't give up male secrets, now can I? Gives you women an advantage over us; you never answered my questions." He could be stubborn when he wanted to be and that small shimmer on her wrists concerned him a bit. He needed to know this information if it meant finding those siblings of hers; he wasn't sure if he wanted to, when she was back with them, she would try to leave him and he hadn't yet tide her to him yet.

"Yes, I would have tried to use them to find the others but again they haven't really been tested for long distance; and they only glow one at a time unless we are all together then yes, they all glow. This one," she pointed to her thigh, "Is for Daina it will light up a soft aqua when she is around. The ones on my wrist are for Taurtis they will glow green when he is around, it looks like a glow stick to be honest."

"A glow stick? You learned that from our DVDs, man we need to update the collection."

She was laughing as he finished applying the bandage to her thigh, the movement brought him closer within a breaths distance. One of the crimson strands of her hair was attached to the side of her mouth; he reached up and brushed it aside locking eyes with Lilith he leaned in and took her mouth.

Mark licked and sucked at her lips coaxing them open so he could sweep inside and duel her tongue. She tasted like passion and sin. He laced his hands in her hair and tilted her head to deepen the kiss; his cock grew hard and he feared he would burst. Lilith didn't do anything half way as she dove into the kiss, clutching him and panting against his mouth as he lifted his head. He kissed and nipped at her neck making her moan his name; one hand wandered to the laced-up portion of her shirt and he slipped his hand inside finding her hard nipples.

"Please, Mark." Clutching him she began rubbing on him in quick jerky movements. At the sight of her arousal, he lifted her shirt to have better access to her beautiful full breasts; his mouth watered as he saw the most perfect nipples he had ever seen: they were rose-tipped and the small little peas were hard. He sucked one in his mouth, pressing the nipple flat against the roof of his mouth, he pulled and stroked it with his tongue, his other hand flicked her other nipple making her suck in a breath. She cradled his head to her and arched into his mouth, they were on fire, passion taking over as the room echoed with moans and the sound of his name coming off of her lips.

Someone cleared their throat and he looked up into the doorway; his brothers were their grinning like morons. Throwing a scowl their way he hoped they would just leave it be but knowing them, he wouldn't be hearing the end of this anytime soon.

"Thought you would like to know we think we found your sister." Jase kept his eyes on the ceiling but his grin was still in place.

Lilith moved then pushing him away and fixing her clothes in place she jumped up and went to Jase all business, he on the other hand was still in a lust filled haze: he didn't even realize he was exposing her breasts to his brothers. He stood up and directed his gaze at his brothers showing them the fury that was riding him after they not only interrupted but saw her; *They better fucking forget what they saw!*

"Where did you find her?" Anxiety filled Lilith's voice.

"We didn't find her but there was a rumor about a hot brunette hiding in the catacombs of France. It's best if we gather more information before we head that way."

"That was the only description of the woman you have? That could be anyone."

"That's why I want to get more information first."

61

"Any word on Taurtis? Why hasn't anyone seen him yet? You couldn't miss him!" She was anxious and worried; he reached out and snagged her arm dragging her back into him.

"*Draga*, when we have a word on them you have my word, we will tell you. Until then just focus on getting better." Lilith nodded and rested her head on his chest sighing. She had to be exhausted with the day she had. "Why don't you take a shower and go to sleep in my room? I'll be there in a bit."

She just nodded and wandered out of the room leaving him with his brothers. She was breaking his heart; this woman was strong and the defeated look did not help settle his fury. If anything, it made him want to take his anger out on the first enemy that he came into contact with. Despite what others thought, he could be a mean son of a bitch and for his woman he would cross through hell just to make her smile; anything she wanted, he would make happen.

"She shouldn't ever have that fuckin' look in her eyes." Fury was over taking him, "Why do you think you found her sister in France, Jase, she is very protective of that sister of hers from what I can tell."

"Like I said, Mouse spotted a hot brunette on his way to the Southern castle." Mouse was his overgrown hawk of a familiar, it was a powerful bird with a wingspan of five feet and stood at three feet tall.

"You didn't mention Mouse, why was he out that way?" Normally familiars didn't stray too far from their coven, that's why the coven house had an aviary attached to it.

"He was hunting. Anyway, he was resting by one of the entrances to the catacombs and he saw a woman with similar tattoos and the same jade green eyes coming out of it. Mouse let me know as soon as he got back but the lazy fuck could have let me know when he was there but you know how he is."

"That doesn't just sound like it could be her sister, that has to be Daina. Why didn't you tell her all of this?"

His brothers looked at each other sheepishly before Jon spoke up rather sympathetically, "We weren't sure if you wanted her to know just yet, were worried she would bolt after Daina and not look back. You can't say you're not worried, and despite what we walked in on, not sorry by the way, it doesn't look like you clipped her wings."

He knew they were just trying to help but the fury inside him boiled over and he turned in one quick motion and slammed his fist into the wall. Silence stretched in the room. He was pissed no other word for how he was feeling; this was his woman. His. Woman. She wouldn't be leaving him; she couldn't, he wouldn't allow it, but she had to know her sister was found. If he was lucky, he would manage to make it a few days before he had to tell her what they had found. *What was this bullshit Jon said about clipping her wings?*

"Listen closely. Her wings will never under any conditions be clipped. Never. Even metaphorically. She is a fighter, fierce and protective. Her wings bring her great joy, you saw how she was when we asked her to hide them. I will never, nor would I ever, allow anyone to take them from her so shut the fuck up about clipping them." His breath was heavy as he tried to regain his legendary steady calm persona.

"We wouldn't dream of clipping her wings that would be like clipping Avis or Akand's wings. We only wanted to let you decide how to handle it."

"I'll gather more info before I tell her."

The border alarm blared throughout the house; it was a high squealing sound that signaled an intruder on their lands. All heads went up as they scattered throughout the home to weapon up and within minutes, they were out in the mountain terrain, familiars in the air, working as a solid lethal force stalking the mountainside. According to the magical barrier the alarm was triggered on the southern side of their property.

The southern portion of the property was covered in thick foliage of trees and bushes making it hard to move about without being spotted; the mountain terrain would also add as a buffer for someone unexperienced to approach the coven house. They searched the mountain terrain along the border looking for a shift in the thick vegetation or birds taking flight. It was silent tonight, nothing moved the animals seemed relaxed, not as if there was an unknown presence in the area. Mark and his brothers were scattered around the perimeter of the breach looking for something, anything, to indicate the intruder. They each had a com piece in their ears for updates but so far nothing; this person was skilled in stealth that was for certain, it was a waiting game it appeared and unfortunately for whoever was out there his coven was trained from a very young age to wait out an enemy for days if necessary.

"Ah....fuck.... guys...bac...."

The com in Mark's ear went live as he heard Danny struggling to get a message out but couldn't; there was a gargling noise on the other end of the link that had everyone franticly running to get to Danny. He was under attack. With the com link active they could hear the sound of fist slamming into bone as well as his youngest brothers' grunts of pain. Danny was at the far right of the perimeter and Mark was the closest as he tore through the thick brush; it wasn't just in the com link that he could now hear the sounds of the brawl as he sped into the clearing. As he cleared the entrance of the small clearing Danny was stationed at Mark witnessed a man slam Danny into a tree by his throat; adrenaline pumped his system as he tackled the man off of Danny. They grappled on the ground fighting for supremacy; the man was on top off him, he was overpowering him, pushing him into the earth trying to get at his throat. Mark let off a small explosion from his palm hoping to injure and dislodge the assailant but the man didn't budge, like he wasn't even hit at close range. Ice rained down on them fallowed by a streak of lightning that collided with the man's side. His brothers had arrived but it didn't appear enough to budge the man; with him momentarily distracted by the assault, Mark opened his palm and let loose six quick mini bombs that sent the man flying off of him. Danny had regained his footing and they regrouped together.

"What the hell is this guy? I tried strangling him, stabbing him, and shooting him. He doesn't have a scratch on him." Danny's voice was hoarse after being in the chokehold but he looked pissed and out for blood.

"He was able to take me down and I was at full strength trying to get him off. He was like a mountain, unable to budge."

"What the hell..." They looked at him full of fury trying to find a weak spot as a wide grin formed on his face.

"Stephanie said this coven was strong but all I see is a bunch of weaklings. Perhaps I got the wrong place? That's too bad I needed a good workout." The man rolled his shoulders back and forth stretching them out.

STEPHANIE?!?! That traitorous bitch has something to do with this? Mark looked at the man, really looked at him. He was a big man, bigger than himself, he had a lot of muscle and scars were apparent on his bronzed skin. He had dark and hauntingly jade eyes that looked familiar to him but he couldn't place them with the wealth of midnight black hair that hung shaggy around his face. There was a tattoo that circled his neck in and intricate pattern. His eyes were mocking and the grin didn't reach his eyes. His face pissed him off, it was condescending and he would have bet he tricked many women with that grin.

Mark looked to his brothers who just nodded as the air became electric with energy surging around both sides as they prepared to launch a powerful assault. The man set his feet apart bracing for the attack, he seemed to believe he would be able to hold his stance. Letting loose the magical energy the ground started to explode around the man's feet as lightening and hail rained down on him, Danny created spears made of shadow and began to fling them through the air at him. There was so much debris it was hard to see their target the explosions had made dirt and dust fill the air and shield the enemy from their sight.

A mocking laughter filled the air as the man stepped into view, he hadn't sustained any injuries. *How is that possible?*

"Is that everything you've got? You are never going to take me down with that level of...." His words were stolen from him as a large gale of wind came crashing down on the clearing; it threw him back away from them. The force of the wind pushed them back away from the man as if creating a barrier between the two opposing parties. Mark's heart dropped as the wind let up and Lilith dropped from the sky and landed with her arms outstretched.

Her hair was still wet and she was wearing just his tee shirt again, but the thing that caught his attention was her wrists glowing a bright green. She shifted her feet and launched herself into the man's now outstretched arms with a wide grin on her face. *Oh hell...don't tell me...*

"Taurtis!" She laughed while barring her face in his neck.

"Oh fuck." Jase watched the reunion with amazement as the aggression melted away from his brother's features.

"Yeah...It's her brother..."

****

Taurtis had barley caught the glimmer of Lilith's tattoos before the wind had knocked him back. His sister was the only one to ever be able to not only budge him but to also cut him; and over the years the two had spared countless times so he was well versed in what her abilities could do.

Joy filled every fiber of his being when she dropped from the sky and catapulted herself into his arms. Lilith was whole and safe. Taurtis couldn't help himself as he spun Lilith in a circle clutching her tightly. While she was hugging him, he noticed three things. One: Her wings were hidden and she never did that...ever. Two: She was wearing only a man's jumbo shirt. Three: The man the shirt belonged to was staring straight at her ass.

Taurtis released her and fixed the shirt so she wouldn't expose herself to the man as he sent him a death glare. Who was this man to her? Did he miss that much? He couldn't trust that they wouldn't take this opportunity to attack. Lifting Lilith once more he placed her safely behind him as he watched the threat in front of him. The group was related, had to be by the way they looked and reacted with each other. They were indeed skilled and if he wasn't as strong as he was, they may have overtaken him; but, unfortunately, he was also a well-seasoned warrior. The one that was still trying to look at Lilith was the biggest and seemed to be the oldest of the bunch was in his opinion the most dangerous with the ability to make things explode the others Taurtis knew he could take down relatively easier.

"Taur?" Lilith tugged on his shirt sleeve as she walked around him to stand in front of him once more. She had her hands on her hips as she gazed up at him all business. Her hair was wet and stuck up in wild curls as some plastered to her face; her all business face was usually intimidating but right now she looked like a wet dog.

"Lil, you need to either stand behind me or fight with me. These fuckers could hurt you in your current state." Something he had said looked to have prickled her nerves as she straightened her spin and lifted her stubborn chin. *Shit.*

"Taurtis! They have been taking care of me and have been letting me stay with them, to them you are the trespasser. So, in your words, stand behind me and maybe you can stay, alright?" Lilith waited for his nod before she summoned one of the men over, "Jon?"

"What's up Lil?" One of the men, Jon, approached them with a cocky grin as the others followed closely behind, Taurtis wanted to punch the man in his smug looking face. But he did just agree to behave though he was finding it hard to settle down. The other men looked on in guarded suspicion as Jon approached. They were ready to resume fighting if need be, not that it would help them. Though Lil was on their side by the looks of it so they had that to their advantage. Shaking his head Taurtis rejected the thought. Lilith will always side with him at the end of the day. Always.

"I humbly ask you, the coven head permission for my brother to come stay at the house with us for a while." *What the fuck??? Was she sick?* He had never seen Lilith ask anyone other than Daina nicely for anything. *What is happening around here?*

"Of course, I have already said your siblings are welcome as long as there is no trouble." The man he now knew to be Jon turned his cocky stare at him, "There isn't going to be any trouble is there?"

"As long as I don't have any trouble there won't be." Yeah, he really wanted to punch this guy but the look on Lilith's face made him stop. She was smiling. Lilith grabbed his hand and began leading him towards the house he had seen from the top of the mountain. It was only then that he noticed the bandages that covered her thigh and arms. Lilith was worse than he originally thought as the scent of blood drifted to his nose; one of her wounds must have opened slightly.

"I warned them that you would cause a scene," Lilith sounded so proud of him as she pulled him along. She looked regal as she continued on her way back to the home. She had a slight limp that caught his eye. She had always been the smallest of the siblings and with her hurt it worried him even more.

"Lil, come here." Taurtis bent and lifted her in his arms as he continued walking, he cradled her closer to him.

"Just this once...." Lilith breathed out softly as she circled his neck and cuddled into him. *How tired are you Lil?* Taurtis chuckled to himself as he passed the men, he knew she must have given them hell about this at least once by the look of amazement on their faces. The taller of the group looked at him sternly as they passed; *Fuck them I've got what I came for.*

7.

Taurtis had carried her back to the coven house and was sitting with her on the couch surrounded by the Fleming coven. The living room was massive and could easily fit the coven and then some; it was filled with comfortable chairs and a massive couch that was posed in front of a huge flat screen TV. Everyone had come in and selected their usual spots allowing the pair of siblings to sit on the couch. Jase was tending to Danny's wounds in the corner of the room, he had denied medical attention saying he would be better after a good rest and Jase had fetched the medical kit from the TV stand and began to work quickly to fix up his brother. Mark had taken up post across from her and Taurtis, to get a better look at him she surmised from the way he was looking her brother over, if he was looking for weak points, he wouldn't find any. With them safely back indoors she finally was able to give him a onceover to make sure he was in one piece. Thankfully he looked like he made it there okay and wasn't injured, not that he would be.

Lilith had been in the shower when an alarm went off throughout the house, the guys had been out of the house with the alarm off in moments so she figured everything was okay. While she was in the shower, Taurtis' tattoos that was on her wrist glowed, they also sent a slight shock to her and she knew he was the one that set off the alarm as he came to get her. When her brother was on a mission, he would go through anyone to get what he needed to do done, in this case: get his youngest sister out of a house full of men. She grabbed the shirt she had brought with her and took flight after them, she was worried what her brother would do to Mark once he caught her scent on him. Thankfully she got there before he retaliated too much, she wished she had gotten there before he had gotten ahold of Danny but she was grateful she was able to arrive before there had been a death.

"How did you know where to find me? I haven't really left this house since I landed, still am pretty injured from that."

"Spain." He was grinning and damn if it wasn't good to see his cocky ass again, even if he wasn't making sense.

"Spain? What's that?"

"You landed in northern Spain dumbass; I saw the crater you put in ground on the news while I was in America." His voice filled with distain when he mentioned his whereabouts at the time.

"What's wrong with America? And you know we aren't in Spain, right dipshit?" She laughed at the familiar name calling and bickering she missed. They had only been separated a week but it felt like a lifetime, and where they come from the world knew the triplets didn't do so well away from each other for long.

"I landed in fuckin' Houston, Texas! It's hot as hell there and the women are loose and unattractive; plus, they don't know how to make a good cup of tea," he whined while looking for support. Taurtis's features softened as he looked to Lilith. He looked much younger when he pouted like this. *How badly did they fuck up his tea?* She looked over at Mark and laughed at the look of disbelief on his face, she didn't think he was believing what he was seeing.

Mark looked away from her brother and straight at her, affection was apparent on his face. He made her heart flutter and if not for his brothers' earlier interruption she would have willingly given herself to him. Lilith fought the urge to squirm. Mark shouldn't look at her like that, like she was the only star in the sky. Her clit throbbed under Mark's seductive gaze. Jon stirred from his perch against the wall breaking the sexual tension that was beginning to form in the room.

"Taurtis, how do you know Stephanie?" The question was asked so politely that you could nearly miss the suspicion in his voice. The room went electric as each brother turned and watched Taurtis. His expression had hardened once more. Taurtis looked murderess as Lilith reached out and held his hand. Softening ever so slightly at the contact he turned his gaze to Jon.

"That *canis* slid into my booth at this cafe I was at and tried to manipulate me into wiping out your coven. Not a big fan of a woman who relies on mind manipulation to solve her problems where diplomacy is concerned."

"*Canis?*" The confusion filled poor Danny's hoarse voice.

"Bitch," the pair of siblings said in unison before breaking into wide grins.

"Did that horrible woman actually try to manipulate your brain?" Lilith grabbed Taurtis heads and inspected it as she asked with curious amusement. "I didn't realize you had much left to manipulate."

Taurtis smiled slightly as he ignored her last comment. "Yes, I felt her sending electrical surges into my brain trying to compel me to do what she wanted. I was bored and she had the means to get me on the same continent as you so I humored her and faked being manipulated to get a free ride over here. I was originally just going to bail on her but then this," he lifted his shirt to expose a glowing red tattoo that was on his lower left side of his abs, "I knew you had to be close by so I went in the direction she wanted me to go. If I would have known they were allies, I wouldn't have struck out at them."

"Don't lie to them Taurtis." She indicated the men in the room with a grin on her face, Lilith would have placed a bet on that. "He would have struck out to test you anyway."

"Not going to say that you're right, but anyway, she said you killed everyone she cared about and stole an heirloom." Shrugging his shoulders, he looked around the room and sniffed the air to test the scents.

"That's bullshit, that woman posed as an ally with that bastard of a husband and tried to use us to murder our king. Then when we figured out what she was up to, we killed her husband, mostly because we saw him stealing family treasures from our vault. Then the bitch went and killed our mother and sister! She is lucky she stayed off the radar this long or all of the witch community would have been on her." Mark sounded like he was seething, his hands were shaking in fury and without thinking she crossed the room and hugged his waist, sharing comfort to him in hopes he would calm down.

Never had she gone out of her way to give someone outside her family comfort let alone let a member of her family see it. She was unsure what she was doing, she couldn't watch him grow increasingly upset and the unexpected and unusual urge to comfort him was strong. This man was stealing her slowly away from the life she once was comfortable with and replacing it with new experiences and feelings she had long forgotten about. The overwhelming urge to rub her face on him surprised her, this was hers for now at least. Without caring that his brothers and hers were watching the interaction she rubbed her cheek against his chest leaving behind a magical scent that could be detected by all showing that he was taken. She knew that both Mark and his brothers thought she did it out of comfort but she was shocked that the scent appeared between them, she buried her face in his chest to avoid Taurtis's prying eyes.

"I'm okay, *sufletul meu*, she tried to ruin the coven name and we are still upset about it is all." Mark bent and kissed the top of her head as he circled her waist and brought her to him, she could feel Taurtis's speculative gaze drilling into the back of her head.

Tension began to fill the air as she heard her older brother stand up from the couch. It wouldn't be unlike him to pull her away from something he deemed out of character or weird on her part. By definition everything about the situation was weird for both of them: hugging a strange man, check, Lilith showing interest in anyone, check, Lilith leaving a magical scent on said strange man, double fucking check. It's a wonder he hadn't already taken Mark to the ground and strangled him. Her eyes darted to Jon as he cleared his throat.

"So, Taurtis is it? What is your full name?" Jon diverted her brother's attention long enough for Mark to move her protectively beneath his shoulder. Silence stretched in the room as her brother continued to gaze at Lilith; he looked as if he contemplating ripping Mark off of her himself. He remained silent for so long before looking at her and nodding.

"My name is Taurtis the Impenetrable and, with irony, I am the Guardian of Land, apparently someone thought it was an amusing fit." Her brother never took his eyes off of Mark's hand that was wrapped around her, his scowl was reappearing on his face as he began to pace the room in agitation. His jade eyes had flickers of red appearing in them. "I am the eldest triplet by a few minutes and am Warrior class just as Lilith is, now, for the safety of those around you. Get. Your. Fucking. Hands. Off. My. Sister."

It wasn't all that surprising that Taurtis brought up both of them as warrior class. However, her eyes grew wide at the menace that filled his voice, she knew Taurtis was just trying to look out for her, after all she was his youngest sibling and he had been the one to always watch her back. When he was angry, he always had a problem with seeing things from a logical point of view and it was one of his biggest shortcomings. *Well, that, and he was stubborn as fuck.* Taurtis was used to seeing Daina with a man all over her but it wasn't every day that he would have seen her in a man's embrace, he would have to adjust his view of her when Mark was around but for now, she just had to appease him. She tried to pull away from Mark but his arm was like a steal band holding her in place; she glared up at him and he bent his head and brushed a soft kiss upon her lips before finally releasing her. Mark had to have lost his mind. No one directly taunted Taurtis like that. Lilith jerked her head to face Taurtis's murderous glare.

"He doesn't mean anything by it, brother, he just wants to make sure I don't get injured any more than I have already been. With the way my wings are, I wouldn't be able to fly far out of the area so I am a sitting duck for now and Mark has been taking care of me." She knew it had been a mistake the moment the words escaped her lips. Taurtis had stopped his pacing and focused on what she had just said.

"I'd bet my spear he doesn't mean anything. What the hell happened to your wings?"

Summoning energy, she shifted the air around her drawing out her wings from their hiding spot. It didn't hurt nearly as bad as it did the previous time she had put them away and she was delighted to see her massive midnight black wings broken or not. Secretly, while the men were away, she had taken her wings out and had inspected and rebandaged them so she knew what her brother saw when he looked at her mangled wings, and it wasn't a pretty sight.

With a sharp intake of air, Taurtis approached her to inspect her wings. His fingers were gentle as he stretched them out and brushed over the injuries, he was meticulous as he inspected each wing. Extending them and repositioning them he tested the wings, searching for any missed injuries, she winced at the sharp pain that ran down her wings; his brow was furrowed and the house began to shake.

"It's not as bad as it looks, they are actually a lot better than they were a few days ago. I would give it another week or two before I can take the bandages off and they should be good to go." The house continued to shake even as she hid her wings from view once again. "Calm down, Taurtis, you'll bring the house down."

"Those bastards will pay for what they have done to us but not all of those injuries are from a fall or the whip." Taurtis's eyes fixated once more on Mark, "There are burns and breaks that would match being caught in an explosion. Surely you realized that dearest sister."

Truth be told she hadn't realized it until she was looking them over without the men around, she had chosen to believe that she had simply gotten a majority of her injuries from impact. Some of the breaks were congruent with an explosion not a fall and some of the feathers where singed in places along some of the breaks. Lilith thought nothing of it as it must have been an accident as she was hurtling through the sky at a fast speed unknowingly headed for a collision on a battlefield in Spain. She wouldn't blame a warrior defending his own if an unknown was coming at them from above, she would have done the same thing, still it did bother her when she looked at Mark's guilt-ridden face as he gazed at her. He could break her heart with that look. "Be at peace deliciae as if I will never fault you for protecting your family," the tension began to melt out of him so she added with a grin, "I would have done the same though I must admit I would have finished the job and not taken an unknown home with me. Though I doubt you could have finished me off."

"Would you have rather I had left you there?"

"Hell no. I wouldn't have known what to do."

"You could have found the nearest horse to feed and ride."

"Hell fucking no! She would not have murdered another poor innocent bike." Jase could have been struck he sounded so hurt with just talk of her going near another motorcycle, clearly, he wouldn't forget so easily. She could feel herself flush crimson at the memory as the room erupted into laughter and the men looked almost boyish as they poked fun at her.

She tried to look dignified as she flipped her crimson hair over her shoulder and spun around jutting her chin up, she walked out of the room ignoring the men as they roared with laughter as she heard them explain to Taurtis what had transpired with the motorcycle days before. She was slightly self-conscious as she left the room; she could feel Mark's eyes trained on her ass as she walked out of the living room and headed towards their bedroom.

****

*God look at that ass...*He watched her leave the room her hips swaying in that come-hither way that she always moved. He could watch her walk around in his shirts forever, he didn't however want his brothers to see her in the shirt or how he couldn't help but be led around by his cock with her. The shirt dropped to just above her knees but it was so big around her shoulders that it fell off on one side. She was sexy and adorable; and she had terrified him tonight. Absolutely terrified him, she had been fearless when she dropped into the fray. He had never seen anyone control the wind to the extent she had been controlling it; even air type witches struggled to get the wind to do more than one thing at once and here she is not only having it levitate her at a high speed but had it parting the men, rather accurately, just like the Red Sea. There was still so much more to learn about their kind and he hoped to be able to learn more about them before the king found out about their existence, or before they left once they found Daina.

He still hadn't had a chance to look into her whereabouts but if Jase's information was correct, he would find her in the catacombs under Paris, France but until he knew for sure he wouldn't tell her. There was a lot to think about if he told her: Mark was certain she would run off without him and he didn't want her to be away from him; he would go mad without her; her smoky ash scent was intoxicating and had become a drug to fuel his very being. He couldn't tell her they had possibly found her sister since he hadn't captured her heart yet; he was aware that he was being selfish but he couldn't bring him to tell her until he was sure she would never leave him. Never had he felt so insecure where a woman was concerned, he had many women over his life time too many to count but all of them paled in comparison to Lilith she was meant to be his and he would never let her go far from him.

"Enjoying the view, Mark?"

"Absolutely," returning focus back to Taurtis who had resumed his position crossed legged on the sofa looking content to watch Mark make a fool of himself. "What can we do for you, Taurtis?"

For the first time Taurtis softened visibly without the presence of Lilith; a small smile teased the corners of his lips. "I wanted to thank you for looking after my little sister and for keeping her out of trouble. I also want to know what all is being done to locate Daina. She is practically powerless and extremely vulnerable I would like to find her as soon as possible."

Looking around the room to his brothers who each dipped their head to him; they had each angled themselves to come to his aid if need were to arise and had tried to make it as subtle as possible as to not tip off Lilith. The question he wanted to have the answer too was why they were so concerned for this Daina, surely, she was like them only slightly weaker than the others?

"Our coven has put out an alert to the lesser covens to be on the look-out for her, and you for that matter so we will have to take you off that alert. If anyone finds her they will let one of us know of her location and we can get to her in minutes."

"Why are you so sure she can't handle herself?"

"She isn't a warrior she is too soft. Daina has literally never hurt anyone physically ever." Taurtis looked upset as he sighed loudly and covered his eyes with his arms. "How long does it take to find one female? She would stick out like a sore thumb with her looks."

"Given that there are over seven billion people in the world and of that include succubus then I'd have to say pretty damn hard. Plus, there are sirens, nymphs, and other beautiful creatures out there that we have to sift through." Jase was always one for numbers but he hated having to repeat statistics to people and his annoyance was obvious in the tone of his voice. "We aren't errand boys, you know?"

"Peace, Jase, he didn't mean anything by it he is just worried about his sister. How would you feel if Danny went missing?"

Jase relaxed and let out a long sigh. He rubbed the back of his neck as he watched Taurtis wearily. "Point taken, Jon. I'm going outside if it's okay with you, I need to check the perimeter, make sure there aren't any other surprises."

"Take Danny with you, just in case; and Mark I want you to head to your room and take a shower, you're smelling up the house."

"Of course." There was no arguing with a coven head and if Jon wanted to deal with Taurtis on his own he could have at it. Besides, Mark took a deep breath and inhaled his shirt. He smelled like a hard workout and really needed a shower. He would have better things to do afterward, like trying to romance the big guy's sister, grinning to himself he headed towards the showers as his cock grew harder with every step of the way. *Oh, the things I want to do to that woman...*

****

Jon wasn't one who usually drew attention to himself but with everything going on it was best for him to handle Taurtis; or at least that's what he had first thought before everyone had left the two of them alone. Alone, this man was intimidating. Jon had seen his fair share of battles, but he had never truly looked at death in the face, and make no mistake this man reeked of death. As head of the Fleming coven, he refused to back down to a guest of the house and Jon had to force down the sudden unease and pasted on his most cocky grin, he turned back to Taurtis.

"I won't bite you know." The man had moved his arms away from his face as he watched everything.

"I know I just wanted to be able to walk you to your room without having a parade follow us down the hall."

"No offense, but I think I will sleep outside." Taurtis was already on the move to the backdoor. Clearly, he didn't discuss much of anything other than what he wanted to know; still Jon followed him out the backdoor and came to an abrupt stop.

"Where do you plan on sleeping? It gets cold out here at night and we wouldn't want you to freeze."

Looking over his shoulder the Taurtis rolled his eyes and lifted his hands, "Shut your mouth and watch."

He tried to keep his jaw from popping open as he surveyed the yard. From the ground came giant stones as they began to shape themselves into walls, vines and branches came down from the trees to add a protective layer over the top of the stone structure. Stones moved and rearranged themselves into massive doors and windows; the fullness of the moon made it easy for him to locate Taurtis in the middle of it all with his arms crossed over his chest surveying his handywork. The man was making a small house in his backyard. *He doesn't camp, he is into glamping. Who would have thought that?*

"You could have just saved yourself the trouble and just stayed inside. That doesn't even have plumbing."

"Don't feel comfortable inside those types of houses, plus who wants to hear their sister with a man. To be honest I'm used to far less than this, let Lilith enjoy it for a little longer before we have to leave."

We're street trash. Filth of the streets of our home world, Lilith had said that hadn't she. That means that this was probably one of their first experiences with things like a sofa or a soft bed, it made him want to go inside and hug Lilith. If Mark had it his way, she will be married to him by the end of the week; sadly, if Taurtis' words were anything to go off of, that wouldn't be happening anytime soon. He had promised Mark he would help him court Lilith and he would be damned if he broke that promise because her brother was stubborn, his brothers happiness always came first. Mark had given everything for his coven and it was fine time to give something back.

"What if she doesn't want to leave, would you make her go with you?" Jon was glad he had sent Mark away, if he had heard talk of Lilith leaving him, he would have gone ballistic.

"If she wishes to stay, she would stay, though I highly doubt it." The confidence he was showing was a little unnerving considering the topic.

"She will stay you know."

"Oh? How are you so sure?"

"She will fall in love with him." He could feel the ring of truth in his voice, it was going to happen, she would be one of them.

"Care to make a bet?"

"You're on."

A grin broke on Taurtis's face. Shit what have I agreed too.

****

She watched him slip into the room trying to be stealthy but the smell of his excitement gave him away. Lilith had been waiting for him to come back to the room since she heard the shower turn on across the hall. She had slipped into the matching wine-red bra and panty sets he had looked excited about and awaited him on his bed. The nights that he was away on his mission she had taken over his room, she felt the most at ease in this room and their scents tangled together in this room now; rain and smoke filled the air. Strangely their scents mingled spectacularly, it made her reminisce of her home plane and the bon fires in the courtyards during their never-ending rainy days. She had come to consider this room theirs, even added her clothes to the closet and dresser. Now, as Mark entered the room with a towel wrapped around his waist, she felt like she had come home for the first time.

He was still dripping wet from his shower and steam came off him in waves as he stood in the closed doorway attempting to dry off his hair. His eyes were glued to hers as she watched him towel-dry his disheveled hair, lust was etched into the fine lines of his face as he drank in her form. Water droplets glimmered as they traveled down his chiseled chest and disappeared into the towel that was wrapped around his waist. The towel clung to him emphasizing his strong thighs and powerful legs; when he turned in the moonlight, she could see the bulge that was forming between his thighs. He was hiding a monster under the towel as the thick bulge lengthened. The moonlight highlighted his well-muscled chest and abs making her mouth water with the need to trace him with her tongue. She knew she was looking at him like she was a starved animal by the mischievous glimmer in his lust fill eyes, a cocky crooked grin formed on his lips.

"My eyes are up here, *draga*."

"I'm aware but there are other, more delicious parts to look at as well." She pitched her voice low, sultry even. Bating her eyes at him she flashed him the best come get me face she had ever made, "You do realize where mine are as well right?"

"No idea all I can see are the most beautiful pair of breasts in the world; I was right by the way. You look incredible in red." Mark made his way across the room and let the towel slide from his waist onto the floor revealing his thick monstrous cock as it became fully erect; his cock was thick and intimidating.

Her mouth watered further at the challenge before her as Mark climbed onto the bed; his eyes looked like the turbulent sea as the blue in them flowed like a liquid lust. The mischievous gleam never left his eyes as he paused at the edge of the bed, "If you want it come get it, draga, show me you want it." His voice was husky and sexy as he tilted his head daring her to come to him.

Never in her life had she ever given herself so freely as she did to Mark. Lilith crawled to him, she reached out and stroked his cock gently to get the feel of him, leaning in she captured the pearly drop that began to form on the head of his magnificent cock and she heard him suck in a hard breath. He tasted like sex and sin, the perfect combination of rain and spice as they blended together on her tongue; she wanted more, like a starving cat wanting milk she began to lick and caress his cock. Learning his shape and girth as she did so. Mark let out an encouraging moan as she wrapped her mouth around his length; he stretched her lips as she suckled him drawing more of him into her hot mouth. Flattening her tongue so she could fit more of him, Lilith stroked her tongue along his shaft as she did so. He was almost too big, as his cock cut off air the more she took him in her mouth. She could feel him at the back of her throat as she devoured his masculine girth. Hands fisted her hair as Mark began to move against her mouth, pressing farther than she had expected him to go, tears formed on the corners of her eyes as he fucked her mouth.

"Look at my eyes *draga*...I want to watch you." Lilith opened her eyes and looked up; Mark was beautiful as his lust filled gaze connected with hers. The sure erotic pleasure sent another wave of moister to drench her already soaked panties. "That's it..."

She was burning up from the pleasure, her feminine core was hot and dripping moister and her nipples were aching for his touch as more of him spilled into her mouth. She couldn't help the strangled moan she let out around his cock as he pushed faster and harder into her all too willing lips, rolling and squeezing his balls amped him up further as he pulled from her mouth. The bra rubbed her needy nipples as pleasure shot straight to her clit. Her moans mingled in the air with the sound of his bliss as he stilled. "Fuck..." Gripping her hair Mark threw back his head and let his seed fill Lilith's mouth. Lilith swallowed taking him all into her, she licked the length of his still hard shaft cleaning him as she prepared him for her.

"We aren't done yet *draga*. I want to see you wreathing under me."

Mark's eyes were glued to her mouth when she pulled back and licked them, "Well come get me already Hercules, don't make me fuck myself."

His breath hitched as he rose above her. He looked like a sex god as he flipped her on the bed, he had ripped off her bra and panties before she had realized it. He said nothing as he licked his lips hungrily and buried his face in her feminine sex; he lapped at her like a starving man.

Her moans where like music to his ears, plunging his tongue into her and tasting her unique feminine flavor he reached up and pinched her nipple causing her to spill more of her juices onto his tongue. He nipped and bit at her thighs and clit driving her higher and higher stopping just short of her climax then he began again letting the sensations build as he devoured her like she was his last meal. She was coming to meet him with each thrust of his tongue her mewling noises muffled by her hands as she tried to stifle the sound. The way her eyes had met his when he was fucking her silky mouth had pushed him over the edge and had him losing control of this fast, he wanted to be inside her but he needed to prepare her for his massive size, he didn't want her to be in pain. He continued to fuck her with his tongue and pinch at her nipples as she laced her fingers threw his hair, she gave a slight pull catching his attention. Looking into her face, eyes showing trust and a lust that made his cock jerk, her hair was tossed around his pillow her lips swollen slightly and her nipples were hard and pointed into perfect twin peaks.

"Next time you suggest fucking yourself I'll take you up on it; you would be so hot playing with this perfect little clit." Mark flicked her clit one last time as she let out a whimper.

Mark slid up and captured one of the dusty little peaks in his mouth rolling it with his tongue, with one of his hands Mark inserted a finger into her pulsing vagina. Her hungry sheath strangled his finger as he stretched her to fit another. She was so fucking tight. Lilith's involuntary movements was making her vagina clamp down harder on his fingers as she rode his hand. She was the most beautiful thing he had ever seen. The passion had overtaken them and her skin glistened with sweat. Her skin was flushed a rose pink as she tossed her head back. Mark circled her clit building her higher and higher until she came apart crying out his name. He was nowhere through as he withdrew his fingers and lapped up her sweet cream. Mark licked and suckled her clit. She tasted like heaven to him. Lilith jerked as she rode his face hard. Each shift brought his tongue deeper into her. His cock was throbbing and he was worried he might burst before he was able to enter her. She was his angel. Tempting and sweet as she let out her sirens call of a moan. His cock jerked and ached as he slowly lost control.

"Please do something, I'm burning up." her voice was husky and sexy as she attempted to pull him over her, he gave in and spread her legs wide enough to encompass him as he slowly eased the tip of him inside her smoldering sheath. He almost came as he entered her, her sheath hot and slick, he eased into her slowly as to not hurt her. With each new inch inside her she made a cute little moan which encouraged him further inside her, it wasn't until she began writhing beneath him demanding more did his control finally snap. Mark pulled almost all the way out before slamming home. She felt like heaven her heat all-encompassing his cock as he moved inside her, her nails bit into his back as the pleasure built between them, he could feel her climax build as he took them over the top.

"Hang on just a little longer *draga,* just a little longer."

"I can't..."

He quickened his pace as her vagina convulsed around his cock, her orgasm was strong as she milked his cock. He was kissing and biting the side of her throat moving quickly as his cock grew fuller with his seed. She was squirming to meet him, dragging her nails along his back, she felt like she was made for him. A sharp prick on his throat was the last thing he knew before he pulled back and surged into her one last time a shout leaving his mouth as he emptied everything into her.

It was a few moments before he could pull out of her as she cradled him too her sleepily. She could feel their mixed juices leaking down her thighs. Brushing a kiss to her lips he slipped from the bed and gathered a wet cloth to clean up he reentered the room and he paused at the door. She was naked in his bed half asleep from exhaustion. He couldn't help but grin as he approached the bed and she reached up to touch him. Lilith filled a void in him he didn't know he had, she made him feel warm and happy not a battle-hardened witch that lived for the next mission. She stirred as he began to clean her off, tomorrow he will have a bath ready for her but for now he would do this.

"You are an amazing man, Marcus Monroe."

"Doamne te iubesc. Your sleepy draga, get some sleep we have much to do tomorrow." Chuckling he gathered her into his arms and slide the covers around them. That had been the first time she used his full name and with her accent it was sexy as hell as it rolled off her tongue.

"What does that mean?"

"Don't worry about it now, I can tell you about it later."

He kissed her upturned mouth sweetly not at all like earlier when he was demanding her attention. She needed gentle now as they drifted off to sleep.

8.

Lilith stretched contently in bed as she awoke from a night's rest, or; lack thereof; Mark was much better than she had anticipated and she was still gloriously tender from their love making. She couldn't believe he had cleaned her up afterward, he had looked so focused and so happy. It was an odd feeling being so happy; truth be told she had never felt so happy in her long life, so much anger and bloodshed that had been a big part of who she was, absent. One week and she was forgetting a life of struggles, maybe she could finally let go of this anger that had plagued her for so long. Could she finally settle down and be happy? She heard a rattling sound coming from one side of the room and shelved the thought as she stretched and found the cause of the sound. The rattling had come from Mark who was in the closet getting changed. Currently he was in sweat pants and sneakers; Lilith hadn't realized she had clawed his back but she could see where her nails had dragged down his back. Watching him from behind was mesmerizing; his muscles moved like flowing water. *Oh, I could watch that man's back move all day; he is so yummy to look at.*

A sports bra and a pair of leggings came flying at her from Marks direction, "I can feel you watching; come on, get dressed we are heading out." He was grinning ear to ear, the most boyish grin his happiness was contagious because he had her smiling with him.

Fighting to put on the clothes he had thrown her she noticed he had grabbed a thin looking pair of shoes and was putting them on. *Honestly, I will never get used to humans, why the obsessive need to have clothing for every event get one or two universal pieces and your good to go. I don't think I owned a pair of shoes until Mark bought me some.*

"Where are we going?"

"For a run; I've missed a few days of training and I need to catch up or I will combust." Winking he brought her a box that contained similar shoes to the ones he was wearing. "Come on put on your shoes and let's go."

Laughing she took the box and placed it to the side, Lilith darted to the door and out of the house. She was surprised when she saw that Mark had not only followed her but kept up as he engulfed her in his arms and swung her in a circle. He laughed with her at their childish behavior as it had her yelling, "Never!"

"Come on *draga* you need shoes or you will look like a crazy mountain woman." The smile that lit his face could melt glaciers; his deep blue eyes shone bright with excitement.

"Not to come off as too much of a barbarian but I'll pass on the shoes deliciae they restrict my feet too much. Nothing on the ground will hurt me so I'm good to start running whenever you are." Mark set her back on the ground and began to stretch out. Was he ignoring her? Before she could say anything more, he turned and smirked before he took off into the mountain side. Was that a challenge? *Non hodie he will not be leaving me behind.*

They had been running for hours the sun had fully risen in the sky and the wildlife had woken up to go about their daily tasks; clearly, they were used to Mark's routine and were ignoring them as Lilith and Mark took a short break. They had started their run as the sun peaked over the mountainside and the view only grew more spectacular as the sun rose. Lilith hadn't really realized just how far into the mountains that the Flemming coven house lies until now.

The house was cradled by the vast spread of mountains; from her vantage point she could see the bird atrium as well as the massive brick structure, with its large bay windows and wooden oak doors it looked like the kind of house that would house a lord; not four larger than life witches. The stone structure outside the house was new, Taurtis must have settled in nicely during the night, the smaller structure would have blended in if you hadn't been looking for it. The lush trees where painted into the landscape as birds zoomed through the air. Some were on the ground capturing their food for the day before flying away back to their homes, or to do whatever it was that birds did....it was a good day. The ledge that they stopped at was slightly wet from a storm that had taken place prior so she had to take care not to slip; out of habit she levitated slightly above the ground, maybe an inch or so, her love for the air had always been present but something about this place called to her. The air here was so clean and crisp. It carried the smell of pine and oak along with other vegetation. It wasn't at all polluted and putrid like the air often was back home. With the blue sky and the warm rays of sun Lilith felt at total peace.

"*Draga*, if you float too far away, I'll lose you."

"You act like I wasn't winning that race to begin with." Lilith let her feet touch the ground as a mischievous thought entered her mind. Getting closer to Mark she let her grin spread wide; he looked smugly amused by something, *let's see how long he will be smiling after this....*

"Bullshit, I hit that bank three miles ago before you did and I don't recall seeing you when I reached the river back there." Mark clearly believed he was in the right and he was she had gotten distracted watching the river but unfortunately for him he would not win this war.

Lilith pitched her voice in a childlike sing song pattern as she sung, "Tag....Your...IT!!!!" Pushing with all her might she managed to knock Mark into a pool of mud and sludge before laughing and running in the direction of Taurtis's make-shift hut satisfaction filling her. Mark's face when he hit the mud was priceless; he had sat in a stun stupor just looking at her as she had run away. Faintly she could hear him stomping through the brush behind her unaware of where she was heading. She ran full speed into the clearing and right into her brother who was hurling boulders it looked like.

Taurtis took in her appearance and grinned, "What's got you so sweaty in these woods Lil? Getting chased by a ghost or something?"

"Shut the fuck up you moron, if you must know I wanted to bring someone to spar with you."

"Who you calling a moron dip shit," Taurtis jerked his head to the entrance of the clearing as Mark walked into it covered from head to toe in mud and grime. Leaves and twigs matted his blonde hair as the mud dripped off of him; he looks like a swamp monster. Lilith choked on the laughter that was bubbling up in her throat.

"What happened to you?"Taurtis looked beyond amused and pleased with Mark's appearance; his grin was blinding and the sound of his booming laughs filled the clearing. Mark on the other hand looked less than pleased at Taurtis's reaction and was flinging mud in her brothers' direction.

"Ask your sister...She seems to love to play with mud"

"Is this true Lil? I didn't realize you played with mud" Sarcasm and innocence could be heard in his voice; it was a little too innocent though and for the first time in a long time Taurtis looked relaxed and playful. It had been a while since they were able to fully relax and be themselves and that Taurtis felt relaxed around Mark made her overjoyed.

"Who? Me? I would never get my hands dirty; did you forget who I am Tart?"

Mark looked on in confusion at the siblings as the pair exchanged playful banter, "What do you mean "who you are"?"

"She is a princess...didn't you know? She doesn't do mud that's Daina she just loves the stuff." The clearing erupted into laughter; Lilith was double over laughing. Daina in the dirt, never going to willingly happen. Taurtis turned slightly to her and winked. Just like that the ground swallowed her up and a familiar feeling swept over her as Lilith was pushed through the ground.

****

CRASH!!!

She was furious! How dare a man defy her will? That pompous fool was supposed to destroy the Flemming coven, wipe them clear off the map; but no. He joins them...and for what...a fuckin WHORE!!!!

Stephanie had watched from outside the barrier as Taurtis made his way through the thick brush that surrounded the Flemming territory, she had watched as he beat Daniel Monroe to a bloody pulp and laughed with glee as the rest of the coven had shown up. Stephanie had been overjoyed when the attacks that where being thrown were ineffective. Their time had come and then out of nowhere a bitch comes flying from the sky and hugged her mindless meat puppet. How did she break my spell? The whore. Getting close with all of those men and then stealing one more. What was she even wearing? Just a t-shirt?

Pacing around the circular cottage she had rented for a time Stephanie gnawed on her fingertip as she looked over what had gone wrong. The cottage was located away from the enemy coven lands and closer to a stream giving it and easy escape route and easy access route for her allies to find her. Her familiar was lounging on a chair lazily watching her pace; the small wild cat never was one to get even a claw dirty unless she had too. She had contacted Gregory days ago letting him know her whereabouts and the plan to take out the Flemmings. With them out of the way it would leave a massive territory needing to be claimed and that is what they were planning to do.

It was a small worry that Gregory hadn't reached out to her after she had made several attempts to contact him. What can you do? All men are assholes. Gregory was probably fucking some random bitch; the man had a bottomless appetite when it came to his grotesque sex life. *Whoever willingly got into bed with him was crazy.* She had taken a small moment to stop pacing as she hurried to her phone that had begun ringing out Gregory's ringtone, Highway to Hell. Hissing into the phone as she stroked her small bob cats head hoping it would calm her down, "Where the hell are you Gregory?"

"Watching a little mouse run through the sewers, I take it your plan didn't work?"

The bastard dare ignores her messages and seemed rather smug about it as well. *The fucker!!! Wait...a mouse? He ignored her for a mouse?* "What the hell are you talking about?"

"You aren't as good at payback as you think my dear. It's rare when one of your little plans actually work and as for the mouse, I'm watching the most peculiar woman run around in haunted tunnels."

"A woman? Well, that's rare, what's so peculiar about a woman?" Gregory wasn't interested in much of anything and she couldn't help but feel envious over his attention being drawn away from her. Still, it was curious that a normal woman would ketch the eye of a powerful mutt lord like Gregory.

"She has scales on her arms that shine like little rainbows and her scent doesn't match anything from this world. Also, she has the most unique eyes I have ever seen. They are a bright ja...."

"Jade green? Does she have long brown hair and multi colored tattoos?"

"I believe I saw something that resembled tattoos on her but I can't be sure if I did, she was moving in the dark a little too quickly. Why do you want her for something as well?"

The excitement was back if this was the female that the youngest Flemming boy was looking for her plan hadn't failed yet. There was still a chance to get back at that blasted coven and to steal their territory, all she needed was that damn woman. Smiling to herself as she struggled to rein in her joy, "Where are you we have much to discuss?"

Gregory chuckled from the other end of the line before hanging up he added, "France and before you say it, I will keep a close eye on the little mouse."

Hanging up the phone Stephanie turned and looked at her bob cat, who was standing up and stretching lazily, "Let's pack our bags Lenna we are going to France."

****

Coming out of the earth was not usually all that bad, so why was Lilith's stomach turning as she entered the kitchen ready to vomit. Taurtis had practiced that maneuver on them often enough that it had become a very pleasant feeling as the ground beneath one's feet would open up and be swallowed by dirt as it would cloak you in a protective shell that felt a lot like a weighted blanket. Once fully enclosed the ground would pull you safely and quickly to a different location and spit you out gently allowing the person to be able to join a battle or escape from one safely.

Sniffing the air as she entered the kitchen Lilith caught a whiff of a salty acidic scent that smelled delicious. She rounded the corner to find Danny sitting at the table eating a strange green food. Danny lifted his hand in greeting as he continued to munch on the food and read his magazine. "Eros, what is that?"

"What's what?"

"That thing in your hand."

Looking up from his magazine he flipped the book over exposing the contents and it wasn't all that shocking to find it full of nude models. Danny wiggled his eyebrows at one of the more attractive blonde women on the page, "This is Maggie Summers she is from the States. Gorgeous right?"

"She is okay I suppose but that's not what I asked you, what is that green thing you are eating?"

"Just okay? You need glasses Lil," Danny sure was great at adding a dramatic flair as he pinched the bridge of his nose and sighed heavily. She couldn't help but laugh as he peered over at her to make sure he still had her attention before dramatically waiving the pickle in the air. "It's a pickle...wanna bite?"

Lilith took the food from Danny's outstretched hand. It smelled very vinegary as she slowly took it to her mouth, biting down on the pickle the salty taste assaulted her taste buds. As she slowly chewed the food a thought came to her, "Eros, do you speak Romanian like Mark?"

"Lil, I am Romanian...did he say something weird?" Concern and amusement entered his tone as Danny's eyes shown bright with youthful amusement.

"He did last night after we...ah...you know..." Lilith could feel her entire body flush as the image of Mark's naked flesh and memory of how hot he was last night as he took her. She didn't realize she had broadcasted their love making to Danny before it was too late and he was looking at her with pride and slight embarrassment at what he had just seen. Her flush deepened and Lilith wouldn't have been surprised if her skin was the same crimson of her hair. *Maybe I should go back to Taurtis and ask him for a nice hole to go die in...* "Shit, I'm sorry I didn't mean to show you that."

Danny cleared his throat and grinned his cute childlike grin, "Oh I wish I could say that's the first time I saw something like that from one of my brothers. Jon used to parade his one night stands around the house whenever he felt like it, believe me there were a lot of them, Jase had to put a stop to it because that's how you bring trouble to the coven house. Never seen it from Mark though if it makes you feel any better." Danny sounded confident but color too began to fill his cheeks. "He better be treating you with respect or I will fuck him up on your behalf angel. "

Smiling Lilith began to laugh, the two of them had become fast friends and Danny was easy to talk too. "I'm glad we are friends Eros." Crossing the distance, she leaned down and hugged his neck as Danny sat shocked in his chair. He was surprisingly solid as he reached up and awkwardly hugged her back, "Believe it or not I deeply enjoy your company and am glad that out of all the places I could have landed, I landed near your family. Mark is absolutely perfect and you are my very first friend outside my siblings. I trust you with my life and more importantly the lives of my family..."

"Hey, what's gotten into you Lil? You're not acting like yourself. I think of you as a friend as well, closer even I feel like you are family, so tell me what's eating you." The concern in his voice made her realize how sentimental she was sounding; he was right she did sound sappy. *What the hell was with her today? It was just very good sex...sex with an amazing man... one that she may be falling for...* Shaking her head to clear it Lilith leaned into Danny's ear and whispered, "I wish your brother was." Before laughing at the dumbfounded look on the man's face.

"Psshh, girl keep it in your pants." Danny erupted into laughter, "So, what did Mark say that he isn't translating for you maybe I could help?"

"Daemne ti iubec? No that doesn't sound right." Lilith knew she was butchering the language as she tried a few more times with the words. She knew she was getting nowhere with it.

Amused Danny laughed. "What was that angel? Kill me not my language."

"Oh, shut up Eros..."

"Don't be mad."

"Doamne te iubesc." Danny stopped laughing as Lilith beamed. She was positive that was what Mark had said. They had such a hard language to pronounce, but it was all in rolling the syllables.

From behind she heard a swift intake of breath as she turned and found Mark, still covered in mud, standing like a statue in the doorway.

****

His face frozen in shock and slight anger as he took in the scene before him. He had been outside chasing down Lilith when they had run into

Taurtis. The man was stubborn as hell and had refused to tell him where he had sent Mark's woman, Taurtis said he would tell him if he sparred with him. Worst decision he had made to date. Taurtis kicked his ass; if they had kept sparring, they would have leveled the mountainside with their bombs and rock slides. After all the effort it took for him to find out where she went, he walks into his own house to find his little brother and the women he was falling in love with hugging over an open playboy magazine whilst Lilith is proclaiming her love for Danny. Damn, right he was confused and angry. *Maybe I heard wrong? Nope Danny looks too guilty...he was a good brother it's too bad I'll have to kill him.*

Danny had jumped up and away from Lilith throwing his hands up in surrender. The only sound that could be heard in the kitchen was the sound of the wooden chair falling to the floor from were Danny had jumped up too fast. A few moments stretched out as Danny began to back slowly towards the window; too bad it was open and Akem was waiting on the other side. Lilith moved slowly between the brothers effectively planting herself in front of Danny in an effort to shield him from a building wrath. Mark spoke slowly and softly in an effort to control his emotions, "What did I miss guys?"

"It's not what you think she was just wanting a translator for something you said to her." The look on his face was a mix of happiness and fear as he understood what she wanted him to translate. "I hadn't told her the meaning when you walked in; I swear I'm innocent."

Mark had managed to take one step in Danny's direction before his little warrior had blocked his path. In her eyes for the briefest of moments a red glow flashed, her eyes had done it once before in the shop in town when she took down the armed man. Like before it had happened so fast, he normally wouldn't have noticed the warning it gave as she jutted her chin up in defiance. His little warrior was beyond adorable as she attempted to block his path; and there was a nagging feeling in the back of his head that if she wanted to, she could very well do so. Tilting his head, Mark inched his finger summoning Lilith forward, "You are mine *draga*. Do not speak those words to anyone but me."

95

Lilith looked puzzled as she inched forward, she stopped inches away from him and with a pouty face she countered, "How am I to know what that means if you do not tell me? Mark, I hate to be the one to tell you this but I belong to no one. I am free to make my own rules."

"No, that is where you are wrong. In this world you make your own rules and you get hurt or worse you die."

"I'd like to see someone...."

"I wasn't done," Mark cut in and gave a mischievous grin. Leaning down he claimed Lilith's mouth roughly; almost immediately Lilith's hunger leapt to the surface joining his burning need. Wrapping his arms around her waist and jerking her closer to him as he devoured her lips; she tasted like passion, hot, burning passion. The kind that could burn down cities leaving nothing but ash. Mark was only slightly aware that Danny had retreated out of the room to either hide or give them privacy; most likely both.

Mark licked and sucked Lilith's plump bottom lip tasting the lust and desire as his one of his hands roamed under her shirt to cup her perky breast; he kneaded her firm heart shaped ass earning an eager moan form Lilith. She parted her mouth and Mark swept inside, their tongues twined and danced, Mark wedged his knee between her thighs to separate them as his hand slid down to her hot little mound. Plunging a finger into her slick pussy he began to pump in and out building her need higher. Her moans increased as she began to grind on his finger; Mark's dick was already hard he hadn't thought it was possible to get harder but the more Lilith moaned the harder he seemed to get as his shaft pulsed with an eager desire to penetrate her feminine core. Lilith reached down and found the seam of his sweat pants; sliding her hand inside she circled his cock and began to pump his cock in a vigorous rhythm, her hands felt like heaven as she pumped in time with him. Lilith seemed to know what he wanted as she slowly rolled his balls and stroked his cock building him closer and closer to the edge. He could feel the need to cum build and was worried he may climax before her.

Lilith tossed her head back and moaned exposing her neck to him; a reckless power surged through him as he slowly licked the hallow of her neck. Mark nipped and suckled as Lilith shifted to cradle his head to her throat. The power grew until he could no longer ignore it; breathing the words softly Mark sighed, "You are mine..." The power flowed from him onto Lilith as she clamped down on him and gave into her relies, a strangled moan left her as she shook from the strength of her orgasm.

They were breathing heavy as Mark looked into Lilith's eyes; she may not be aware of it but they shone bright with affection and he hoped one day she would look at him with something more. At the moment though his woman was covered in the same mud that must have come off him; serves her right but dammit all if she didn't look more beautiful. Laughing he started to brush the mud off of her. "Look who is covered in the mud now."

"Shut up Hercules you still are the one who sat in it," chuckling to herself she spun and she headed to his room. Mark's eyes focused on the way her hips swayed in to each side like a seductive dance. Lilith tossed her head to the side and laughed over her shoulder, "Stop staring at my ass and come take a shower with me Mark."

*Was that? Shit it had to be...*we were burning so hot I should not be surprised to see it. There on the hollow of her throat was the beginnings of a claiming tattoo. The small marking was a deep crimson and the intricate knots formed his family crest; once it is fully formed and the pair is brought before the king, they would be a married pair in the eyes of his people. Maybe she wouldn't notice right away. Mark followed Lilith with an anxious heart as he knew he would have to tell her about his culture and the story of the mark.

****

*Damn he looks like a god...*Mark had his back to her as he rinsed his hair of mud; the man had the witch warrior look down. With his hands running the mud out of his hair water ran down his muscular back; his muscles flowed like liquid grace with every move his hands made. Lilith bit her lower lip as she remembered where his hands just where; she had thought his cock was good but damn his hands were fantastic also. Her eyes hungrily took in Mark's appearance as he continued to was off the mud; Lilith's eyes roamed lower to his rounded firm butt and before she could stop herself, she found herself wrapping her arms around his waist and reaching for his still aching cock. Mark started but relaxed into her with a sigh as she began massaging his throbbing penis, her mouth watered and Lilith really wanted to taste him again.

"*Draga*, what are you doing?" Mark's voice was huskier than usual and held a note of raw masculine need.

"Hmm," she released a seductive purr, "Doing what? This?" While squeezing and rubbing his cock she lowered her right hand to fondle and roll his balls. Mark stiffened as he made a sound of pure pleasure; he was getting close to climaxing. He hadn't reached climax when they were playing in the kitchen. Mark groaned as he turned to face Lilith in the shower, steaming water pelting his back, her feminine channel grew hot and slick as she gazed upon Mark's lust stamped face.

Mark looked positively devious as he licked his lips and gripped Lilith's shoulders, "Drop *draga*. I have a job for you."

Pushing her shoulders urgently, Lilith went to her knees, eyes leveled with the thick broad head of his engorged cock. She gripped his base and licked her way up to his tip; repeating the action over and over again until she saw the white pearly drops of precum form at the crest of his cock. Lilith pulled back and blew cold air along the tip making Mark shudder in delight. Triumph filled her as she took his massive erection in her mouth; he stretched her lips as she suckled and rolled her tongue around his length. Hands became fastened in her hair as Mark grabbed her head and rammed himself in her mouth. Tears formed in her eyes and he reached the back of her throat; Lilith flattened her tongue to accommodate his size as she continued to suckle and pleasure Mark. "Damn, I'm sorry *draga* I can't hold back...your mouth is heaven..." He sounded breathless as he began to pump into her mouth, finding his rhythm Mark let out a breathy sigh, "*Sufletul meu*, don't let me be the only one being pleasured."

Greedily, Lilith suckled harder as lewd noises left her stretched lips, running her hand down her flat stomach seductively she reached for her soaked mound. Lilith dipped her fingers inside her channel and swirled, tears filled her eyes as he picked up a brutal pace. She closed her eyes as her fingers pumped in time with his thrusts. Never had she experienced pure sexual ecstasy like this until she had been with Mark; he had her pinching and rolling her clitorises, she was drenched and hot with need. She suckled harder as he thrusted roughly, almost painfully, into her open mouth; Mark was groaning as he grew even more desperate for her to pleasure him. Lilith could feel the need release grow and grow in both of them until she flicked her clit and erupted; Mark gripped her hair, shouting out his release he expelled his scorching hot seed down in her throat. Lilith swallowed him up readily as she continued to circle her clit.

"Shit woman you get me fired up..." Mark lessened his grip on her hair allowing her to pull back and lick his length to clean he is seed off. He sighed as he stroked her hair, Mark's hands felt fantastic as the massaged her scalp. The man had ways of making her relax around him; almost as if he was made for her. Really girl?!? Made for you?!? A soulmate is a thing of myth and if there was such a thing, he would have come for you sooner...Lilith had zoned out for only a second when she was suddenly lifted and carried out of the now turned off shower. When the hell did he turn that off?

"*Draga*, we are nowhere near done so I hope you got enough sleep last night." Mark's voice was still husky as he whispered those words and carried her to the bedroom.

"Bring it lover," leaning upwards Lilith bit and tugged Mark's lower lip.

"Oh, it's on now, get ready for a long day." Laughing he tossed her on the bed and mounted her.

****

99

Mark stretched his muscles as he woke up. Lilith had worn him out after four more rounds of steaming sex he was finding it hard to believe that he had completely forgotten all his responsibilities to roll around in bed with a beautiful woman. Speaking of the lady in question, Lilith had curled herself against his side with her head on his naked chest. Her breathing was even and relaxed as he ran his hand gently down her small pixie like face. Her arm was stretched around his middle as she cuddled into him holding him close; he was one lucky man. Lilith's hair, he noticed, was all over the place as he picked a piece out of the crease in his mouth with his free hand. This was peaceful, his eyes were drawn to Lilith as he heard a sigh escape, Mark continued to rub her cheek as she slowly began to wake.

****

What's going on? Lilith was sitting in a field with both Taurtis and Daina; the field was massive and there was a slight breeze bringing in the familiar scents of her family. The three of them were sitting around a small table enjoying herbal tea, it was peaceful. Daina was talking in her very soft voice asking some odd question but Lilith's attention was pulled elsewhere searching for something, someone.

"Lil? Are you listening to me?" Daina sounded concerned brining her attention back to the table. Daina looked to be herself, no injuries to be seen. She was always concerned about her looks with her long beautiful brunette hair, and her tall curvaceous figure. Daina had the kind of body any man would kill for; she was model type material but didn't have a strong enough will to do it. It was a relief to see her older sister in front of her whole and healthy.

"Of course, I am listening to you." Taurtis snorted into his tea earning a slap from both sisters as they looked at each other and laughed. It was like old times, well the more peaceful times. A gentle breeze filled the space tasseling her hair and carrying a faint scent of rain. Wait, rain? A strange feeling filled her as she tried to focus. The sky didn't look like it would rain. It was a clear blue. Daina sighed loudly reclaiming Lilith's attention.

"What were you saying Daina I'm sorry I had zoned out. I feel like I have forgotten something." Lilith turned slightly to take in the beautiful field as Daina began to speak again. Her voice turned into background noise as Lilith took in the scenery, it had always been a bad habit of hers. It looked to be around noon at the latest; they were sitting on a hill that had long grassy fields and flowers of all kinds scattered around. The flowers and tall grass stretched out as far as she could see; shadows flickered around the skies as birds flew about. Breathing in she could smell a pond nearby and the smell of winter frost, which was odd since it had to be spring or summer. Lilith sipped her tea and closed her eyes as she tried to pinpoint the scent and another odd scent caught her nose; there in the breeze very slight was an ever-changing scent, it was as if it wouldn't decide, the two scents were blending together as if they were next to each other moving through the fields of flowers and grass.

Taurtis grinned and pointed with his cup, "Incoming Lil. It looks like your husband let the little monsters catch critters again." Husband?

"What are you...." Confused Lilith turned around to see what Taurtis meant, she had no husband and what little monsters. The breeze carried those odd scents to her nose accompanied by the smell of spice and rain. Husband? Was he talking about Mark?

They came into her view moments after the scents reached her nose. Two little boys came running up the hill towards her each holding a very large toad; the sight had a large grin form on her face as the boys drew nearer. One of the boys had short spiked out strawberry blond hair, he had the same jaw as her and there was no denying with the red in his hair that he was hers. He had Mark's smile though and the same deep blue eyes. The boy tried to hold up his toad but it jumped out of his hands causing him to run after it. Mark caught up to the boy as he ran back down the hill after the toad leaving the other boy with her.

This boy looked just like her. He had longer hair for a boy, defiantly shaggy, but it was the same blooden red that her locks had. His eyes where angled like a cat with the same jade green that she possessed. He was lanky and had an energetic boyish grin as he held up his toad for inspection. The boy looked to be seven or eight, just like the other boy, but that meant nothing for a Custos child. He could be a few months old for all she knew; Custos children aged abnormally fast and could be fully grown within a few years. "Look Mom! I caught it faster this time."

Smiling to the boy Lilith looked up to see Mark carrying the other boy on his shoulders, "Did you? Well, that must be a new record, did you help your brother?"

"I didn't need help mom...I froze it so I could catch it..." He clutched the same poor toad in his hands, this time the legs were frozen so it couldn't get away. The boy had zoned out as he stared at the sky at Akand as he flew by. Ah, looks like the boy had the same habit for zoning out she did. That is unfortunate for him it'll get him into trouble.

Mark looked as handsome as always with his cocky grin. His hair was a little longer and he was covered in dust. His white shirt clung to his broad chest; his arms lifted to the boy as he tossed him in the air catching him. The boy squealed with laughter alongside Mark, "Looks like your uncle Jase needs to teach you not to let your prey thaw out before you reach your destination Jordie."

"Don't call me that papa, that's not my name..."

"Momma look at mine!" squealed the other boy. He was holding up his toad with a huge mischievous grin. He looked so much like her it was uncanny. "It's bigger than the last one!"

A sense of pride swelled up inside her as she made a show of inspecting the toad that was in the boys outstretched arms. "Yes, sweetheart it looks like you have a new record to beat next time."

This was nice. She had her family and everyone was happy. The boy had run back to show his brother the toad. Nothing in this moment could make her happier.

Lilith's happy thoughts fell short when the wind changed; the hair on the back of her neck prickled and rose as the wind sent signs of warning to her. Jerking around she saw Taurtis clutching Daina, now on the ground, the two weren't moving and looked like still statues as she rushed over leaving the dream family behind. As she approached Lilith saw blood running from Daina's haunting eyes as they stared back at her. Healthy moments ago, her sister now looked like skin and bone. Her face was covered in filth and her once flawless skin was marred with cuts and bruises; Daina looked like she had been through a great battle. Almost as if the earth mourned clouds opened up and rain began to pour, just like the blood that Daina cried. "Daina! What happened to you?"

"You have beautiful children Lil, I told you that you would make a wonderful mother someday." Daina smiled a sad smile as the words escaped her mutilated lips, the words where barely audible. "It's too bad you know...you traded me for them...did you stop loving me sister? Was I too weak to keep up with the two of you?"

"What are you talking about? We love you; don't you know that? Taurtis and I will always love you and we will never stop looking for you." Panic rose like crashing waves inside her as she franticly tried to reassure her sister. Surely this was a dream for her Daina would always know that she would stop at nothing to find her. Her Daina would have known that they loved her. While she was running around having new experiences was Daina learning new things as well. Her Daina. Their sweet sister who wouldn't hurt anyone? Would she soon suffer? Is she suffering now?

"If that is true, uni carissime, then you shouldn't trust your mate for he is hiding something from you..." Daina's words faded out as her eyes turned dull and she moved no more. She was so injured but she still called Lilith her dearest one; tears welled up and spilled over her cheeks as Taurtis and Lilith mourned the loss of their sweet sister....

Lilith awake with tears running down her face. She smelled the scent of rain and spice as the scent surrounded her. Lilith found herself in Mark's strong embrace with him stroking her hair; burring her head into his naked chest Lilith tried to wipe the feel of dread away. Daina's words echoed threw her head over and over again; Was Mark hiding something from her? Something that could help find her sister? He wouldn't hide something from her...would he? Determination and resolve filled her as she made the decision to stop letting her broken wings be a handicap in finding Daina. She would find her and soon.

"Good morning *draga*, what's wrong? Did you not sleep well?" Mark's husky voice sounded damn sexy first thing in the morning and brought a slight smile on her lips. They had turned his bedroom into a love nest for their love making very quickly. He was becoming her world and it scared her just a bit, but made her happier than a fairy in a field of flowers. Still the feeling of dread was there marring the happy moment.

"I slept well; I had a good dream for the most part..." Her words cut off as the memory of Daina's bloodened face emerged in her head.

Worry gleamed in his eyes, "Happy dreams shouldn't make you cry like that *draga*. What happened that made you upset?"

A sudden lurch in her stomach had Lilith wiggling free of Mark's embrace and rushing to the bathroom as bile rose up in her throat. Lilith ignored Mark's concerned face as he hurried behind her; before she could tell him to leave Lilith clamped a hand over her mouth and made her way to the toilet where she spent the next few moments emptying the remaining contents of her stomach while Mark held her hair back.

"Is everything okay? Did I push you too hard last night?" His concern soothed her worries that he may have been hiding something from her, dreams were just that; dreams.

"You could've pushed me harder to be honest." Lilith looked over her shoulder to see his piercing blue eyes staring back at her full of concern, "I'm telling you the truth, I'm okay. I just had a vivid dream was all; it could also be the pure air around here."

"Something bad going to happen?"

"No, it was only a dream. It started off good I think, can't really remember much of the beginning, but the end wasn't so great. It turned my stomach is all." Slowly she stood and caressed his cheek, "Thank you for worrying about me Hercules."

"Hmm...I will always worry about you." As he purred the words in her ear, her sex clenched and began to pool in between her legs. A cocky grin tugged at his lips. The man knew exactly what he was doing. "How about I bend you over and let you watch me make love to you in the mirror?"

Turning slightly Lilith noticed a strange marking the hallow of her neck that wasn't there the last time she had seen it. The mark looked familiar but she couldn't place it.

Suddenly, the bedroom door flew open causing both of them to jerk in its direction, Jon entered the room with searching eyes. He was taking in the crumpled sheets and blackened windows; the smell of sex was still tangent in the air as Lilith watched him sniff the air slightly. Jon's head turned in their direction and he froze mid-step into the room. Lilith had all but forgotten that they were both naked and her face warmed, wishing she had thought to bring a bed sheet with her but when the need to vomit calls one would best go running. Jon's eyes fixated on her throat as a wide cocky smile lit his face. Mark, a little late on his que, stepped in front of her blocking her from Jon's sight. "What can I do for you brother?"

"Congrats bro! I didn't think to see that mark so soon but..."

"What is this symbol, Jon? Do you know it?" She began to peer around Mark before caught her up behind him. Jon's amused laughter filled the room.

"He didn't tell you?"

"Tell me what?"

"Oops....well you see..." Rubbing the back of his neck Jon glanced to Mark.

Mark spun around and clapped his hands on her shoulders, "Before he ruins it let me. That symbol is the crest of my coven, it means that you can be one of us. It's like a marriage mark but only when it is completed." The words rushed out of him in a hurry as he surveyed her face for something. Rejection maybe?

Confusion and flattery consumed her as Lilith reached up to touch the small symbol, *he wants to marry me?* Mark had given no indication that he was even thinking it; sure, she was dense sometimes but she hadn't thought she was this dense. Remembering how happy she was in the dream she got the feeling he was a part of it. It had made her happy and that warmed her inside. She could have that...she needed to find Daina but then when everything was done; she could have it? Maybe he didn't mean to leave the mark. "You wish to marry me?" Even to her she sounded perplexed.

"Well no... yes dammit." Mark balled up his fist and rubbed the back of his head as he struggled to get out what he was saying. It was adorable the way he was struggling to decide what he was going to say but at the same time confusing. Jon's booming laugh erupted in the room as he watched Mark. "Shut the fuck up Jon."

"Or what you will blow me up? Good luck it didn't work the last time you tried; when are you going to cover up. You're shamelessly showing your ass and I'd much rather see hers to be honest." Jon laughed as he threw a blanket over the pair.

"Wasn't expecting any company."

"You should always expect company; or did you forget your training?" The room grew serious as Jon's features turned to stone, "Where is your phone Mark?"

"Shit, I forgot to charge it what's going on?" Within seconds Mark was in motion. He draped the blanket around her making sure Lilith was fully shielded from Jon's gaze; as he walked away Mark caressed her cheek and headed to the closet. From the outside she could hear his getting dressed and the clicking of metal as he assembled his weapons.

Looks like the we are losing marriage conversation. I will have to bring it up later after I speak with Taurtis.

The king is sending us to Rila. There has been rumors of mutts gathering in that area and we have been told to survey the area by air and confirm the rumors or put them to rest."

"And if the rumors are true?"

"Eliminate the problem."

"Understood."

Mark walked out of the closet clad in black. He looked delicious. He wore his favorite biker boots with black jeans that hugged his firm ass; the shirt was a black form fitting shirt that clung to his thick muscles, as he was pulling on his leather jacket a silver glint caught her eye. At his waist sat a small string of daggers, by the way they looked they had been used many times and screamed death. "Where the hell is Rila by the way?"

Jon snorted, "It's in Magyouitsa, Bulgaria. The king thought it best to send hawks to check it out."

"Fucking Bulgaria? I thought he had banned Danny from going there again after what happened last time."

"Times change."

At the very sight of him Lilith grew hot with need, this man could be both a fierce lover and even fiercer partner. Without a second thought Lilith summoned energy and focused it on her forearm, elongating her nails slightly Lilith drew a line down her arm where she was focusing energy. The familiar slice into her flesh accompanied by the pull of magic had her smiling as she reached into the already healing cut and pulled out a large jaded studded dagger; by the time the dagger was out the wound was sealed with no evidence of a slice. The dagger was eight inches of black steel, it was cold to the touch and sharper than most blades she had seen, it was light weight and easy to wield. This dagger was special, it could not only cut through metal but it could also cut into a person's truth. Lilith looked back to Mark with the dagger outstretched to him only to find both brothers looking at her with amazement.

"*Draga*? How the hell did you do that?" Mark's jaw was slacked open and he had a boyish twinkle in his eye, Lilith could see the curiosity flowing from him.

"Do what?" Giggling Lilith walked past Jon and placed the dagger in Mark's hands, "This is for you, I have a feeling you will need it, but I want it back. That thing is one of a kind and I don't want to have to make another one."

"It's beautiful, but what do you mean I might need it? I have plenty of knives on me," Jon had stepped beside Mark and began to inspect the blade as well.

Jon, she noticed was more meticulous with his inspection, pulling the blade out of the sheath and testing the weight of the blade. He glanced up at her briefly before he placed the blade on his palms and sent sparks throughout the metal. Sparks flew but the knife remained intact, was he seriously testing to see if it would break under high stress? Her knife? Please... The sparks died and Jon hooked the knife on his belt and looked up at her. "I'll barrow the knife and I promise to give it back, in exchange I will let you keep this." Jon held out a gold card, it looked like the one that Mark had used in town, reaching out Lilith took the card from Jon and turned it over in her hands inspecting it. "Use that card to get food or clothes or whatever it is you would like. It is connected to our family account and most people will give you anything you need if you just hold it up."

"Your rich?"

"Loaded sweetheart," Jon flashed his cocky grin as he pecked the top of her head and headed for the door. "Mark hurry up and tell her you want to marry her so we can go; it's best not to keep this mission waiting I have a bad feeling about this one. Be safe sora mai mica."

"Shut up dumbass," Mark's ears were red and blush crept up his neck as he rubbed the back of his head and looked at her with those piercing blue eyes. "If the mark completes itself that just means you accept me and we will become one in the ways of my people. If it doesn't complete itself, I understand, but just know I will stop at nothing to win you to my side. You are mine Lilith and in time I hope you see me in the same light." Leaning down Mark took possession of her mouth; the kiss was rough and demanding as he claimed her. As quickly as the kiss began it ended; "For luck..." Mark had spoken so softly it was barely audible but his eyes spoke volumes.

He loved her. She could see it clear as day; Lilith began to fill uneasy a Custos mated for life. She hadn't known him long enough to really know for certain if she loved him enough. Her uneasiness grew as she remembered the words Daina spoke in her dreams; her sister was never wrong not even in sleep and if the dream was correct, she needed to hold onto her heart or lose her sister forever.

"Be safe out there Hercules!" Lilith called after him as he turned to leave. Mark glanced over his shoulder and saluted her before he joined his brothers; she was alone well almost alone Taurtis was around here somewhere. Maybe he will know what to do...he had gone through something like this before. Lilith's stomach gargled and rolled again. Her hand flew up to her mouth; *but first back to the toilet, what did I eat?*

******

The air felt crisp as they soared threw the air on their familiars. It had been a while since Mark had been sent on a scouting mission and even longer since the last time he rode on Akand. A familiar was an amazing creature, they grow to soot the needs of the witch and in his hawks' case that meant literally as Akand carried him through the sky. Mark loved his bird, Akand was big to begin with but grown to the size he would need to be in order to carry Mark he was terrifying. The hawk's wings were long and powerful, he was a mahogany brown with silver flecks dusted along the tips of the wings. Akand's talons were the same size of Mark's palm and could cleave muscle from bone in seconds. The bird was well mannered and laid back most of the time but like all familiars Akand could get very temperamental if rubbed the wrong way.

Bulgaria was beautiful. It had so many different terrains, Mark noted, as they flew high in the evening sky. He could picture Lilith's face if he ever brought her here; he knew her eyes would light up with glee as she would take in the beautiful snowy peaks and the sun kissed lakes of Rila. This was one of the most beautiful places he had ever been the lakes were crystal clear and had lavender and lilies growing along the shore line; the higher you looked the weather seemed to change from a spring like breeze to the crisp of winter as they climbed higher. Mark felt a little uneasy as he picked up a faint distress signal from an old friend that was said to have been incognito for the last two years. There was a gentle gust of wind pugged at Mark's shirt as he soared; a grin tugged at the corner of his lips as he imagined Lilith impatiently calling him home. He knew she wasn't there but he would never again think of the wind without thinking of her; Lilith was the wind, wild and free, the thought of her smothered the sense of unease and strengthened the resolve to get this mission done and get back to her. The town they were told to investigate was just on the other side of the mountain, nestled into a remote valley that can only be reached by train. Jase had researched the town before they left, it was an odd place to put a town and according to Jase the town's only real source of income was a ski resort that kept people coming back every year.

Akand swooped and let out a screech as he warned about what he saw ahead.

Plumes of smoke became visible as they reached the top of Mt. Rila; it wasn't noticeable from the distance but the closer to the town they soared the thicker the smoke became as it blackened the sky. Jon signaled the group to cover their faces with jackets to create a barrier against the onslaught of fumes, smoke, and gas when they grew closer to the town that was now ablaze. Mark closed his eyes and focused his energy on Akand's eyes as he blended their visions together so he could get a bird's eye view of the ground through the smoke, his eyes burned with the sudden assault but he could see the ground at least. The snow was littered with ash and rubble due to the taller buildings from the resort collapsing from the weakened structures. Looking at the ground there where strange shapes covering the ground leading all throughout the town; doors were knocked open and hanging off the hinges in some doorways. Lights were left on in store fronts and windows were shattered the shards scattered about. There was so much debris and destruction in such a small amount of time; Ash Wolfpaw, the king, had said that his informant in town had reported a large gathering of mutts that they were to investigate and exterminate if possible, but this… They were too late to help anyone that much was apparent to him when he spotted mutt tracks leading away from the resort; *Where are the people?*

A high pitch two toned whistle cut through Mark's concentration; his head turned to look at Danny who had given off the sound, Danny was pointing at a movement on the ground. In silent unison the group split into two groups, Mark and Jase glided to the ground. The moment their feet silently hit the ground the two ran in practiced unison in the direction the movement was coming from.

Blood was smeared along walls and the ground. The smell of burning flesh gave Mark pause in front of a bakery that was ablaze; there was a young female body hanging lifeless out of the shop window, she couldn't have been in her mid-twenties, terror was etched into her features and her mouth was slightly opened from the final scream she would have made just before her untimely death. The fire obscured everything inside making it impossible for him to see how many bodies like hers where inside. There was no helping her or anyone else in this god forsaken town. Mark nearly tripped over Jase as he turned to continue to the courtyard; Jase was brushing snow off of one of the oddly shaped mounds uncovering the body of an old man. The man's throat was ripped open and the body mutilated.

Mark watched as Jase counted the bodies in the snow, his younger brother's features hardened into the battle-ready warrior he was trained to be. They all went through the same training but something had happened to Jase that he wouldn't speak of and that worried him. Jase had been as care free as Danny at one point in time and now he was hard and cold to the world, always skeptical of what others were doing or planning. Jase finally spoke breaking the silence that had stretched around them as the fires crackled and buildings crumbled. "This is over kill Mark, there had to be at least a hundred mutts here, I would guess, to do this amount of damage."

Mark nodded as he looked closer at the damage to the town itself, "Did you notice the damage to the buildings?"

"No what did I..." Jase eyed the nearest building closely, the burn pattern on the building wasn't touched by flames even though the shop next to it was burning. It was as if some of the buildings were protected by enchantments against the flames; it was rare but sometimes witches branched off from their covens and became nomads and it looked like there was a few that had lived here. "Damn, they were over run here. Do you think one of them was the one to tip off Ash?"

"I don't just think it, I had heard Nathan moved here a two years ago after his girlfriend died, he wasn't taking any more missions for now so he could raise his daughter Karryn. He had been off the radar for a while and I picked up a distress signal from him on the way here."

"There isn't any sign of a distress signal now..." A child's scream cut Jase off as both men turned and ran to the sound, Mark's heart dropped when he realized the scream had come from the courtyard.

The vile stench of mutt grew stronger as Mark grew closer; the streets were deserted making it easier, and faster, to reach the courtyard. Jon and Danny would be coming from the opposite side of town. They always stuck to the same routines while on scouting missions. The plan was for Danny and Jon to round the corner of the other side of the courtyard and corner the mutt and by the tracks and the strong scent that was coming from dead ahead there was only one target left for them to round up. Mark hoped that if he willed the child to hold on till they got there that the child would be alive but even one mutt spelled trouble for a town such as this one. Mark was moving fast as he hurled himself over piles of bodies as he finally cleared the final block necessary for them to get into the proper position.

Surveying the area Mark held his breath as he saw a huge pile of corpses stacked on top of each other in a large pile in the middle of the courtyard next to a marble fountain. There had to be at least a quarter of the town stacked in that pile; blood poured from the pile into the fountain turning it into a scene of absolute horror as the blood was replacing the water as it continued to flow in its eerie way. The smoke turned the snow from a white to a grey soot like color as it continued on and in the midst of it all was a single female mutt crouching over a male body that was separate from the pile. Blood covered the ground; the attack had clearly started here then spread to the outskirts of the town. Mark couldn't see any sign of the child that had screamed. Think. Children did one of two things in this situation, they either run out into the opening or they make themselves small and hide. There wasn't a child's body so they would have hidden themselves. Searching the scene in front of him once more Mark focused on places that a child could have hidden. His eyes kept focusing on the pile of corpses, to be sure the child wasn't hiding among the corpses. It was slight but sure enough there was a breaths movement from the middle of the pile. *There you are little one.*

They needed to move fast; the movement from the pile had caught the attention of the mutt. Mark gave a two-tone whistle and immediately everyone leapt into action as he made a mad dash to the pile. The female mutt barely had time to drop the corpse she was devouring before Danny slid out of the fountains shadow and was on her in moments. Jon and Jase stood on either side of Danny as he wrestled the mutt to the ground and pinned her at knife point.

Mark could hear the mutt's frustrated growls followed by skin against bone, as he could only assume Danny got fed up with the sound and knocked her unconscious. The pile was just in front of him now and he could see where the child had wedged itself as to best not be seen.

Very gently, Mark reached up to collect the child but it had scrambled back a bit in fear making it hard to reach, "Come here sweet thing I won't hurt you. My name is Mark, I was sent to find you and bring you home safely."

No movement. The child was too terrified by everything that was happening around it. It was no surprise a strange man would scare the kid more.

"Mark! It's Nathan...this little fucker was eating him after the kill." Jon sounded pissed and discussed as he heard a kicking sound and a grunt come from behind him.

"Are you sure Jon?" Mark hoped it wasn't true, Nathan was a good man and a great witch. Nathan had fought alongside him many times and he had saved his ass on more than one occasion. He knew it could have been a possibility, especially since the town had only one survivor that they were aware of.

"Pretty damn positive. I see Ash's seal on his collar bone...it's Nathan," it wasn't hard to hear the rage in Jon's voice.

"Is your name Karyn?" Mark could hear Danny curse under his breath from where he stood only five feet away. The child could see everything. Every gory detail. He hoped like hell that this child was Karyn; yes, she would have seen the mutt eating her father's remains, but she would be alive and that was more than he could say about the rest of the town.

Big brown eyes appeared from the pile and peered down at him; Mark knew those eyes, they belonged to a dead man. Mark remembered what felt like not long-ago Nathan had shown him pictures of his baby girl. He had been gushing over how cute she was going on and on about how much he loved her. This little girl was Karyn, she was alive and for that he sent up a silent thanks to whatever god or goddess had watched over her. Though he knew that her father would have fought even in death to protect his daughter. *Nathan...Don't worry we will get your little girl somewhere safe.* He hadn't realized that he was holding his breath until a soft bell like voice reached his ears." I'm really good friends with your dad. Please come down we want to bring you someplace safe."

"Is she sleeping?"

Mark sighed with relief as Karyn wiggled her tiny body out of the pile and into his outstretched arms; "Yes sweetheart she is sleeping and will not try to hurt you again, I promise." He cradled the child close and walked over to were the others stood; turning her he made sure that she wouldn't see any more of this nightmare he handed her over to Danny. "Danny could you please get her out of here while we take care of this? I know you want to be here but she needs out."

Mark pleaded with his eyes as Danny nodded, "We will be in the valley's below. Be careful." With that Danny called down his bird and flew off carrying Karyn to safety, with Danny nothing would happen to that little girl he was sure of it.

Jon walked over to Nathan's corpse as he called down Avis. Nathan was still in one piece for the most part nothing torn off of him. His face looked so peaceful. Jon looked calm only his voice gave away his turmoil, "He needs a peaceful burial. We owe him that much, after all, he was part of the guard...one of us...I'm taking the corpse down to the valley where Danny and I will give him a proper witch burial you too take care of this. Make it as brutal as possible." Jon laughed as he looked to Jase who gave a grim nod.

A witch burial. Not much of a burial more like a silent fire memorial. *Rest well Nathan we will make them pay for your loss.*

Together the pair hoisted the unconcise mutt onto a nearby wooden restaurant table. Jase produced four ice sickles and jammed them into her wrists and ankles securing her to the table. A pain filled scream came spilling out of the now very conscious mutt as she fought to get loose. Jase jammed a small blade in-between the mutt's fingers and, with a grin on his face, began splitting the fingers apart. Blood spirted as her fingers were slowly separating from her palm. The knife cut through nerves and small ligaments inside the hand. The mutt's screams and howls filled the air. Jase's laugh boomed over the mutt's screams as her terror became tangent in the air. "What is it? Does this hurt?"

The screams came louder as Jase wiggled the ice after a while, she grew quite but pain was etched into her face, "Now tell us, where is the rest of your hive going."

"I would rather die bastard!" Her voice was gravely and animal like as the words spewed from her lips. She looked up and spit at Jase as he got closer, her spit was mixed with blood from earlier and could be seem on Jase's shirt.

"I didn't say you would live." Jase closed in on the mutt with the small blade in hand he began peeling off thin layers of skin...this was going to be a long night.

****

Jon had found an open space that was covered in lilies and lavender in a valley below Mt. Rila. It was beautiful and would make an honorable spot to lay Nathan to rest. Softly Avis placed Nathan's body to the ground and landed next to him. Jon had instructed Avis to spread out his large wings to hide the body from Karyn's sight until they could cover his body properly. Danny landed next to him still clutching the girl close. She hadn't shone any indication that she was frightened or that she was going to cry. *Poor girl is in shock.* Sliding off of Avis Jon walked over and held up his arms to collect her from Danny; she didn't seem to want to leave him.

"Karyn sweetie I need your help picking flowers for your papa. Can you help me with that?" He tried to sound calm and kind all the while rage boiled inside him.

Karyn pressed deeper into Danny's side, the man had a way with children they always flocked to him, she clutched his leather jacket and peeked slowly around her small fist. Danny hugged her close and sat back; the smoke hadn't helped his damaged voice as huskily he sighed, "You don't have to you know? You can stay up here with me but I would love to be able to give your dad respects for protecting you, will you help me do that?"

She shook her head when her eyes looked too Avis, the girl knew her dad wasn't coming back; she probably thought she was alone and that nobody would take care of her. *She was wrong.* Her dad was on the royal guard like he was, they wouldn't let Nathan down like that. Jon pulled down his t-shirt collar revealing the dark green circular pentagram that had swirls coming off of it, it was Ash's personal mark claiming him as a member of his guard. Karyn's eyes grew big when she saw the mark and slowly left Danny's side with her arm's outstretched. "You're like my papa."

"Your papa was often my partner on assignments in the past little soldier, he would be so proud of you." Reaching up he pulled her off of Amaan and placed her on the ground, "Can you pick lots of flowers while we gather wood and branches for the pyre?"

"Yes sir..." Staying in sight she began inspecting and picking flowers.

Danny hopped off his familiar and helped Jon drag large pieces of wood from the surrounding woods. Jon's mind kept wandering to his last months working with Nathan. The two of them had been on so many back-to-back assignments they had practically lived in the winter castle, every night they had off they would get drunk and hit on the castle maids. One of those maids had been Karyn's mother and Nathan had fallen head over heels for the woman. He had talked about marrying her and raising their child together, after Karyn's mother died Nathan lost it for a little while and had asked for time off from the guard so he could raise her on his own. Jon hadn't seen him since he got drunk with him the night before he left, they had been good friends, partners, and now as he dragged Nathan's body over to the pyre, he regretted not checking up on him. Danny helped raise and place the body on the wooden slab arranging him to appear like he was sleeping, Karyn walked over with her arms full of flowers and together they placed the flowers all over the pyre.

"Step back Karyn, we don't want you hurt when I light this."

"How will you do it?" She asked in a sad small voice, she was hiding her pain well, he wished she would let it all out.

"You will see." Danny said as he took her hand and pulled her a few feet away so Jon can begin the traditional witch burial. "Quite now and pay your respects to your father little one."

Sparks surrounded him as he stepped up to the pyre and placed his hand on the wood. Jon looked up to the sky and began channeling the lightning that ran through his veins out his palm creating sparks on the wood as small flames began to eat at the wood. Jon rose his hands and spoke into the valley as he connected with every member of the guard through their marks. Once he had all twelve remaining members present in mind and shadow, he projected everyone's thoughts to Danny and Karyn. In a solemn voice he began, "We have gathered here to bring respect to this man. Nathan was one of us and died showing his fierce strength as he tried to protect a village from a massive mutt hive by himself. Their numbers were too much for a single soldier to handle but he held them off long enough for us to get here. He protected his most beloved daughter and she will be safe in the guard's protective embrace. To Karyn, we are sorry we weren't here to help your father and we have failed you but we will not fail you again." Each guard member gave their confirmation as Jon turned and saw her gazing in awe as she saw the shadows of everyone in the valley. They had projected their shadows here for her. "Nathan was fiercely loyal and fought with everything in him. To you my friend we will look for the bastards that did this and we will have vengeance. To you we promise. My coven will bring your child safely to the castle and she will be taken care of. Rest well in the Goddess's embrace. Karyn do you want to say anything?"

Slowly she looked up at the now blazing pyre, "Papa take care of mama...I love you..."

Slowly one by one the shadows vanished leaving them in the valley while the pyre blazed high. *We are coming for you, you fucking bastards.*

9.

Dancing about with her cup of sweet and salty bliss Lilith and Taurtis had made their way back to the small town that was a few miles from the coven house. The pair had stopped at a weird store that sold flavored ice and both got a snow cone using Jon's card. If the man had given them the card, they were most definitely not passing up free things.

Lilith was so happy she couldn't contain it; this was a good break, she needed it after all the stress she had been under recently. She had this feeling in her gut that something wasn't quite right and she wasn't feeling it was only for her sister. She kept throwing up and just this morning she thought she saw the unmistakable pouch forming around her stomach. Spacing out she remembered her dream. As the day had gone on pieces from the dream came back to her. There had been two children. She had been hoping she had been seeing things but when she got out of the shower, she had seen the small bump forming. She had been so stupid. Mark hadn't been wearing a condom and she hadn't thought to protect herself. *What was she going to do?* With the dream she had she wasn't so sure how much she should trust Mark; even if he did claim to want to marry her. It was all happening so fast. Lilith hadn't had the chance to speak with Taurtis about any of this but her brother had just looked at the mark and gone about his day. He knew she would eventually talk about it. What was she going to do about Mark?

Sure, she was starting to fall in love with the man but could she trust him with her children. Lilith was certain that he would never hit her or hurt her children for that matter but the nagging feeling that he was hiding something was there. When they had returned from their last mission Jase had said they have a possible lead but it wasn't much to go on. Come to think of it they hadn't brought it up again either. Mark wanted to marry her so what could he be hiding?

Then throwing in the chance of kids. Not just any kids. Custos children would be weird for him. They grew fast and were typically pretty powerful depending on the parents. Then there was the fact that depending on how strong the child's parents are it shortened the length of pregnancy. A custo's female could be pregnant anywhere from one to six months on average. With her already having a small pouch forming. Lilith was certain she wouldn't have long to worry about telling Mark. She knew she would be meeting her child soon enough. She had so much on her mind with everything that was going on. Between everything going on with her sister and now with Mark's announcement this morning she didn't know how she would throw a baby into the mix. Lilith knew that even if it didn't work out with Mark, she would still keep her baby; her family would always protect their own. Having trouble processing everything the only thought that came to her mind was that she wanted to find Daina before the baby got there.

The pair of siblings had originally come to town to look around. Taurtis hadn't yet got the feel for the area yet and when they had gotten to town they saw the snow cone shack. The place had over one hundred flavors anything from cherries to toothpaste. She had saw the pickle flavor and craved it instantly so as they walked down the street Lilith licked at the salty treat.

"That has to taste like shit." Taurtis looked grossed out and slightly affronted at her snow cone.

"Surprisingly this is better than sex," Lilith wiggled around while she enjoyed the salty sweet treat. The baby must like pickles that is all she had been craving all day.

She liked that she could walk down the street and zone out as she was going. This life was peaceful. It was an appropriate atmosphere to raise a child; nothing like the filthy streets she had grown up on. Truthfully, she had never pictured herself every becoming a mother. Always fighting, always careful, Lilith truly had never let go with anyone. Mark was special whatever he was hiding she could handle it.

Taking another bite of her snow cone Lilith wiggled again with happiness as she walked alongside Taurtis. He had selected a cherry flavored cone and seemed to be enjoying it while he was looking at shop windows. Window shopping. Who would have thought they would feel safe enough to do this? Remembering how Mark had bought her a new wardrobe she looked Taurtis over. He was wearing the same clothes he was wearing two days ago when he showed up at the coven house. Excitement filled her as she happily took her brothers hand and dragged him along with her.

"Where's the fire Lil?" Taurtis looked happy as he kept himself from dropping his frozen treat.

Smiling up at him, "It's time i did something for you! We are getting you your own clothes so you can ditch the stolen ones."

"Do you have a place in mind?"

"You will have to trust me. I know a great place and it's up ahead."

Taurtis was grinning now. As they passed a trash can that was on the street the pair tossed their trash. Mark had taken her down this busy street before so finding the store wouldn't be a problem. Cars were driving along the two-lane street. Shop windows shone their goods but she knew Taurtis had similar tastes. Only the best for Taurtis. He had never been spoiled like this before and he deserved it after taking care of his two younger siblings by himself all these years. Mark shouldn't mind either after all if he married her then Taurtis would be his family as well. They continued down the street and rounded the corner. Standing on the corner was the cute little boutique that she got her clothes from. The sign read The Marsh. As they approached the store Taurtis stopped to look at the window. It looked like they had changed their display since the other day. Taurtis looked at her and his grin widened.

"You know me so well." Taurtis laughed as he pointed to a black leather jacket that was on display. "I really want that."

"So, let's get it for you. We will get that and other clothes. Hopefully they have your size."

Entering the store, a friendly chime sounded signaling new customers to the worker at the counter. The store was deceptively large compared to how small it looked from the outside. There were several rows of clothes throughout the store. There were actual rooms in the back used for trying on clothes and a love seat in front for anyone waiting. Full length mirrors ran along the walls and ended just before the changing rooms. The radio was playing soft welcoming music as they walked through the rows of clothes looking for the men's wear. It seemed like they had gotten to the store at a good time as they were the only customers in the store at the time making it easier to locate the row they were looking for. Dancing along to the music Lilith began searching the racks for something that would fit Taurtis, he was tall and muscular which made it a bit hard but she was finding a surprising amount of clothes in his size. They had just found the jacket he had seen in the window when they heard the sound of shoes clicking on the tile floor as the sound grew louder with the persons arrival.

Lilith turned to the sound to find the familiar face of the elderly woman from before. She had been expecting the young lady that was at the desk but Mark had let her know that this woman owned the shop. The elderly woman was coming closer with a large warm smile on her face; Lilith couldn't help but smile back at her. "Mrs. Marsha, it's nice to see you again."

If it was possible the woman beamed bigger at the both of them. "Welcome back dear. I am happy to see you again." Marsha eyed Taurtis with much curiosity. "Who might this be?"

Taking the lead from Lilith, Taurtis smiled and held out his hand. "I'm her brother. My name is Taurtis."

"Taurtis? That is a peculiar name." Marsha looked at Lilith and smiled. "Is there anything I can get for either of you? I still haven't thanked you enough for taking down that mad man."

Taurtis held up the jacket, "Do you have this in brown as well?"

"Yes, in the back we just got it in today. I'll get it for you and you can have them both free of charge." Marsha smiled wide, "It's the least I could do."

"That's not necessary Mrs. Marsha you already gave me all of my clothes last time I was here." Last time she had been in the shop Marsha hadn't let Mark pay for anything. This time she had hoped to be able to spend enough money to make up what she had gotten then and now.

"Nonsense I insist," with the wave of her hand Marsha dismissed the topic.

"I'm glad my sister chose to help such a beautiful young woman such as yourself." Taurtis took possession of one of the older women's hands and brushed a kiss on it. *He is such a flirt.*

Blush crept up the older woman's neck as she patted his hand. "Oh, my. You are a charming angel, aren't you?"

"Don't be fooled ma'am. Even the devil was once an angel." Lilith glared at her brother after she smacked him hard in the stomach. "Be respectful to her, you aren't here to woo her."

"I can't help myself around a pretty lady, you know that Lil." Taurtis winked at Marsha.

Before she could say anything, her stomach lurched. Quickly scanning the room Lilith spotted the restroom sign and bolted to the room. She had just barely made it to the toilet before she dropped her hands to her stomach and hunched to vomit. What kind of a child would tragedy produce? What kind of title would they have? The thought terrified her as she stayed hunched over the toilet. A gentle pat on her back startled her as she turned with protective hands over her stomach. Her eyes locked with the knowing hazel eyes Marsha possessed. The older woman glanced at Lilith's belly then looked at Lilith's eyes. She knew that Marsha could see the terror in her eye she was feeling with the timing of a child. Marsha gently brushed Lilith's hairs out of her face and opened her mouth to speak.

"You know it's strange." She began in her calm aged voice. "All my life I have lived in these mountains. I have seen many strange things. One of those things are those boys. They aren't quite human but they hide it well. I turn a blind eye to that fact because they are good boys. They watch over us here in this village much like you did the other day. I know you aren't at all human yourself. You said you were a warrior and showed me your beautiful wings. I don't know how things work with your people but Marcus is a good boy and he will take care of you if you would let him."

"What are you saying?" Lilith knew what she meant but wanted to hear an outsiders' logic. She couldn't stop the worry from showing through her words.

"I'm saying that I saw the way that boy looked at you the other day. He looked at you the same way my Marvin used to look at me; god rest his soul. I'm not blind dear just old. I see you in her hunched over the toilet and can't help but remember what it was like with my first child. I was as sick as a dog most days and Marvin would bring me soup and take care of me." Marsha made a face as she appeared to be remembering her first pregnancy. "I thought it was horrible at the time and most days I thought I was dying because of all the throwing up but do you know what? I had Marvin to take care of me."

"How did you know Marvin was the one for you?"

"I didn't at the time but it all worked out for the best. He was courting me quite seriously. He couldn't keep his hands off of me most days and when we found out I was pregnant we were worried. He went to my father that night and asked him if he could marry me. Back in my day getting pregnant before marriage was quite the scandal. We were able to hide the pregnancy until after we were married and my Marvin had taken care of the both of us. He was such a good man. I lost him last winter to old age."

Lilith felt a small nudge inside her stomach. It felt like a gas bubble but she instinctively knew it was a small kick. Her eyes grew wide when she looked down at her hands still covering her belly. Marsha reached over and touched her hands. Maybe she should ask her? "What if you knew Marvin was hiding something from you? Would you still have married him and trusted him with your child?"

Surprise glimmered in her eyes, "Is that what's stopping you from giving yourself wholly to him dear?"

"I believe so. That and I need to find my sister."

"I see. Well to be honest I would have fussed with him until he told me what he was hiding but I would also have trusted his judgement. If I felt what he was hiding would hurt me or my baby I would have gone back to my father's home. The important thing during this time is to feel comfortable and safe. I say this because this may be the only time in your life when you have to stop being the warrior for a little while and be a nurturer for your baby. They need to be loved and cuddled often. I would trust your partner until they give you a reason to not be trusted dearie. Marcus and his brothers are good boys and will look after you. I also get the feeling your brother would set the boys straight if anything was to harm you or your babies."

"She is fucking right Lil. Nothing will come near you or your children while I'm around." Lilith jerked her head up and saw Taurtis blocking the doorway. He had heard everything which was okay. She was going to talk to him tonight about everything anyway. "We are a family and more than that you are my partner. I would go to war for you. If you are feeling uncomfortable just tell me and I will get you out of there."

Tears filled her eyes as she looked at both Taurtis and Marsha. The emotions came from nowhere but she was glad for them as she was so confused. "I was going to tell you when we left here. You're going to be an uncle soon." Rubbing her stomach, she looked hard at her brother. He would understand, "Very soon and they will need both their aunt and uncle around so we best find Daina. Mrs. Marsha we never really had a mother but I thank you so much for the advice that you just gave me. It is something that our mother should have been here to tell me but I am glad it was you. You helped me clear some things up. I do have to ask a huge favor though for both of you. Please do not tell Mark or the boys until I sort everything out. I will be forever in your debit."

"Of course, dear that is your news to tell them and I can't wait to have a baby shower for you." Marsha looked excited again as she helped Lilith off the floor.

"You don't even have to ask Lil. I always have your back." That was all he said before turning and went back to shopping. Looks like he was happy spending Jon's money.

"Come on dearie let's get you over to the love seat to sit down." Marsha smiled at her.

"Okay." Was all she could say as she felt her stomach hoping to feel another little kick. She shouldn't be able to feel it so soon and that was slightly concerning. *Slow down my little warrior, I'm not ready yet.*

****

Akand flew over Glittertind, one of the highest mountains in Norway. They had arrived in the country an hour ago and had to go the long way to the castle due to a storm. It rained often up here in the mountains so it wasn't much of a problem. A couple days had passed since they left the coven house, at least three days. They had gotten some good info from the mutt. By nightfall they had all the information from the mutt and she was begging for death. Mark had slit her throat and watched her bleed out after she had revealed her hive was headed to France. The mutt wasn't sure why they were gathering there just that they were. They had caught up to Jon and Danny, they had gotten to the valley just in time to watch Nathan's ashes drift away. Mark had sent out a silent prayer to Nathan promising to get Karyn proper care and a good family to watch over her. The little girl was crying now and had refused to let go of Danny so she was flying with him. She must have been tired as hell; she hadn't made a sound since the had flown over England.

The group finally had their destination in view. Ash had gone back to his winter castle in Scandinavia. The castle was a massive stone structure that rested on a cliff overhanging the Norwegian sea. The castle was built out of the cliffs itself over a thousand years ago by the head of the Wolfpaw coven at the time and the coven has ruled the castle and all of the witches since. The Wolfpaw was the strongest coven of witches ever and under their rule witches have flourished. They were strong warriors and fair rules; despite their small numbers they are still the strongest. One Wolfpaw was worth at least a hundred witches. They were there to pay their respects and to report to the king, Ash; he would want details and lots of them.

Mark was flying point and he signaled the descent from the air. Circling the courtyard, he had Akand land by the wolf statue that was erected in the center of the yard. Despite the cold temperatures the courtyard was covered in plants and grass; this was due to the many enchantments that were placed on the castle grounds. Ash liked his gardens so he made sure to take care of them no matter the climate. The high castle walls blocked out the outside world but Mark could still hear the crashing waves from the bluffs. Looking up he watched his brother's decent one by one into the courtyard. Danny landed last with Karyn. There was a place for their familiars to rest on the castle grounds and knowing what was coming Akand took off in the direction of the rest area. Mark turned to Jon all business, "Is Ash expecting us?"

"Looks like it." Jon responded as he pointed to the courtyard entryway where a maid had just appeared. To the maid Jon nodded and approached her. "Does he wish to see us now or would he like us to wait?"

The maid bowed at Jon's approach. "Welcome back, my lord. His majesty wishes to see all of you in the garden plaza at the back of the castle. If you would follow me please."

Statues of wolves were everywhere in the castle; some were on pedestals and others were scattered about was something that always stuck out to him as they headed to the king. With all the statues one would think it was tacky but here in the castle it looked elegant. The castle was beautiful but the corridors at times could be narrow and had sharp turns.

When Mark was younger, he had gotten lost a few times to due to all the winding corridors. Rounding the final corner, the corridor opened up the brightly lit courtyard. The garden plaza was a favorite place of the kings. It was covered in lush vegetation that acted as a defense for him. He had all of his favorite plants in that area; most of the plants there could be found in every botanist's wet dreams. There was a small stone sitting area in the center of the plant circle that he had meetings in. Right now, the yard was empty with the exception of all of Ash's many rare plants.

Bowing once again, the maid backed out of the courtyard. "Please wait here and his majesty will be with you after his current meeting."

"How long do you think he will be?" Jase chimed in curiously. One never knew how long the king's meetings ran.

"I'm not sure. Goodbye." The maid turned to leave again. The king's staff loved to stay hidden when guests were on castle grounds unless you were a guard member that lived on the grounds or the king it was hard to get ahold of the maids.

"Wait!" Danny called out to the maid. She looked at Danny who was still carrying Karyn. "Is Marie here? This little one...."

"That won't be necessary Daniel, thank you for the thought though." Whirling around Mark found himself face to face with a massive white she-wolf. Her master stood a few yards behind her at the back entrance.

Danny placed Karyn down and the little girl coward behind him. "With all due respect your majesty; Karyn has been through enough and I believe she shouldn't have to relive it when we debrief you."

Danny was calm and respectful. His hands were clasped firmly behind his back as he stood at attention. Danny was still and looked totally serious as he waited. Mark noted that Danny rarely got like this outside the king's castle. The she-wolf stepped around Mark and slowly paced closer to the child; Ash walked into full view. Ash looked tired as he ran a hand threw his dirty blonde hair.

"Do you think so little of me Daniel?" Ash asked quietly.

"No sir. I was only trying to remind you that she was still only a child."

"I am very much aware of that." Ash, like his wolf, got a closer to the child and dropped to his knee in front of her. "You are Karyn Rose, am I right? No need to hide from me I don't bite."

Slowly Karyn slid out from behind Danny. She eyed the wolf as she approached the king. "Your doggie won't hurt me?"

Mark froze. Nobody called Ash's familiar a dog. The Wolfpaw's took great offence whenever someone was brave, or stupid, enough to do it. Wolfpaw's took great pride in their familiars; they all thought that their wolf was the best didn't matter how old they were. The previous Queen, Ash's mother, had been the same way with her wolf. What was more surprising however, was the slow smile that had formed on the king's lips.

"Anieua isn't a doggie. She is the most beautiful winter wolf alive," laughing Ash quickly added, "but no sweetie she won't hurt you. She loves children and do you see Kira over there?" Ash pointed to the maid who still stood at the entryway. "She will take you to the kitchen and look after you for a little while until I get done with these guys, okay?"

Mark watched as slowly Karyn took a deep breath and reached in her little pocket. The little girl with trembling little hands clutched a slip of paper. With a trembling voice but focused eyes Karyn looked forward at Ash. "You are King Ash?"

Cocking his head to the side politely Ash stated, "At your service little witch."

Nodding at Ash's affirmative, Karyn held out the piece of paper. "Papa told me to only give dis to you. Told me to hide it well. It's my first mission."

Ash looked surprised as he took the paper. He had just barely glanced at it when he signed loudly and awkwardly hugged Karyn close and patted her on the back. Releasing her he slowly walked to Mark still looking at the paper; Ash crinkled his nose a slightly when he handed the paper over to Mark.

Concerned. Mark looked at the crumpled paper, it only had one word that looked to be quickly jotted down. *Gregory.* Mark's head shot up in time to see Ash's concern blend with raw fury. The man quickly hid everything under a calm demeaner as he turned back to Karyn. Mark passed the paper to Jon so it could be passed around the group. This little girl had amazed and surprised them all. At such a young age she had completed her dead father's final assignment.

"You did great on your first mission little witch." Ash started. "Your papa would be so proud of you."

Karyn began to tear up at the praise. "I'm...sorry...king."

"Why are you sorry? I heard from one of my guard that you helped make a beautiful pyre for your dad." Ash peered at the girl in concern. Mark noticed that it was the wolf that cuddled and licked at the child to comfort her.

"My...fault..." she mumbled in-between sobs.

"What's your fault?"

"Papa...got hurt...cuz he was...tecting me..." She was looking at her little feet as tears streamed down her face as the sobs racked her little body. Ash knelt once more in front of Karyn.

"Karyn Rose look at me." Nobody could mistake the command that rang through the air as he waited. Once she was finally looking at him, Ash continued. "Your papa was one of my most trusted guard members. He wouldn't have made the cut if he would have run. He protected you because he loved you very much. He probably didn't run because he felt it was his duty to watch over that town, he always stood his ground with his head up even if it wasn't good for him. Your papa gave you a mission I would have assigned to another guard member. He trusted you were strong enough to get to me and here you are; you aren't even of age to get a child's mission. Do you understand? Your papa got hurt doing his duty as a witch. It wasn't your fault. You're a smart girl, you should know that."

Karyn nodded as Ash motioned for the maid. "Take her to get something warm to drink and look after her for a little while."

Ash managed to wait for Karyn to be taken away before he whirled and faced the Flemming coven. Fury was etched into his features as he paced about the courtyard. "I need that report now!"

Jon stepped forward as they lined up at attention. "There is one thing you should know before we get into anything further."

"What else is there?"

"Stephanie Greene has resurfaced sir."

Ash looked surprised, *had he thought she died quietly?* "Where? I can send out two guard members now to go collect her."

"That's the thing. An ally of ours ran into her in Houston, Texas. She had tried to convince him to kill us so that much has not changed. Furthermore, I believe she may be working alongside Gregory."

Maintaining continuous eye contact, Ash waved his hand over his shoulder and a chair sprung to life; out of the vines it formed, bending and hardening so it could be sat on. Pacing to the chair Ash sat propped forward with his fingers intertwined on his lap. The tension in the room increased as Ash sat staring at them with a perfectly practiced blank expression. Mark quickly took a breath he had not realized he needed to take as Ash finally spoke. "Gregory again. He will be a problem for me in the future."

"I agree..." Jon continued with the king but Mark was too focused on the wolf to pay attention.

Mark grew still as Anieua prowled closer to him sniffing the air. *Shit.* He had forgotten he still smelled of Lilith slightly. She had been all over him just before he left and he hadn't had time to shower. Even with all of the smoke and blood he knew Anieua smelled her on him. Ash's eyes kept glancing at him as Jon explained what all they had seen in that decimated town. Mark shifted slightly trying to move away from the she-wolf but from her first appearance in the garden she had been focused on cataloging the new scent for Ash.

Mark looked away and retreated to a corner of the garden where he pretended to look at all the new plants that were recently added. He had only been there a moment before someone leaned over and sniffed his shoulder. The sudden presence from behind caused him to spin and lash out his arms. Anieua growled and the room grew silent as Iblis jumped back dodging his fists. Iblis smiled back at Mark as he walked over to where Ash sat watching.

"Good evening." He said in a traditional ghoul like greeting in a cool voice. The ghoul was tall and tanned, which was odd for a ghoul. He looked to be made of rope after rope of muscle. Typical of ghouls, Iblis had long shaggy hair that he was pulling back into a long messy man-bun. He was dressed in his usual dark jeans and a pale green tunic, while in the castle he liked to wear older styled clothes. His cold empty smile did not bode well for him as his stomach dropped. Iblis stopped close to Ash as he

132

dropped a hand to the king's shoulder. "Sorry I'm late my lord but I had to finish my meal before it ran off."

Ash grunted but did not remove his eyes from Mark. The wolf marking his next target. "Glad you enjoyed it Iblis."

"I do however agree with Anieua. Mark does smell particularly delicious today." Iblis turned and looked at Mark once more, scenting the air once more he cocked his head to the side he added, "Wonder why that is?"

Mark tensed as Anieua growled. Jase and Danny stepped forward to him trying to help but Mark had waved them off. "Call off your wolf your majesty. I do not wish to fight. We have had a long flight here and I don't wish to add wolf bites to the list of things that have happened while on this particular assignment. Jase and I obtained information from the mutt that was eating Nathan."

Ash sat back and gave a low two-tone whistle that had Anieua slowly walking back. Mark let out his breath he had not realized he was holding. With a raised eyebrow and slightly amused look Ash breathed out, "Do share then."

Mark looked at Jon who nodded and stepped back leaving room for Mark to speak. "We have determined that the mutts where heading towards the German border. She was ordered to hang back and pick off any survivors that may have come back to the town. She wasn't sure why they were told to gather there just that Rila was a great gathering point. They have gathered over a hundred mutts but the lower ranks are clueless. She only knew that our new best friend Gregory was leading it. I would also like to add that she had been mumbling about a traitor helping them. By the description that was given of the traitor helping them we had surmised that it if Stephanie. End report sir."

"Jason, anything you would like to add to the report." Finally turning his piercing crystal blue eyes away Ash switched his attention and relaxed as he sat back in his chair.

"The bitch died slow and hard." was the only thing Jase contributed to the conversation.

"Good. I will think on what to do about Gregory but I also have one more thing I want to go over with you. Mark, who is the female that's been all over you and why haven't I met her yet?"

All eyes turned to him as he shifted uncomfortably from side to side. Mark opened his mouth to talk his way out of answering. He had hoped the smell of smoke and blood would have masked her scent enough to chuck the smell up to the female mutt. Sadly, Lilith's scent smelled like sweet ash and not burning mutt. If he could tell the difference he knew he couldn't trick the nose of a wolf, Mark was willing to bet his left nut that Ash had been waiting to ask. Ash looked too amused.

"While you are at it you can also explain the APB that was placed by your coven looking for a tall brunette with strange tattoos and emerald green eyes. That was a very specific description." Amusement and curiosity filled his voice and Iblis was laughing at Mark's obvious discomfort.

Lilith flashed through his mind. Her laughter and enchanting eyes filled his every thought. She deserved more than a man lying about his love for her to other people. She deserved better. The king would eventually meet her anyway. He might leave stuff out about her for now but for Lilith Ash needed to know. Rubbing the back of his neck Mark blushed. "Her name is Lilith. As of three days ago I placed my mark on her throat. The other woman is her sister and she is missing. We wanted to help Lilith find her and thought it would be the quickest way, it was just easier if there was an accurate description of her to make it easier."

Within a moment, Ash was out of his chair and clapping Mark on the arm. He his wide grin flashed his dimples, "Finally! Some good fucking news. The first I've heard all day. When do you want me to officiate? I would go anywhere you two wanted the ceremony to take place at; hell, you could even use the main garden here if you would like."

Mark found himself laughing with the men. Lilith in a castle? *Not a good idea.* "First i need her to say yes and I know she wouldn't go through with anything until we get her sister back for her."

"When we find her, we have to put a big red bow on her and give her to Lil." Danny added thoughtfully with a rueful grin on his face. "She likes the color red, doesn't she?"

"Are you kidding? She obviously loves the color," Jase was grinning as they made fun of his little red head.

"Before we do that, I also have to talk to her brother about marrying his baby sister." Mark sighed out. That was one conversation he was dreading having to have to make. That man loved his sisters and would probably take his head.

"You marked her without asking? Scandalous." Ash hit him one more time before Iblis walked over to shake his hand.

"Congratulations man. If you need help passing the word about her sister around to the darker corners of the world, I'd be more than happy to lend you a hand and put out some feelers to my contacts." Mark was sure his jaw was slacked open. Had hell frozen over? Iblis was never this helpful to anyone other than the king. It had to be because Ash was here, they would have to expect a surprise visit from Iblis to collect on this debt in the future.

"If you wouldn't mind doing that it would be truly appreciated and our coven would be in your debt." Jon chimed in with a huge grin on his face. Now that everything was reported it seemed that the atmosphere out in the garden had lightened up quite a bit.

"Will do," with that Ibis vanished into a puff of smoke.

'Why don't you boys stay here for the night and drink with me? It would be fun and we can finally celebrate Mark catching a girl." Ash sounded excited.

"Sorry your majesty but we need to head home it's around a three-day trip from here and a storm is rolling in fast." It was unfortunate but they really needed to get a move on. "Maybe next time we can all have some of your famous wine when we report here again. I heard that your last year's wine was fantastic."

"It truly was a good year for the vineyard." Ash clasped Jon's forearm, his grin never faltering. Ash was a strange man; he could go from a terrifying foe to a good friend very quickly. Lately he looked so stressed, but even mixed in after the bad news, the good news Mark had brought him made looked happy and much younger than his usual haggard looking self. Still, it was odd how he was smiling. The smile didn't quite reach his eyes. "I would be happy to have you over anytime and next time I want to meet your girl Mark. I'll call on you if I have any updates that need your attention and don't worry about the girl. I have a long list of families that want a child; I'll make sure to put her with the best family."

"Please find someone nice for her Ash not just the best family she will need someone to love her. It sucks to watch your parent die like that in front of you." Danny sounded so sad as he looked at his feet and cleared his throat.

"Of course, now if you don't want to get stuck here and have to stay the night, I would advise you leaving now. I can smell the rain on the wind and it's only a few miles out."

"Shit." Mark bowed. "Thank you for having us. We will be taking our leave now." The others each bowed and gave their goodbyes as they each filed out of the garden courtyard.

"You think those two will be at the okay at the house by themselves?" Jase sounded tired as the headed back the way they had come.

Jon smirked over at his brother, "It's a little late to ask that don't you think?"

"Don't be a dick Jon," Jase sighed, "It was just a question."

Danny laughed, "He doesn't know how to not be a dick."

"They should be fine. We had given them one of the credit cards so they shouldn't starve at least." Mark shrugged.

"So... ugh...will we be alright? You gave the card to two people who doesn't understand how earth money works."

"Yeah, they should be fine Lilith will keep it in check." *Lilith. Fuck.* Worry creased his brow and his footfalls quickened as he summoned Akand from the aviary that was connected to the west wing of the castle.

He heard his brothers keeping pace behind him as he rounded another corridor and nearly tripped over a wolf statue that was in the hall. Mark knew his words and actions weren't lining up but he didn't care. The need to get back to Lilith was overwhelming. Mark could hear the familiars land as they entered the great hall. He was just about to reach the door when Jon caught up to him and grabbed him by the arm slowing him down as he gestured to the others to go ahead. He had a perplexed look on his face as he studied Mark's worried expression.

"Slow down Hercules the house isn't going anywhere." Jon paused as he thought about that, "Maybe." Jon was smirking as he tried to lighten Mark's sudden tense mood. Mark knew he was trying to fix things by calling him what Lilith did but it didn't stop his worry. Jon searched his eyes and could see it too. Looking over his shoulder Mark saw that the others had left the great halls door open. "What are you not telling us? Is there a reason we should be running home so quickly?"

Blowing out a breath, Mark patted Jon on the shoulder as they walked outside to their awaiting familiars. "It's nothing I'm just worried about Lil. She wasn't feeling well when we left the house and I feel horrible that I hadn't even thought about how she was feeling."

"Do we need Maverick? We can pick him up on the way home." Jon had visibly relaxed.

"No but can we stop on the way for medicine? I think the clean mountain air may have shocked her system. Lilith had been telling me that the air at our place was cleaner than the air in Domus Meus."

Grinning Jon walked to Avis, "You worry too much. She will be at home ready to kick some ass but if it would ease your mind of course we can stop somewhere and get something for her."

"Thanks guys." Mark climbed onto Akand and they took off into the air. Maybe he was overreacting a bit too much. Grinning to himself Mark was overjoyed his brothers had his back no matter how crazy he got over that little female. His little warrior. Steering Akand in the direction of home Mark could think of nothing else but holding her in his arms.

****

Ash watched the coven take to the air and leave the castle grounds. Their familiars were truly beautiful when the final rays of light hit their feathers. Clouds had begun to overtake the sky and rain threatened to fall at any moment. *Not as beautiful as Anieua,* Ash thought as he scratched behind her big fluffy white ears. As soon as they had left the garden Ash had headed towards the bluffs below the castle where he could better watch them leave. He may have the title of king but sometimes he felt trapped in his own prison.

The waves crashed below along the boulders but wouldn't reach them where they sat in the shade. Anieua had wanted to stretch her legs and meet him at their favorite hiding spot. Her snow-white fur had blurred down the rocks as she made her decent to where they were now sat together. Ash was propped on her side as they both scented the wind once more. The winds smelled different in the last few week. As did Mark. He had a strange scent unearthly ash scent that filled the air around him. The wind had been carrying the same scent two weeks ago when they had been reporting in from Spain.

They were hiding something and knowing them it shouldn't affect him or his people too much. They were too good of soldiers to do that and two

138

of them were on his guard. They could be trusted but this female was an unknown variable and he was positive she was causing the ash like scent. What had he called her, Lilith?

He knew no one by that name and that made him all the more curious. Iblis will just have to get more info on both her and her sister. She was no witch that much he was sure. Ash could tell that by scent alone; it was figuring out what she was without looking at her that was almost maddening to Ash. He liked a good puzzle but damn this one was hard and this woman was hard to pin point scent wise. He was a little irritated over the situation but happy for Mark.

Ash may have been crowned the youngest king ever to grace his coven. He was only thirty-two but he had been ruling his people since his early teens. He had remained king for so long by using his coven's monstrous strength and his superior intellect to outmaneuver his foes. He was focusing too much on the woman when he also needed to divide some of his attention on how to best handle Gregory as well. Ash couldn't help focusing on the woman though at the moment. Something about her he couldn't let go and he was beginning to find some enjoyment in her mystery; her sister would make for a fun game as well.

Anieua licked his face as she went to bop her nose on his. She was always fussing over him but he enjoyed her affectionate side. They only acted like this when they were alone with no prying eyes. Anieua was special, most familiars communicated with pictures to their witch but not his, she spoke to him; Ash could hear her words fill his head as her unique growly voice spoke through there telepathy link.

You're overthinking again.

"I know." Ash sighed.

If you were going to worry so much about the female, we should have made them talk. Her scent was tickling my nose and I didn't like it.

"No neither did I but if we had made them talk, we wouldn't now have the perfect excuse to leave this place and go somewhere outside one of our castle grounds." Ash smiled slowly. They both needed to get fresh air. He felt Anieua shake with her barky laugh as she laughed with him.

This is why everyone thinks you are a bastard you know. You're always plotting something.

"Hmm. I'll have to disagree with you; it's because of all the prisoners who have never left my sight alive." Ash grinned as he stood up and stretched as he looked over at his she-wolf. "Though I do suppose I should at least help our friends find the other woman. What kind of king would I be if I didn't help?"

You would be yourself.

"And I'm the bastard?"

I'm a bitch not a bastard Ash. Anieua smiled her wolfy grin as she too stretched as she stood. Droplets of water began to rain down and the sea grew rougher. Thunder could be heard approaching in the distance.

"Fuck it let's go find Iblis, we have lots to discuss with that ghoul."

Don't forget we still have the little girl to look after.

"I'm not going to forget about her," Ash sighed and looked over at the now stormy horizon once more, "actually I think I already have the perfect place for her. Come let's go inside before we catch a cold. No good plotting if you can't finish the plot."

****

Lilith found herself back in the field. A gentle breeze tugged at her hair once more as she sat with a hot cup of tea watching the two children once more. The children no longer played with frogs. She watched with her siblings as Mark ran after the two young boys. Her little mini-me was tormenting his brother. He really looked like a male childlike version of herself with his mop of blood red hair and his cat like green eyes no denying she was his mother. Moments before the boy had surprised her when he started mimicking his brothers voice flawlessly. It seemed like he was a cute little chameleon; she watched as he slowly morphed his shape into a wolf pup and began chasing his brother around. The second boy was the same size as her mini-me he had such a likeness of both her and Mark. His short strawberry blonde hair was blown by the wind as his little body ran playfully away, his deep blue eyes were carefree and full of joy to be out playing. Mark had been sitting with her before the first child morphed. Mark had gotten up and abandoned her at the table as he ran off mumbling, "Not again."

It was so peaceful and perfect, but she knew this happy scene wouldn't last as she looked over at Daina who sat chatting away. Last time she had been here in this dream world she had watched her sister die in front of her and she hadn't been listening to what Daina had been saying. She wanted to know what she had been saying last time before the dream turned bad, even in this dream world she yearned to hear her sister's slurry sweet voice.

This time in this dream, she turned away from the playing children and listened. Daina looked at her and smiled, her half dimple flashed and the wind played with her hair. Daina reached and tucked hair behind her ear as she tilted her head, "You finally want to listen to my story Lil?"

That's an odd question, it had caught her off guard. Wait. Lilith's eyes widened like saucers as she grabbed at Daina's hand. Daina had always been adept at dream walking, had she found a way around the elders' physic block? Daina would most defiantly have figured it out if there was a way around it. Maybe she can fix it. Permission. She always asked for permission. It was Daina!

She hadn't realized she had frozen; Lilith pushed the words out of her lips before she realized it. "Of course, what is your new story Daina?"

Daina's smile widened and she closed her eyes. The sky opened up and rain washed over Lilith, closing her eyes like her sister, she felt the water wash away the scene before her as a new scene began to form. Lilith felt the moment Daina took control of the dream as slowly she made way for her sister to come forward. She could see and feel everything her sister felt, her sister was not smiling anymore. Daina was terrified and cold.

Rushing through the catacombs' Daina fled these monstrous flesh-eating creatures. She didn't understand, Daina had been down here alone since she awoke in a man-made lake not too far away. She had celebrated finding this place. Since she had gotten to this plane Daina had been scared and worried as she frantically had been reaching out to her siblings. They would be coming for her and goddess help whoever got in their way; their unique bond was weird to most people but to them they depended on it.

The elders had done a number on their mental link with time she would be able to fix it but for now she was glad she had been practicing dream walking before they were banished. Now on this new plane she was cut off from her siblings for the first time; she had quickly learned to hide her scales from the humans and hide while she tried to reach them in their dreams. Once she had reached Lilith but she had been too overwhelmed with the enormity of the dream that she hadn't paid attention to her asking to let her in.

Daina could slip into a dream as easy as water could fill cracks; she had always had an affinity with water. Lilith had always left openings in her dreams for her just in case of emergencies unlike Taurtis. Even if he wanted too, he would just build an unbreakable wall in his sleep that would keep her out. She had been unable to reach them and now found herself being chased in the catacombs of what she recently found out was France. It was a perfect maze down here and tunnels crumbled and changed all the time.

Nobody had been down here in the newer parts of the tunnels for the weeks leading up to this one terrifying moment. She had been asleep on the cold wet floor when she was unexpectantly awoken by the scent of blood. Jolting upright she had spotted two odd creatures with sharp looking teeth and razor-sharp claws closing in on where she had been asleep with her one thin blanket. Daina had scurried to her feet, scraping her leg open badly on the bricks as she ran out into the narrow corridors and tunnels. The creatures were closing in on her fast but with the now throbbing leg she couldn't run as fast as she wanted too. All she could do was hope with all the twists and turns they would get lost as the newer bricks turned into the older cobblestone ones as she crossed into the older section of the tunnels.

From behind she could still hear their panting breaths as they closed in on her, panic swelled inside her as her heart clenched. They were getting too close. She had been in this area of the tunnels a few times and the way she was running would lead to a dead end. There was only one way out ahead and that was through a narrow hole that was high on the old cobblestone wall. The walls in this section were crumbling in places and risked collapsing, it was dangerous but if she got a running jump, she should be able to reach it and get out of there.

It was so dark as she reached the end of the tunnel. The cobblestone had piled up and sealed off the rest of the tunnel what looked like years ago; Daina frantically searched for the hole as she squinted into the dark. A sliver of light peaked out of a crack. There! Daina backed up just enough and with a running jump she launched herself in the air. Reaching out she caught the edge of the hole as her body slammed hard into the stones and her breath wheezed out of her. Hope filled her as she regained her breath and she hurried to pull herself through the hole. Her leg throbbed as she tried to use it to brace herself on the slippery rocks. She heard the creatures close in as the smell of blood grew closer. In a panic Daina lost her footing. Thankfully she had a good grip on the ledge as she used her arms to try and pull her upward. She was too nervous to check where they were as she concentrated hard on moving her muscles. They sounded closer than before.

Pain shot through her good leg as she felt something slash into her achilleas tendon, her scream filled the air as her leg went completely limp from the pain. She couldn't move her foot and the creatures had her cornered. Daina's hands were sweaty and she was quickly losing grip on her only means of escape. Sharp claws came at her again as white-hot pain flashed across her back and she lost her handhold. The creatures were there below her ready to slam her hard and pin her to the ground. Daina's mouth clenched hard with the impact, her sharper canines' bit hard into her lip and her mouth tasted metallic with blood. Without thinking Daina's skin glimmered as her scales reappeared on her hands and the side of her neck for added protection as she tried to kick and punch her way free; but it was no use, they had her now.

"Calm down, bitch." The big toothy creature hissed. It was terrifying with its yellow oversized eyes and its sharp animalistic teeth that was on a muscular humanoid body. Her blood dripped from its now blood-soaked claws as he raked her back once more.

Her blood spirted all over the tunnel as over and over the creature drove his claws into her. Pain was all-consuming as blood curtailing screams left her throat. This wasn't enough to kill her but the pain was driving her to madness. The creature lifted her and slammed her back into the ground, what little air she had left in her lungs flew out of her. Tears burned her eyes and sobs racked her slender body. Pain was all over her and she was sure more was to come.

"You smell delicious bitch," the creature leaned in and breathed in her now bloody scent, "Your lucky we were told to not kill you only make you mind."

"No more or Gregory will get pissed David. He wanted to play with this one too." She couldn't see the other creature with the way this one held her down. All she could do was sob and pray help would come.

Feather soft, she felt a man's masculine consciousness brush with hers and disappear as quickly as it had come. Daina feared the pain was making her hallucinate.

Human footsteps could now be heard echoing off of the old tunnel walls and a torch came into view, it lit up the area and now her blood was visible all over the walls. Daina had just managed to calm herself enough to quell the sobs that were swelling up inside her as a man appeared. The creature that was pinning her stood and backed away at the new man's approach. This must be Gregory. Shutting her eyes tight Daina tried to make herself small and hoped he would just leave her there.

A soft velvet voice filled the space, "Look what you boys did, was all of this really necessary?"

"She was trying to get out of that hole up there, sir, I thought it would make it easier on us to transport her this way." The one who had slashed at her had said sheepishly.

"Oh really?" Everyone fell silent, suddenly her head was wrenched upwards by her hair. Her scalp burned as the tears rolled down her face and mingled with her bloody face. Her eyes slowly opened as she locked eyes with the devil himself. He was smiling and his black hair was perfectly in place around his handsome face. His grey eyes were filled with joy at her pain as he dug a finger inside one of her wounds; extracting it he licked the blood he had collected. "We are going to have so much fun little mouse. I guarantee it."

Bile rose up her throat and her vision went black.

****

The wind howled and raged as Danny and the others got close to the house. They had gotten caught up in the storm almost as soon as they left the castle but the wind here was much stronger. It was truly brutal and he struggled to keep Amaan in the air as the wind pelted them downward. His palm prickled as he caught the end of the vivid dream Lilith was having; his since of guilt raged in side him as Danny remembered the report Mouse had given. They had waisted so much time in retrieving Lilith's sister and they had known where she was almost the whole time. If something happened to Daina....*best not to think about that.*

Danny urged Amaan to fly faster as he blew past his brothers, Amaan kept his wings tight to his side as he zoomed through the air. The house should be coming up over the next mountain.

Lil are you okay? It was quite now until he felt her softly brush his mind. Suddenly he felt a stir in is stomach. What was that?

Ignore that Eros I'm not feeling well. Are you almost home?

We have some medicine for you and we will be there soon just wait for us.

What do you have to feel guilty over?

Shocked Danny hadn't realized he was letting his guilty conscience leak through their link. She didn't need this on her mind right now and he didn't want to give away Mark's secret yet.

This was a tough mission and we found an orphan in a burned down town.

Oh no, is the child okay.

I hope so. We left her with the king. I just feel bad about leaving her. There that should throw her off his actual thoughts for a little while.

I'm sure your king is kind and wise. He will find a place for her.

Danny snorted. *I really hope so, but don't tell the king you think those things he will get a bigger head than he already has.*

With good reason from what I've gathered. Besides, don't all kings and queens have a big head?

True though Ash doesn't have a queen yet. I've heard he is hard to live with.

He felt his stomach flutter once more as she slipped away from his mind leaving him alone with his thoughts as the rain pelted down.

****

Lilith shot up from the sofa and ran to the trash can in the kitchen. Bile and her last snack spewed from her mouth as Taurtis appeared behind her to hold her hair back for her. He had been staying in the guest bedroom while the men where away and had been helping her whenever she needed it. He was such a good brother as he made sure she rested and drank lots of fluids. She was showing a little more obviously but was able to hide it under a baggy shirt. Lilith was sure Danny had lied about the cause of his guilty conscience, but she was glad they were able to save a child while they were away at the very least. Lilith had been throwing up a lot lately but this time it was due to her dream about Daina that had caused it.

Taurtis grabbed a wet cloth and knelt down in front of her to wipe the sweat from her brow, he had a stern face as he contemplated something. "The little one is strong Lil. It'll be a fighter like it's parents; I may end up kicking it's ass when it gets big enough for putting you through all this though."

Lilith leaned into the cool cloth, "I wish it was the little one," she sighed.

"What do you mean?" Concerned now, Taurtis picked her up and carefully carried her the short distance to the kitchen table. A bird's crow mingled into the sound of the downpour of rain, the pair tilted their heads as they heard the faint sound of the coven's giant birds touching down out back. Shaking her head Lilith ignored them, this was important.

"I think it's Daina."

The back door flew open as wind and rain rushed on outside; Taurtis stood protectively in front of her hiding her from view. Lilith couldn't help but roll her eyes and peer around him. *I'm pregnant not an invalid.* Water splashed as the men walked in, she could hear their boots slosh on the floor as water dripped off of them. They looked wet and tired but otherwise okay. Mark's eyes searched the room then locked on where she sat behind Taurtis; Mark completely ignored him as he crossed the distance and placed a scorching hot kiss on her parted lips. Mark looked at her concerned when he pulled back and saw the sheen of tears that were in her eyes. Reaching up she hugged him around his neck and peaked over at Danny as Mark hugged her tightly. He was getting her some water and placing something orange inside the glass, stirring the glass he turned back to her and handed her the strange liquid.

"Here drink this there is medicine in it that should help your stomach." Danny looked worried as he glanced back at the trash can. *He must have seen the vomit.*

"I'm okay just had a very bad dream."

"Are you sure you are okay, that was some strong wind out there." Mark was defiantly worried as he pulled back to look her in the eyes.

"She was just about to tell me about Daina." Taurtis cut in as he took the chair next to her. Lilith watched as some of the color leached from Mark's face at the mention of her sister. *He is hiding something from me.* Lilith pulled out of Mark's arms and stood up to go to the sink. On the way she passed by the other brothers, to avoid looking at them she gulped down the liquid Danny had given her and washed the glass in the sink. Lilith could feel anger and confusion bubbling up inside her.

"What about Daina, *draga*?" Mark sounded funny, not like himself.

"She is hurting."

"How do you know?"

"I saw it happen. She was hurt and dragged off of a wall before she was slashed to a bloody pulp." Tears rolled, ignored, down her face. "She was bloody and in so much pain."

"Where Lil?" Taurtis was already in motion on the way to the still open back door.

"In the catacombs. France, I think," she was uncertain until, "Jase, mouse saw a woman near there, hadn't he?"

"I believe so. A little over a week and a half ago," Lilith caught the quick glance he gave Mark.

What the fuck was that look for? Doubt pushed through her as she slowly looked around the room. Taurtis had switched his path and had crossed the room to shadow her. Mark watched and appeared to be deep in thought. It was Jon that cut the silence, "Are you sure it wasn't something that will happen in the future?"

Was it? "Maybe but it felt different," Lilith glanced at Mark in confusion. He was looking at her with love and worry in his eyes. How could she doubt him when he looked at her like that? Maybe it was just the pregnancy hormones that made it feel weird.

"*Draga*, you look like you haven't been sleeping. Maybe it was a future prediction but you can't tell because you are not sleeping. It could also just be a nightmare and not even be happening. We can take a few days and prepare for the trip and in a week, we will head down there and check it out. How does that sound?"

Lilith found herself nodding along to what Mark was saying. It made since, she could have just been having a nightmare and since they had talked about the possibility of her being there before it just stuck. They needed to prepare first then when they are ready, they will head out. Lilith heard Taurtis head for the open door again. "I will head there first and...."

Wind whipped through the door and slammed Taurtis into the countertop. Red hot anger filled her suddenly and erratically. She could feel her eyes change red with the anger as she slowly turned to him. "Wait for everyone else to move you idiot," she hissed as she closed in on him.

The wind stopped as she stood before him now. Taurtis was smiling at her sudden outburst as he looked down at her, "It would be in Daina's best interest to have someone down there sooner just in case." Bending down so no one else could hear what was heard, Taurtis whispered in her ear, "Get ahold on those hormones or it will give you away before you even tell them about the little warrior. Keep wearing those oversized shirts for now until you calm your doubts about the man. You are showing but you should be able to hide it for at least another week but don't let him have sex with you. He would notice in no time."

Flushing red Lilith quickly assessed her mood. She had calmed down quite a bit after releasing the wind but now was embarrassed by her sudden outburst. Over reaction was an understatement she realized as she turned around and was forced to face the men's concerned looks. She had never been this moody before all this; tossing her hair over her shoulder in the attempt to look regal and composed. Taurtis was right she was starting to get noticeably pregnant but because she was so physically fit, she was hiding it well. *Thank god for my spartan like workout schedule.*

"I see your point but what if something happens? How will you let us know if something is wrong?"

Digging through his back pocket Taurtis extracted a small black phone, "You are still thinking like we are back home. I will call you Lil, I promise. Besides you are so close to being able to fly again. The medic said in about one more week you should be able to fly again," smiling he called out as he ran out into the downpour and away from the diversion he had made.

Lilith's jaw went slack. Had he really just done that? They had agreed not to tell them about the Maverick's visit and the way he ran out she knew he did it on purpose. Raising her voice so he could hear her she called out, "Be safe you fuckin coward!"

The door swung shut with an audible click as all eyes were still glued on her. Danny ran over with a grin plastered on his face picked her up and swung her in a giant wet bear hug. His voice was still husky from his first encounter with her brother but it wasn't that noticeable anymore, "I don't really know what was up with that but thank you for slamming him one for me."

"What the wind thing? He had been picking on me the whole time you were gone and then he suddenly wanted to run off. He had it coming."

Lilith hated to lie to him but something with their glances made her uneasy. She knew she shouldn't tell them about the little one. Not with the uneasiness she felt and now when they were so close to finding Daina.

Warm hands clasped her waist from behind once Danny had released her. Mark stood behind her as he hugged her close and brushed a kiss to her neck. A flash of hot desire shot through her and made her clit clench. Lilith hadn't noticed that he had left the table and walked up behind her. His strong muscular arms banded around her and she could feel his heat like brands, branding her to her bones. This was her man. Once they have Daina back she would tell him about the baby and ask him what he was hiding.

"*Draga*, if you keep wiggling like that, we will have a problem," Mark mumbled against her neck.

Lilith hadn't realized she had been moving around and rubbing her butt on his groin, "Sorry I didn't mean to I was thinking and spaced out."

Mark lifted his head with a groan, "It's worse when you tell me you didn't mean to. It implies that subconsciously you want my dick there."

"Does it? Sorry."

"Are you?" Mark asked as he spun her slowly in his arms to press his forehead on hers. Tilting her head, she looked him in his deep blue eyes, he looked worried again. "From what I just heard Maverick was here and you still haven't told me what he had said."

"Jealous another man looked at my naked flesh?" Lilith teased.

"I was worried but now I want to hit the poor bastard."

He was almost boyish when he pouted like this. "I'm fine. He said one more week before I am aloud to fly with my own wings. He also checked out my bandages and said I'm okay to stop wrapping them up so they can get some air." Lilith stood on her tip toes and kissed his stubble covered jaw.

Mark looked skeptical at first, his handsome features searching her eyes before he relaxed and nodded. Lilith loved how tall and muscular Mark was. He always made her feel safe in his arms. Mark looked like the very definition of what a warrior should look like. His deep voice stopped her from daydreaming, "Good we will see how they are in a week when we head out."

"Of course. Now can I have a kiss? It's been days since my last one." Lilith asked sweetly and was rewarded when Mark pulled her hair to properly tilt her head upward as he devoured her lips. She opened her mouth to allow his tongue inside to slip inside to duel with hers. Someone cleared their throat, reminding her again that they weren't alone in the room. With one more quick kiss Lilith pulled away.

Jon with his messy mop of blonde hair was peering at them with an amused look, "If you would like to continue with that please do so later. We have so much to prepare for so we will be ready to go next week. Don't really have time for all the lovey-dovey shit, you know?"

"Sounds good I don't want Taurtis to have all the fun anyway." This was it, soon they would be going to save Daina.

Soror cara salvus erit. Be safe dear sister.

10.

The week leading up to their trip passed quickly. Everyone was busy preparing what they would need and gathering supplies to evenly disperse and pack so they would be ready to go, even if Taurtis called and summoned them immediately. It wasn't too long of a flight from the coven house to the catacombs, only around a four-hour flight. It would be easy to make a trip like that in a day. She had been doing research all week on the winding tunnels and how they had come to be there below the city of Paris. Once Mark had shone her how to look things up on the computer, she had been doing pretty much nothing but research. She had read every article and watched any documentary she could find on the tunnels and she felt like she had a good handle on what all she would need to bring and also what to look out for. Mark had also been too preoccupied by all the nonstop phone calls from random people and gathering all sorts of supplies for everyone. He had only just gotten back last night from flying back to the king's castle, he had gotten a call that they needed him for a debriefing and he flew out. He had flown night and day to make it back in time to leave. Secretly she was grateful for him being called away, with him away she didn't have to worry about finding excuses not to have sex with the smoking hot warrior. She wasn't sure if the oversize shirts she had bought when she went out with Taurtis would hide her pregnancy very much longer. The baby was growing faster than she had ever seen a Custos child grow, already she looked like she was around five or six months but with how often she went on a run her features still managed to look normal, the only thing that would give her away would be the belly. The only other person she knew of that had progressed this quickly was her mother who took the record for fastest pregnancy. She had them in a month but she had also been having three little ones and with her not being on her home plane there wasn't any easy way for her to know how many she was carrying. She was just assuming it was one based entirely on one set of kicks. Lilith was grateful that the men weren't very observant, Maverick had been right about that.

It hadn't taken him long to figure out she was pregnant in fact he almost just walked in and immediately said she was. It took her nearly his entire visit to convince him not to tell Mark about it, Lilith had told him she wanted to surprise him with the news. Maverick had let up on the issue and had given her special vitamins to help her with the day sickness and since she had started taking them, she had hardly thrown up. He should be back sometime next week to check on her and see how she was doing if he had the chance he had said. Soon she will need new clothes and she was sure her little warrior would need some too pretty soon. It might just be a few weeks until she met them.

"Lil stop daydreaming and grab your duffel bag! We are heading out in a minute." Jon called from the backyard.

They were heading out of the house now and today couldn't have been a better day to travel. Lilith picked up the heavy duffel bag and closed and locked the kitchen door behind her. They had given her a key when she had first brought her into the house in case she wanted to leave while they were away, she hadn't really left the house all that much but she loved having a key. It made her feel like she had a home to go back too. She carried some clothes for Tauris in her bag, her brother had made a closet in the stone house he made outside. *The showoff.* They hadn't heard anything from him in a week which made her eager to head out. "Coming Jon!"

"Take your time *draga* make sure you haven't forgotten anything." Mark called from Akand. The men were fastening their packs around their familiar's necks, each pack had the supplies equally divided between them in case if they got separated. Lilith had been adamant she would carry her own bag.

Smiling Lilith approached Akand, he was a truly magnificent bird. He looked the strongest of the bunch in his fully grown form. The bird was standing at around seven and a half feet if she had to make a bet and his wingspan was slightly bigger than her own, but that wasn't surprising as it had to accommodate Mark's size as he hopped on its back. Mark turned and held out his hand for her to hop on behind him; with lots of discussion Lilith agreed to ride alongside Mark but only because they had been worried her wings would give out since they haven't been used in a while.

Lilith pulled the strap of her bag over her neck and tied back her hair in a high ponytail so it wouldn't fly everywhere, mainly she didn't want it slapping her in the face. With one last look at the house to make sure everything was in order Lilith nodded her head as she reached up and took Mark's outstretched hand. Grinning at him now Lilith quickly pecked a kiss to his cheek. "Ready whenever you are ready *deliciae.*"

"You are in a good mood today." Mark laughed as he secured her arms around his waist. He had been acting weird recently but she was glad he was back to himself for the most part. He hadn't been looking her in the eye much.

"The wind is calling me and i can't wait to get into the air again." Lilith wiggled as a gentle breeze filled the air around her.

"Be patient *draga* we are just waiting on Danny. He went out back to lock up the garage then we will be on our way." Marks laugh was warm and made her laugh with him.

"I can't help it; patience is not a talent of mine."

Eros hurry up will you I'm dying to take off.

"Coming!" Danny yelled as he ran up to his familiar, Amaan. "Had to make sure everything was locked up and turned off."

"Enough commentary over there, is everyone good to go?" Jon looked to each of them and waited for them to nod, "Okay let's take off."

Akand unflared his large powerful wings and kicked off the ground, the joy she felt increased with each powerful flap of his wings, they were finally in the air. *Finally! We are coming Daina!*

They had been flying for around an hour or so; it wouldn't be long before they reached their destination. Lilith had been looking curiously at all the mountain tops and streams as they passed by them but she kept glancing at the familiars envying the freedom they had right now. She would give anything to fly with them, Lilith gripped Mark's waist tightly as the wind beckoned to her softly. Mark looked back at her with a huge grin, he was enjoying this she could tell as he faced forward again.

Lilith felt Danny brush against their bond. *What's up Eros?*

Are you having fun over there? Danny looked back at her with a huge grin on his face as the wind whipped at his hair.

Yes! This is relaxing. I've never had the chance to glide through the air like this before.

Glide? Lil this is flying! He looked smug as he had Amaan do drips and summersaults. *See flying.*

I see Amaan flying and you are hitching a ride so technically you are just gliding along. Lilith teased as a strong gust of wind slammed into Akand; instinctively so she didn't pull Mark off with her she let him go and fell off the back of the bird. She heard Mark bellow out her name as she tumbled down.

Lilith rolled so she could see the ground as she free fell. Throwing out her arms and legs so she was making an X she slowed her decent. Back home she was one of the most feared predators of the sky, and it was about time these men knew what flying really was. The wind whipped at her clothes and the bag kept hitting her backside; focusing on her wings she summoned the energy required to release them from their hiding spot. Her back prickled as her wings shot out unflared causing her to flip, focusing she tucked them to her sides and zoomed downwards before evening out and opening them up again.

Utter jubilation filled her as she watched her midnight black wings flapping away once more, with a few strong beats of her wings she was projecting through the sky. Shooting upwards she zoomed out of the clouds startling the men as they were searching downwards for her, she guessed. Lilith zoomed around them doing summer saults and flips as she tucked her wings and hurled herself forward and backwards. They watched in awe and amusement at the joy she was experiencing. After getting it all out of her system she took her new place alongside the familiars.

That is flying. Lilith thought breathlessly.

Point taken.

Glancing over she saw Mark shake his head and smile in her direction. The wind felt good and she was content.

They had flown a few more hours passing all kinds of cities, towns, and villages. There was so much she still wanted to learn about on this plane that she had never thought she would want to know, so many experiences she wanted to have as well. They had entered France not long ago and where just now flying into Paris as the Eiffel tower came into view, it was much larger than she was expecting and decorated with lights. People were sitting in groups around it having picnics and playing sports with friends. She wanted to see what the tower looked like at night all lit up. It probably looked romantic.

They had circled the city twice before landing in an empty park, Jon had signaled for their decent and one by one they had landed; theirs birds dropping the packs and returning to the size of normal hawks. Lilith was the last one in the air and she hadn't wanted to land; landing meant putting away her wings. She had contemplated just flying around the city and try to look for Daina that way but knew it wouldn't work if she was still underground. Tucking in her wings, Lilith had dropped next to Mark and focused on turning her wings back into the tattoos to hide them. She was a little sore but nothing rolling her shoulders wouldn't fix which showed her progressively getting better at hiding them.

Mark leaned down and brushed a kiss on her cheek, "Did you have fun?"

She couldn't help but smile up at him, he looked like he was proud of her. "Very much, sorry I ended up falling off and stretching my wings."

"You call that stretching?" Mark asked with a quirk of his brow.

"Seriously, you really have to tell me how you do that."

"Deeply guarded male secret remember?" Mark laughed as he circled her waist and brought her over to his brothers. Lilith couldn't help it. She stood on her tippy toes and kissed his neck. She found herself wrapping her arms around his muscular body and hugging him tight. Looking up at his handsome face she was pleased to see his stunned expression.

"I don't mean to interrupt you too but think of this as a mission and let's go," Jon held up his phone, "Taurtis just texted me his coordinates, he didn't give me much to go on but he says he found something."

Jon's serious demeanor had her releasing Mark and looking up. Mark had his soldier look on his face with his shoulders back, he was no longer relaxed and playful. *What did you find Taurtis?* Lilith felt the change in her as well as she stopped thinking like a lover and settled into the warrior she was more familiar as. A soft kick in her stomach made her smile. *Looks like my little warrior is ready to fight alongside it's momma. When this is all over, we will have to tell your dad about you.* She promised as the followed the coordinates.

Danny knew when they reached the catacombs he would be scent in first, with his ability over the shadows he was the best at leading point in dark places. Lilith slid in place right behind him, then Jase, leaving Mark and Jon at the rear. He trusted if anything happened that this little red head would spring into action and cover him. The thought warmed him. *When had she become one of his best friends?* Danny thought as they rounded a crumbling corner.

Lilith had just entered the space when rocks crumbled downwards, with quick foot work Danny reached out and pulled her into him. Jase moved quickly and froze the rocks so they wouldn't tumble on the rest of the group. Lilith peeked up at him and smiled. *Mark is really lucky.*

"Are you okay?"

"Yes, thank you for that."

Danny let her go, as he began to pull away from her, he felt a small bump to his abs and glanced down. Lilith had frozen.

"What wa...." Her hands flew up and silenced him question. *What the hell? Was she... What was that Lil?*

Nothing. She was shaking her head and trying to push him down the tunnel.

No that was something, are you by chance pregnant?

*Please just walk Eros, promise not to tell...*she sounded desperate.

Mark sounded worried as he called up their chain, they had been paused too long, "Is she okay?"

Danny searched Lilith's pleading eyes, "Yes she is fine. Let's get a move on and for god's sake watch your steps everyone." Danny turned and headed back down the tunnel; he couldn't believe he was doing this.

****

Oh no, he knows! Lilith watched Danny's back as he led the way down deeper into the tunnels. It was dark and wet down here. Daina would have beelined straight to this area, she felt that in her soul, Daina would have looked for the safety this tunnel would give her. She had been too focused on not falling on the rubble at her feet that she hadn't looked up and noticed the falling rubble. If it wasn't for Danny she would have been hurt. Lilith was surprised he hadn't noticed she was rounder since the hug he gave her last week; she was well aware she wouldn't be able to

159

hide it another week and now Dany knew. *My little warrior wanted to meet his uncle.* He hadn't said anything to the others. *Why? She was noticeably pregnant,* not that the others were sharp enough to tell apparently. If the others had noticed they didn't say anything and she knew they would have never let her come with them. So, why hadn't Danny said anything? Reaching out Lilith felt for Danny's bright consciousness, once she found it, she softly tapped it to get his attention.

Thank you, Eros...

He said nothing as they continued down the tunnel, they had crossed into a wide-open room and headed back into another tunnel. She was starting to get the scents of both Taurtis and Daina's scent, hope blossomed inside her chest. She heard Danny sigh as he reached out to her.

It was nothing but why didn't you just tell us anything, and don't say it was because you wanted to come with us. I know you better than that and we would have put you in a better position to keep you safe.

That took her by surprise. He sounded hurt; Lilith was surprised at how his hurt look affected her as he kept his gaze forward. When had they become such good friends? She was sure he thought the same. They had grown close in the time she was on this plane, he was always finding ways to goof off and look out for her. He treated her like a part of the family and called her his sister because of the mark around her throat, Danny had almost had kittens when he saw it. He was always talking with the others and they were a very close family, perhaps he knew what Mark was hiding. Would he tell her? Only one real way to find out.

I was scared.

He paused briefly to check the stability of the ground and ceiling. *I get that. Too many new things at once it can be scary but we would have helped you through everything.*

That's not what I was scared of though thank you for the reassurance. I was afraid because I have a feeling Mark was hiding something from me. I can see how much he cares for me but why would he hide something from me? I guess I had a bad feeling about it and didn't want it to hurt me or my little warrior.

Lilith watched Danny's shoulders tense up at her admittance, he was trying to roll them a nervous habit she noticed all of the Flemming boys did when they were unsure of something. *He knew something.* Lilith noticed as she cocked her head to the side taking him in.

Stop.

Stop what?

Don't poke so much. I will tell you but you have to promise not to get too mad at him without a cause, okay?

Of course, I wouldn't, why would I get mad? Worried now she nibbled on her lower lip nervously.

Well, he sort of knew where your sister was and didn't tell you but only because he was terrified you would leave and never come back. He wouldn't do anything to hurt you I swear and he wouldn't want to do anything to hurt anyone you cared about.

She stopped suddenly and Jase slammed into her nearly knocking her over; his arm shot around her stopping her from falling. Jase's ice could do nothing to freeze the red-hot rage filling her; Mark had betrayed her. *How could he?*

Lil...

Jase moved his cold hands to her shoulders as he helped stabilize her footing, he was peering down at her with a concerned look. When had he gotten used to her being around? "Is everything alright Lil?"

Was everything alright? Mark hadn't said much this entire trip and now she knew why. Guilt. He was trying to hide this and charm her at the same time; did he actually care about her? Wait. Don't go down that rabbit hole just yet. She needed calm until they figured out where Daina was, Danny had just said not to get mad. Plastering on a sugary smile Lilith glanced back at Jase and patted his hand, "Yeah everything is fine just thought I finally was starting to smell Taurtis and got distracted."

She saw Mark over Jase's shoulder looking oddly at her, shaking her head she turned back and continued to follow Danny as he ducked under a beam.

Lil, I didn't mean to make you feel upset and betrayed. Mark really adores you and he would never intentionally put you in a situation like this. He is just an idiot sometimes.

Can it Eros, anyway you look at it your brother was acting like a selfish bastard all the while I was worried sick about my sister!

He thought she was safe underground and thought he had time to court you properly. He didn't know that anyone would find her down here, it's a fucking labyrinth down here.

How can I trust him with my family after this? With my baby? Do you see nothing wrong with what he has done by not telling me the full truth?

Danny let the link fall silent for a few minutes with every moment Taurtis's scent grew stronger. Finally, Danny responded slowly.

I know you are upset but he would never endanger you or the baby, he is an idiot for hiding it this long. Please believe me Lil he is over the moon for you and will probably die from excitement when he finds out about the baby; he won't admit it but it's what he has wanted. You call the baby your little warrior, right?

Yes. My little warrior because they are always kicking at me. A small smile tugged at her lips; she patted her belly for a moment before dropping her hand back to her side.

How long until you make me an uncle? She could hear the smile in his thoughts.

Lilith blew out a puff of air. He was trying to change the subject. *Maybe a few weeks? Custos children grow fast and the baby has been growing faster than I've ever seen so I'm honestly not sure.*

Hot damn Lil, how long have you known? When did this happen?

She had to think about that. Every moment she had alone with Mark was often hot and intense, but...*It had to have been the first time we were together, so a few weeks, I think.*

Well, I can't wait to meet him and I'm sure Daina will feel the same way when she finds out. We should have a huge baby shower after we find her.

Why would you celebrate it raining babies?

No, it's a party to celebrate the baby and its mom. Not too sure why it's called a baby shower now that I think about it.

That's so weird. Ducking she followed Danny into a wide-open chamber, it was the same chamber Daina had been sleeping in from her dream. It smelled of absolute terror and unmistakable rage, why was Taurtis so angry? She felt Mark slip behind her as she inspected the small thin sheet her sister had been using to sleep, it was now balled up on the ground. The room was littered in bottles and other pieces of trash, there was a manhole cover high up on the ceiling and a faint scent of sewers nearby. This must have been an abandoned sewer, looking around Lilith saw a small makeshift bed that was in the only dry corner of the chamber. Daina was sleeping in a place like this?

She hated how Mark's rainy scent calmed her nerves, she hated how he touched her gently, she hated how his deep rumbly voice enveloped her in warmth as he spoke into the silence, "*Draga*, I'm sure we fill find some sign of her around here somewhere."

Lilith said nothing as she turned and looked at his strong and handsome features. She felt a sharp pain form in her chest as she couldn't get over the betrayal she felt at the moment. Something had happened to Daina....

****

Lilith had looked tense the entire walk to the cavern. She was sad and worried, he got that, but with the way she looked at him now felt like he had been stabbed. She wasn't saying anything and she wasn't looking at him as much as looking through him, his heart clenched. Mark looked around the cavern for something he missed he was sure it wasn't anything he had said because he hadn't said much this whole trip. Mark bent down and captured her lips with his. Moving his mouth over hers he could feel her resistance and pulled back looking over her face, she just looked sad. "What's wrong *draga?*"

She shook her head and looked away. Mark tensed as he heard heavy footsteps coming from the other tunnel that led out the chamber. Slowly, he gripped the hilt of his dagger only to relax when the newcomer became visible. It was Taurtis. If possible, Mark's heart dropped further when he took in the other man's haggard appearance. He looked like he hadn't slept all week and his pitch-black hair was covered in soot and sweat, his clothes were torn in some places and his shoulders were slumped slightly. All hope of Daina just popping out of the tunnels unharmed left him.

Mark felt Lilith brush past him, he could see the effort she had made to touch him as little as possible when she walked by him. What had he done? She had been so happy before they came down here. She had hugged him and kissed his neck when they had arrived; she had made him rock hard when she had done that. Her small body had pressed on his. It had caught him off guard but now he missed it.

Mark watched the way her hips swayed from side to side in that sexy catwalk she always did as she headed over to her brother. He wouldn't ever get tired watching the way his woman walked even when she was upset, she still could be such a turn on. *Fuck, does that make me a horrible person?* Whatever was bothering her they would have to talk it out in private whenever they got a free moment. He didn't want to put her on the spot and ask in front of the other men, she looked like she wanted to yell and it was best to give her privacy to do so. The last week had gone by so fast he hadn't had much time with her other than coming home and holding her, his phone started ringing off the hook as soon as he got back to the coven house each call came with updates on Stephine. That bitch was still on the move.

Lilith's voice sounded devoid of emotion, her face never giving anything away. "What did you find? Jon said you had found something down here."

The other man raked his hands through his hair and blew out a long breath. This was not a good sign. "Best if I just show you, it's not far from here."

Not good at all.

Mark looked at Jon who was pointing at Danny, his youngest brother was pink in the face and was ignoring them all. He had become Lilith's best friend, hadn't he? That's how they had been acting at least, they were practically joined at the hip. There was a small twinge of jealousy for his brother's close relationship with his woman; Danny would never do anything to hurt him but still. *Why does she always talk to him and not me when she is troubled?* Jon was nodding his head in confirmation of Danny knowing something. *Looks like we are going to have to talk.*

Taking one last look around the dark empty cavern Mark made sure it was clear before he turned and followed the others. They hadn't been walking long before the newer brick turned into old cobblestone walls and floors. The deeper into the tunnels he went the easier he could pick up the scent of blood. Torches began to line the walls and were casting a warm glow down the halls, Taurtis must have set them up.

Nearly falling over Jon who had apparently stopped to check out something on the floor, Mark stooped down with him to inspect the dark droplets that began there, the small drops led deeper into the tunnel. Jon's whisper drifted low to him; Mark had almost missed the thread of sound.

"Mark."

"I know," and he did, this wasn't good.

"If something happens to her sister, she may never forgive you and Taurtis may kill us all for helping you hide this." he sounded worried.

"Let's hope we find her."

The ground started to shift. Mark fell over as he tried to stand up, wind shot through the corridor blowing out the torches. Jon had made his way to his feet and braced on the wall as he pulled Mark to his feet. Jase and Danny had continued down the hallway where the rumbling was more sever. On unstable legs he continued further down as the wind assaulted him and pulled him along; it was pulling at his clothes and tearing small cuts into his skin. The cuts weren't deep but they stung like salt had been rubbed on them. *What the hell was going on up there?* Falling into the wall Mark was able to finally hold himself up as the wind and shaking suddenly stopped. *The hell?* He glanced over at Jon who was supported on the other wall, "What was that?"

"Hell if I know, let's move."

The two took off into the dark corridor and within a few minutes they saw a flicker of a torch, someone had just relit the torches down here. The stench of blood clogged his nose as the walls came into view. They had made it to a dead end. *Oh no. Where was her sister?* There was a small hole at the top of the wall, even from a distance he saw the bloody scratch marks he could tell were made by someone who had been clawing at it for their life. Slowing his pace Mark panted as he surveyed the rest of the area. The walls had high velocity splatters going up the far wall and a deep pool of dried blood was only two feet from the wall with the craw marks.

"What the hell happened here?" Mark choked out, his throat suddenly dry and his conscience was heavy.

Lilith stayed silent as he watched her crouch to the ground; she was poking the dried blood and bringing it to her nose. *Could she track as well?* His brothers stood in stunned silence as they all took it in; it was Tauris that cut the silence, "This is what I found when I got here. I was only hours behind Lilith's dream and the blood had already looked to be about a week old. I've been trying to track her this whole week and have turned up nothing."

"We can have some new trackers down here in a few hours, I swear we will find her." He yanked out his phone and punched in the number to the guard's best tracker.

"They won't find anything." Taurtis sounded a little to matter of fact as he looked sadly at Lilith, "I have been looking for days and haven't picked up much of her past the entrance. It had rained before I got here."

"Maybe we just need a few new pairs of eyes," Mark could hear the phone ringing as he impatiently waited for the phone to pick up; after five rings he heard Matt's groggy hello. "Fucking finally, where are you at right now?"

"Was I supposed to be somewhere with you?" He could hear Matt getting up and stretching, the lazy hound dog.

Blowing out an impatient breath Mark gripped the phone hard as he tried to control his temper. "Get out to the catacombs of Paris, I'll send you the coordinates just be here by nightfall. Bring your coven there is a lot of ground to cover."

He went to hang up and heard Matt's mumbled *who made you king.* He turned and noticed the twin jade green eyes staring at him, "They will be here by nightfall to help with the search."

"They won't find anything," Taurtis repeated.

"It's worth a try." She looked devoid of emotion as Mark hung up the phone, much like a broken doll. He couldn't take her looking like this, he knew she would bottle up her feelings. "*Draga,* honey this isn't your fault; your dream was off by a few days, it happens." Mark hoped he was guessing the reason for her sudden coldness correctly. She had to feel like this was her fault.

Piercing jade eyes glared daggers at him as her stubborn little chin jetted up at him. Her feline like features sharpened as unease settled in him, he wasn't looking at the face of his sweet little lover. He realized he was looking at the fierce warrior he had met in his bedroom when she was pinning Maverick in a kill hold. He braced his feet when she took a step forward, her hand shot out and an audible slap echoed through the tunnels. Mark's cheek stung as he stared at her in shocked silence. His brothers had fallen silent as everyone watched as Lilith poked his chest hard.

"How dare you!" She hissed.

Mark rubbed his stinging cheek in confusion, "What did I do?"

"*It's not your fault,*" she mocked as she repeated back at him.

"It's not," he said quietly.

"Pray tell whose fault it is Marcus Rolan Monroe? If I hadn't had the dream how else would we have ended up here?"

The way she asked made him worried as he reached out to her and gripped her shoulder; he had barely closed his hand around her before she slapped his hands away. His hands fell to his sides, "I don't know."

"Don't touch me," huffing a breath her mocking smile crossed her lips, "Taur, he doesn't know, did you hear that?"

The man crossed his arms as he nodded to her letting his sister keep the floor and vent her frustration. His calculated eyes never left Mark. "*Let me show you my story* she had said. Her. Story. It had already fucking happened and you know what? I sat on my pregnant ass and trusted your guidance. I trusted you!" She was yelling at him as she clutched her stomach protectively. Now that he paid more attention, she did look much rounder when she pressed on the oversized shirt down.

All air rushed out of him as he processed what she had just said. Pregnant. He was going to be a dad? Mark froze in place as he almost reached out to her again, she was too emotional right now and would only grow angrier with him if he touched her.

"You fucking knew where she was this whole time, you bastard!" Lilith had reached back to hit him again. He deserved her anger. She was right, he had known but how did she find out he had known? Shock held him in place, his muscles tense as he processed all the information that had just been dumped in his lap. He was excited for the baby but so very worried about her discovery of his secret. *I should have told her about this sooner.*

With a gentle swiftness Taurtis caught her wrist before she could slap him again, "Calm down Lil, this stress isn't good for you or the little warrior." She was sucking in air fast as she shielded her stomach further from him; Lilith looked at him as if he was a monster.

"We will find Daina and I'll fix everything. I promise just please..." Mark felt cold as she backed away from him. His soul felt like it had cracked slightly.

"No, you won't," She sounded so small now as she shrank behind her brother's arm. "Gregory has her and we will make sure he dies for this."

"Gregory? How do you know that name, *draga?*" Desperation was setting in as he reached out for her.

"Someone you know?"

"He is leading a pack of mutts. We found out about him recently with our last mission." He sounded like a robot. She was his heart. The way she was looking at him made him feel like someone was ripping open his chest. If she left it may kill him. She was blinking back tears as a sad smile appeared on her beautiful face.

"I wish you all the best of luck but Taurtis, I would like to leave." She had let go of her brother's elbow and backed up to the bloody wall. *No, she can't leave....*

With a wave of Taurtis's hand the walls crept around her and swallowed Lilith gently into the earth. Fury shot through him like he had never experienced before. Mark ran and slammed into the wall where she had stood. There was nothing left for him to hold onto. Slowly, Mark turned and gazed at her bastard of a brother. He was furious, he could feel the heat coming off him in waves as he tamped down the need to self-destruct; he couldn't in such close space. "Bring her back," he gritted out with clenched teeth.

"No. You don't deserve my sister as you are right now." The bastard smiled at him sadly. "You know she loves you right? She was so excited about the baby and was going to tell you about it when we left these damn tunnels today. She was just worried you were hiding something important from her and as usual she was right."

Mark had heard enough. He launched himself at the man in a blinding fit of rage; crouching low Mark had planned to punch him in his kidneys. Before he could make the hit connect Taurtis's large arm wrapped around his waist as he flipped Mark into the air and slammed him into the ground. The bastard crouched down next to him while Mark caught his breath. "I had hoped she was wrong for the record. Like i said, she loves you, so maybe with a little time she will forgive you. Either way though I'll be watching out for her and the kid when they come along in the meantime."

Taurtis was looking at Jon now, "Our agreement still stands, she wants out. There will be no looking for us unless you have news or she changes her mind."

"Of course, a deal is a deal." *What? When had they agreed to that?* Mark sat up slowly eyes never leaving Taurtis. Jon paused and looked over at him, Mark could see sadness in his eyes before he quickly hid it and looked at the other man. "One thing before you go."

"What? Your brother has already stolen much of our time."

"She said she was pregnant and I admit I thought she looked a little rounder but with the way you just said you would watch over the baby what did you mean? When will she be expecting?"

Taurtis paused and snapped his fingers. The ground opened up revealing a large black pit right next to the man; Taurtis walked closer to it, "Who knows."

"Wait!" Mark scrambled to the hole, "Answer the question."

"I really don't think I will," turning the man fell back into the hole giving them the American two finger salute. The ground closed up leaving no trace of either sibling, just lots of dried blood and the smell of fear.

Mark clutched at his heart as the pain of Lilith's sudden departure ripped through him. She was his whole world and he had let her down. He had one job, protect his family. Had he not wanted her to be a part of his? *Hell yes, he had wanted her in his family.* She now had his child growing safely inside her; he was an idiot; he should have treated her family as his family. Lilith had embraced his family with open arms and had treated him like a king. Even Jase was fond of her. *What have I done?*

He could hear Danny slowly approach him. Jase's cold hand patted his shoulder and Jon crouched in front of him. Tears clogged his in his throat, "I messed up."

"Yeah, you did," his head shot up to look where Danny stood. Mark's eyes were wide with disbelief; Danny never spoke out like this or called him on his bullshit. He also had never looked down at him with such hardened features with his arms crossed over his chest, he was all business. "You had something any of us would have died to protect and you fucked up man. Now what are we going to do to fix this mess? So you can get her back."

Danny stood with his back straight, his eyes were focused. Somehow, he looked older and so much like their mom. *When did you mature enough to boss me around kid?* He was right, no time for self-pity. He needed to prove himself to his woman. If she wanted effort, he would show it, no more being selfish, nothing mattered more than Lilith and their baby.

Straightening his spine, Mark took a deep calming breath and looked at the men who would die for him. "Matt and his coven will be here today; we are going to buckle down and find Daina or we will die trying."

"Roger that."

****

She could feel him pulling out of her slowly. The man, Gregory, had taken her two weeks ago if she was counting the sunrises correctly. Every night Gregory would come into her cell to sate his perverse needs, and during the day he would go back to beating the holy hell out of her for information she did not possess. At first, she had tried to fight him off, crying every night as she begged for him to stop, but two weeks later she merely hung limply from the raptors he had hung her from. Her once flawless body was not a cup up bloody mess.

Gregory should be getting ready to let her rest now that he had satisfied his needs, *even a monster needs its rest*. As usual, he reached around her and grabbed her throat. His nails pierced her neck as he cut off her air. Daina fought for air as the chains rattled, she heard him laugh as he kissed up her bloody shoulder, slowly he eased his grip allowing her to breath. *This is hell*, she tensed. When she first met Gregory, she had though his voice sounded warm and soft but now, he sounded menacing and cold. "You really are beautiful, my little mouse."

She remained still saying nothing as he pulled the rest of the way out of her. She knew what came next as he walked to the wall and lowered her chains so she would be able to drop to the floor. Not that she had much of a choice. The two beasts from before had ripped open her achilleas, all she could do was fall to the stone ground in pain. Gregory made his way back in front of her and impatiently forced her to her knees. "Open."

Daina opened her mouth as he slammed his penis inside her mouth, she could feel bile rising as she tamped it down. "Clean it." She did as he asked, licking and sucking him clean as her throat burned from the forced entry. Her eyes started to burn as she looked up at his sick grin. His hands were like iron bands as they pulled her hair yanking her head from his cock, she gasped as his fist collided with her face. Her head hurt. Gregory crouched down getting in her face, "You are mine now mouse and I will get you to talk."

"I don't know who those people are," Daina whispered meekly as she shrunk away from him.

"What do you know about a little red head and a large man with jet black hair?" Daina froze. He was talking about Lilith and Taurtis. Gregory felt her tense and his smile widened. "See, I knew you knew something."

Daina watched as he walked back to the wall and jerked at her chains, her arms were yanked upwards as he hoisted her back up into the raptors. She felt the bile she had fought back rise again in her throat, "We aren't done yet little mouse, this is only the beginning."

"No please...stay back"

****

A soft bell chimed as Taurtis walked back into the Texas café he had visited the last time he was in town. He had thought it best to bring Lilith back to the states where they could hide and blend in until they were ready to move. They had arrived in Houston a little over a week ago, Lilith's pregnancy was progressing much quicker than either of them had expected. She had the oddest craving for pickles he has seen. She looked like she would give birth at any time and her hormones were all over the place, she was always cussing up a storm or being super sweet. He could see that Mark's absence was having an effect on her, but it was best for them if he focused on her health and not the coven who had sworn to find Daina. Lilith needed the rest and had asked him to leave her alone for a little while so, he came back to this café. They were still using Jon's card to purchase things and it seems they weren't lying about being loaded.

Walking right up to the host stand he recognized the same slutty server that had served him before. She must have recognized him too, her cheeks flushed and her eyes grew wide, standing up straight she purred, "How can I help you today?"

"Table for one." Taurtis turned his head and indicated his previous table, "Is that one available?"

"Yessir, right this way," she hurried him to his table and ran off to the back area. *What the hell?* He nearly laughed when she had tripped over her feet on the way back.

Classic music played on the speakers as he played on his phone. He had found a plague game on his phone that was addictive and time consuming. Hearing a familiar click of shoes, he glanced up to see Maddison coming his way with a mug of hot liquid and a piece of pie. She smiled politely when she saw him watching her, *she's not eating enough,* he noted at her smaller frame.

"Welcome back stranger," her southern drawl called to him as she set everything down on the table. "Where is your girlfriend?"

"What girlfriend?"

"The woman who came and collected you last time you were here," she was adorable when she looked curiously at him with her eyebrow raised. "She came in a few weeks ago saying you two were an item and to let her know if you turn up. Of course, we won't be letting her know you're here. We aren't a daycare."

"Hmm..." Hiding his expression, he took a sip of the tea she had brought him. *Damn she could make a good cup.* Pondering what she had said, Taurtis gestured to the seat across from him. "Why don't you join me? Would love the company."

She looked surprised but didn't object as she claimed the seat, "So she isn't your girlfriend?"

"No, she isn't."

A curious expression crossed her face as she leaned forward over the table, "Why not? Are you gay or something?"

He had just taken another sip when she asked making him choke on the liquid as it went down the wrong pipe. "Hell no, I'm not gay."

Glaring over at her now grinning face, she was clearly enjoying picking on him, "I figured you weren't but Tabitha was insisting you were because you hadn't been interested in her the last time you were here."

"Ah, I see but you can tell her I'm not interested in *licisci like her*. I much prefer women like you who has a shred of respect for yourself." He watched as color crept up her neck. "Besides I have my hands full with my sisters."

"*Licisci?*" The way her southern accent hung on each syllable made his heart squeeze in an unexpected way.

"Now who has a potty mouth?" He teased as he laughed when she swatted his arm.

"What does it mean, jerk?" She was laughing with him.

"Bitches, I called her a bitch."

"What language is that? I've never heard it before."

"It's Latin, though I don't blame you for not knowing it; outside of my country not many places use it."

"Where are you from?"

"Somewhere far from here, I used to be a soldier in my country but now I mostly run security all over the world," he would have to change the subject soon. "What about you, are you from here?"

Maddison shook her head and stole a bite of his pie, "No, I'm from New Orleans. Only been here for a few months. You said you had sisters, are they as intimidating as you?"

"You think I'm intimidating?"

"Well not me, but my servers were scared to serve you," she laughed as she waved her hand dismissing the subject.

"Well, to tell you the truth," he leaned forward just like she had and lowered his voice, "I'm hiding from my little sister right now she is terrifying at the moment."

Her eyes got big, "You?"

"Yeah, she is humongously pregnant and I'm hiding for a bit before heading back," he joked with her. His phone vibrated and Lilith's name appeared on the screen. She had sent him a text and he laughed at the timing as he showed Maddison the message. "See."

Taur, the baby wants more pickles, please can you bring some home for us?

Maddison laughed as she called over a nervous looking server, "Can you please get three sides of fried pickles to-go for this poor man." She turned back to him smiling, "Does she want any ranch?"

"Please. I really appreciate it," to the server he added, "Just add it to this bill and whatever you and Maddie want to eat for lunch as well."

They looked surprised at his offer, "I can't accept that Taurtis, really we are fine."

"Sorry but I insist. It's a thank you for everything." The young server was pink in the face as she thanked him and hurried away.

"Well thank you," Maddison was looking over his shoulder, "Do you know that man? He has been starring."

Taurtis turned in his chair and froze. Standing by the host stand was one of the Custos elders. Senoi, like all Custos he didn't look a day over thirty-five at most. He smiled that slow smile he always did and waved. Taurtis waved back at the old man. This was the one elder that always had tried to look out for him and in doing so had earned Taurtis's respect. Senoi made his way over to the table and pulled out a chair; in his husky voice he addressed the table. "Hello you two, anything fun going on?"

Taurtis snorted. *Small talk really?* Taurtis looked at Maddison who seemed to get the que to leave. "I'll go check on those pickles for you Taurtis, they don't take too long to make."

"Don't forget to ring up something for yourselves." He called after her.

"I'm sorry I ruined your little chat boy. I'm here because I felt new life coming from one of our kind on this plane and wanted you to take me to Daina."

"Excuse me?"

"Really? I know you have already met up with your sisters. It was idiotic of the council to want to separate you three, so where is the mother to be I sense i will be needed soon to help with the birth and on the title assessments." Senoi sounded so sure.

He couldn't help it, as he laughed at the bold assumption, it was a valid assumption but it was way off. Senoi looked puzzled as Taurtis calmed down enough to explain, "You have the wrong sister in mind old man."

"Lilith of Tragedy?" Senoi's eyes grew wide, "Are you sure?"

"Look, I know that everyone thinks we are idiots because of where we were raised, but even I can tell when a woman is pregnant."

"Of course, I was just in shock my boy." Maddison had returned to the table with a large container, it smelled amazing.

"This should hold her for a little while I think, the cook put a little extra in there when I told him it was for a pregnant woman."

Taurtis smiled and gently brushed his hand on hers as he took the box, "Thank you Maddie. I'm sorry to cut my time here short but we must go back to Lil."

"Of course, be safe and next time bring her with you."

Senoi was already waiting at the door when he turned around. He moved fast for an old man. Senoi pointed to the box, "I could use a snack, thank you."

"Not for you, Lil would kill me if even one pickle went missing."

"I see well if it's what she wants..."

"They are all she wants, trust me. Let's get going they are getting cold."

11.

Mark paced the living room. They had returned home a week ago after turning up nothing. Taurtis was right there was nothing left there, but how? Everyone left a scent even if there was rain Matt's coven should have found something; they were bloodhounds for fucks sake. Matt had stayed behind in the tunnels and was calling him with daily updates. It wasn't until matt asked him why this was so important did Mark admit outload that Daina was family. The other man had buckled down harder to find her. With nothing left for Mark to do Jon had all but dragged him home, he would rather be out there helping. When he led the search from the house his mind always wandered back to Lilith and his baby. Was she doing okay? Was she eating well? Sleeping? The questions were endless and left mostly unanswered. They knew where the siblings were because they were tracking the card they had given them. It took everything in him not to storm over to Houston and shake his stubborn woman. He loved her. She was his one and only. His everything and he would find his way back into her good graces.

"You are pacing a hole into the floor."

Mark jerked slightly; he hadn't heard Danny walk in. "Anything new?"

"Lil really wants pickles is that's what you wanted to know." The smartass said with a grin. They had cornered Danny in the tunnels and made him tell them everything, the fact that he had told Lilith everything and the fact that he had a direct mental link with her. They had been getting updates slowly whenever Danny got anything useful, like the new custos that showed up two days ago.

"Easy now big guy. No need for hostility," Danny said throwing his hands up. *Was he being hostile?*

"What do you want then?"

"Just checking on you, how are you holding up?"

"How do you think? The love of my life ran off with my baby and my baby brother, whom I trusted to have my back, narked on me." *Okay maybe a little hostile.*

"We talked about this remember? It would have been worse if she found out later than she did." He was right. Mark blew out a puff of air and rubbed the back of his neck.

"Yeah, I know. Doesn't make this any better, you know?"

Mark noted Danny flick his nose with his thumb. he only did that when he was thinking. "Well truth be told Lil and I have been discussing everything."

Mark was across the room and gripping Danny's shoulders before he even realized what he was doing. He was shocked, "And?"

"Damn loosen up on the grip," Danny winced.

"Damnit Danny, what did she say?"

"I've been trying to reason with her since she left. I'm not promising anything but it seems like she is listening to me a bit now that she calmed down from shock."

Slowly, he let Danny go, he was stunned silent. Would she forgive him? Hope blossomed in his chest. "Thank you, seriously you have been looking out for us since day one."

Now it was Danny who rubbed his neck, a family trait for sure. "Of course, we are family. Speaking of helping we should probably help Jase."

"What does he need help with?"

"Well, he felt slightly responsible for Lilith leaving so he locked himself in the guest room and is renovating it into the baby's room. I've been hearing him cuss for hours and I think I saw Jon slip in their earlier."

"Really?" He was surprised, Jase didn't usually surprise people like this. It spoke volumes on how fond he had become of Lilith and how sure she was going to come back. A smile pulled at his lips as he followed Danny into a paint covered room. Jon was painting the walls a pale blue while Jase put together a crib. The room was a mess but he didn't care. These were his brothers and at the end of the day he loved these jackasses.

****

When Senoi walked in Lilith had worried that he was here to take her child back with him. It had taken him a good hour for her to allow him to come near her and here they were two days later. She had been having contractions all day and around lunch time her water had broken. The pain was overwhelming as it felt like an air pocket was stabbing her in her womb. It was too early to be going into labor, "It's only been a month..."

Senoi's kind face appeared beside her with a wet cloth, pain pierced her ribs and lower abdomen as her little warrior fought to get free. This had been going on for hours. "Normally I would agree child but, in this case, I really will have to disagree with you, with you having more than one babe and all."

"More than one?" Lilith managed to get out before she screamed. She could feel her bones and insides shift as her little one was preparing for its appearance.

"I would say so. That's the only explanation for you growing so big so fast." Senoi walked around the bed and began to gage how dilatated she was, "they will be coming soon," he smiled up at her. "You are doing great child."

Taurtis was holding her hand as she screamed again. It felt like someone was trying to rip her in two. Taurtis looked at her with excitement and worry, "Are you sure you don't want Mark here?"

Was she? If Mark came so would the others, he had once said they weren't a pack of wild dogs that traveled in a group but she thought of them as a flock of birds. An audible pop sounded and she was no longer listening to Senoi, he had been in the middle of telling Taurtis that it would be a hard birth but all Lilith could think of was Mark.

She had dreamed of him playing with her children. He would be so good with them. She could expect him to be gentle but firm with them just like he was with her...*What am I doing? He loves me*! Sure, he had hidden this from her but he hadn't wanted to lose her. Danny had pleaded with her for days after she had left and had shown her what leaving had done to him. Mark looked rough and rugged but also determined to find Daina. He was referring to her sister as family. Her resolve to stay angry melted when she saw him do that, she wanted them in her children's lives. *Of course, I will kill him if he hid something from her like this again*, she could see him trying so hard to be better. She had seen how many trackers he had summoned to those tunnels and saw how long he had been working in the dirt trying to find something to lead them to Gregory.

Tears streamed down her sweaty face as she felt the baby move. It felt like she had someone breaking her femurs in half repeatedly as she made her decision. "Taur..." another scream ripped through her, "go...get him!" She barely registered him dropping through the earth as the crown of the first baby pushed out of her.

"That's it, I see it." Senoi encouraged, "Come on push for me."

Lilith pushed and pushed all the while the pain ricocheted through her like she had never experienced before. She was gripping the bed so hard she could hear the tearing of the fitted sheet. Screaming she gave another push and she felt something kick her thigh as the sound of a baby's cry filled the room. Her heart melted at the sound as she slumped back slightly int the bed. She could still feel her insides contracting as another baby fought for freedom. "Ah, there he is come on little one, let's wrap you up."

A whine escaped her when Senoi turned away with the baby, she hadn't seen it yet but the other one wanted out. Screaming out she began to push again and felt it crown out of her. This pain was unbelievable but different than the first. This baby was ice cold as she pushed, she feared the worst. Senoi rushed back to catch the baby as it was ushered into the world. The room was silent for a heartbeat before erupting into tiny tired cries as the little one took its first breath. Finally, she was able to slump fully into the pillows, she was panting and covered in sweat and blood.

Senoi was smiling as he took the second child over to the first, she still hadn't seen them. She heard Senoi cooing and cleaning them off as she tried to even her breathing; she wanted to see and hold her little ones. "Elder," was all she was able to say. Her throat was still raw from hours of labor and screaming. The old man turned with a wide smile.

"Congratulations on two healthy baby boys," Senoi handed her the first bundle. "I have already written down his weight and time of birth but this one needs a name now."

Turning the little bundle in her arms Lilith gazed at her firstborn. He had her pale skin and a head full of her bright crimson hair. His face was all scrunched up as he gave a big yawn reveling small teeth that were already pushing through his gums. "Ah, that's it little guy big yawn," she cooed, at the sound of her voice he slowly opened his eyes and she sucked in a breath. Senoi turned around at the sound.

"What's wrong? Is something wrong with his eyes?" Senoi reached forward only to back off at Lilith's eyes tearing up.

"Nothing's wrong," she was looking down into her eyes, only three people had them; her unique pure jade green eyes. He had the same slight tilt in the corner of his eyes that she had and the same slight curl in the corners of his lips. This was her mini-me. Lilith hugged him to her as she looked over at the elder. "His name is Lilium, my little warrior."

Unlike his brother, Lilium wasn't crying, he was just staring silently taking everything around him in. "Can I have my other baby please?" Lilith asked as she watched Senoi come back over to her. Lilith wanted to check on her other boy he had been so cold, she was sure of it.

"Let's trade shall we, he needs a name and Lilium needs some clothes on. He can't very well run around in a diaper and a blanket, can he?" Senoi gently swapped the boys and Lilith looked down and smiled, *of course.* "What is it child?" The elder asked curiously as he pulled out some clothes from the dresser and began to dress Lilium.

"Lilium looks so much like me and this little one, well, he looks just like his father already; see these beautiful blue eyes and the blonde in his hair. I am willing to bet when he gets older, he will have Mark's lopsided grin too," she mused as she brushed aside the blanket that was wrapped around him. His tiny hands reached out and wrapped around her finger as he tried to suckle it. He was still ice cold as she marveled at his tiny hands. "Baby that's not food," she laughed as she brought him to her bare breast; Senoi was right when he said it would make it easier if she stripped, it had made everything easier for her and her babies. As the little one suckled, she reached out for Lilium so he could eat as well.

Senoi watched as he cleaned her legs; he was the elder that gave titles and helped with birthing the babes, he was also gifted with foresight. "Have you chosen a name for the second born boy?"

Lilith laughed at the way he had referred to the child, often times she saw her kind treat any child after the first born as second class. She didn't see him that way, any child is a welcome child and her children will be loved equally. Smiling down at him she scented he had more witch in him than Lilium, she liked the idea of multiple names as she thought about it, "Yes, his name will be Jordium Rowan Monroe. Isn't it cute?"

"Yes, it is very cute and is a strong name child. Do you want little Lilium to have a middle name as well?" Senoi asked as he finished cleaning the blood up, he had snapped his fingers and the blankets absorbed the blood on them and returned to their original pristine white color.

She hadn't thought past Liliums first name, as she watched her younglings, she thought of all the stories she had heard growing up. One of her favorite stories stuck out the most and that was Jason and the Golden Fleece. *Lilium Jason Monroe*...it sounded nice though, the boys would probably think she named him after Jase. *Not hardly,* she mused, "His full name will be Lilium Jason Monroe."

She yawned big as her eyes grew heavy, the elder took her children gently from her as he looked down at her, "Come here boys, looks like you tired your mama out. Rest well Lilith I will watch over all of you until Taurtis returns with their father. When you awake, I will tell you both of their very special titles."

Groggy now that the adrenaline was wearing off Lilith had to force her eyes to stay open, "Wait for Mark to come before you tell me their titles please. It's a special occasion and he will want to be there to hear it."

"Of course, now you sleep well."

The next day went by quickly as Senoi showed her the motherly ropes, which she picked up rather quickly. She had found it rather easy to bounce between the boys and their needs and she had also discovered they loved her singing voice. Jordium cried often and Lilium giggled quietly when she sung them an old song about a fairy and a stubborn hunter who wanted to marry her. Lilith was smiling more often around them, the pain she had experienced was worth it just to be able to see her boys smiling at her. She couldn't wait for Mark to come; she hadn't heard anything from him as she stayed in the bungalow that Taurtis had made. Taurtis had gone out and bought her a bed and other furniture to make her feel more comfortable and prepare for the baby...*well babies.*

Playing with Jordium's feet she talked in a singsong voice as he giggled, "Your uncle Taurtis is late, yes he is. Lilium sweetie where are you going?" Her boys had surprised her, they were only a day old and were already big enough to crawl around and support their own heads. They were going to be powerful when they got older. Senoi had told her that when she was their age, she was already walking around so it didn't really surprise him all that much to see them already crawling. Custos children were amazing.

Senoi caught Lilium and spun him around while cradling him, "You're a fast one, aren't you?"

Lilith laughed as she went back to talking to Jordium, "I wonder if your uncle will fly in with your papa or tunnel in? What do you think Jordium? Do you want to learn to fly?" Scrunching up his faceat the question, Jordium looked like something sour was in his mouth as he turned his head away from her making her laugh. "Oh no, don't give mama that face, let me get your bottle. Elder, do you mind feeding Lilium in the rocker?"

"Not at all child, you have a feisty one over here." Senoi was reaching for the bottle she held out and it looked like Lilium was trying to fight him for it.

"Lilium behave for mama please." At her words the boy stilled and suckled at the bottle. "Come here Jordium, its dinner time."

"Looks like you have a couple of mama's boys on your hand." Senoi chuckled.

"Yes, appears you are right elder, what will their father say."

"I never thought I would live long enough to see you become a mother, I always thought it would be Daina who would be the first out of the three of you." Senoi had silently been watching from the corner rocker as he fed Lilium. "Your mother would have been proud if she was still around."

"I don't remember her but, I hadn't thought this for me either elder, but I must say that I am overjoyed to have these two little warriors with me." Lilith smiled as she looked down at her perfect little boy. He had both of their hair and Mark's strikingly blue eyes, looking to the other boy his blazing crimson hair was poking out around his head. These were her boys, and Mark's sons. Her heart warmed as she thought of him; she had missed the big idiot. They would work through this and raise their boys together. The earth rumbled a warning as the sound of large wings could be heard as large birds descended in the field beside the bungalow. A slow smile tugged at her lips as she counted each touchdown...*One...Two...Three...and Four...they really do flock.*

Senoi was getting up when Lilith waved him to sit down, "It's alright elder no need, Taurtis is back and it seems he brought everyone back with him."

"Would you like to hold Lilium as well" Senoi was being cautious, he was known to protect all custos children, and she knew the situation was odd for him but she couldn't pass up the chance to surprise Mark.

"No sit there," her smile widened when she heard the front door opened, the sound of Mark's combat boots sounded down the hall as he made his way to her room. "Let's surprise papa Jordium."

****

His heart hammered in his chest as he made his way down the hall. His palms were sweaty and his pulse was racing in his ears. Mark had asked everyone to wait in the front room while he went to check on Lilith. He had been stunned when Taurtis showed up in their living room covered in dirt with a huge grin plastered on his face; he had apparently beaten his record for tunneling. The man was rambling about them getting to Lilith as fast as possible, the man had had blood on his hands and it had taken the men a moment to calm him down to find out that Lilith was in labor. Taurtis was a proud brother with a wide grin on his face, they still hadn't been able to wipe the grin off his face as they pulled him on Mouse and flown as fast as they ever had; they broke some records of their own on the way over. The bungalow was nestled into a field of flowers and had the plants growing all around and on top of it. Mark gripped the handle and knocked softly on the door; the room was silent for a moment before he heard Lilith's soft sultry voice, "Come in quietly Mark."

He hadn't seen her in two weeks, her accent caressed his name and every word sounded like it was dripping sex; at least to him it did, the way her voice slid over him made his cock stir but he was nervous of what she thought of him so he hesitated. Taurtis hadn't exactly said she had forgiven him. He had only told them that she wanted Mark there to meet his child. *Was she still angry?* He hoped not, he hadn't thought to bring flowers until he had landed. Quickly, he had picked a bunch of lilies and dandelions to give to her as a peace offering. He was so excited and nervous he hadn't brought anything for the baby, Mark wished he had at least brought a blanket for them. *Your overthinking, move your feet.* Mark straightened his spine and slowly he opened the door.

The room was tidy and surprisingly large and rectangular. The stone walls were cool and kept the home at a nice temperature despite having no air conditioner. A dresser was placed along the wall; it looked like she had turned it into a makeshift changing table. There were three large windows one on each side of the room and the biggest was behind a large four poster bed. There was an earth made crib next to the bed and looked to have been rarely used but a stuffed yellow rabbit sat inside. Mark looked from the crib back to the bed and his breath caught. *Lilith...*

Her small curvaceous body sat perched on a large pile of pillows as she sat with her legs crossed. She was wearing shorts and a tight tee-shirt. Surprisingly, she didn't have any baby weight left and looked to have a flat stomach. Mark marveled over the custos metabolism as his eyes noted her breasts were still a little swollen but no less lush than when he had last feasted on them. His hands twitched slightly from the sight of her pale soft skin and the overwhelming need to touch it. Slowly raising his eyes, he took in Lilith's long crimson hair; it was all over the place and small ringlets had formed throughout it. Her enchanting jade eyes laughed at him as a small shy smile tugged at her lovely plump lips. *Beautiful.* Her accent wrapped around him and fisted his cock as it twitched, "Are you going to come in or stare at me forever?"

"Is that an option?" He hadn't realized he had been staring at her as he now slowly closed the door behind him, "You know I can't help it, you're still the most beautiful creature I've ever seen."

"Cheesy," her face had flushed softly making him feel a bit more confident as he held up the flowers. *Cheesy or not she had liked the complement.*

"These are for you."

"Can you put them over there please?" She asked as she gestured with her chin to place it on the dresser. He had been so focused on her he hadn't fully noticed the medium sized bundle she was clutching close. *Boy or girl?* Danny hadn't gotten word on what gender the baby was ad the suspense was killing him.

"Are you still mad at me?" He had to ask, to clear the air between them before he held his child. His heart drummed harder as he watched her take a small breath.

"Honestly, no. When I was in labor, I had time to think everything over. You were a giant idiot, yes, but you didn't have ill intentions; you just acted selfishly when you hid it so I would fall in love with you."

"Yes, I know and I can't tell you how sorry I am *draga*. I'm beyond sorry. When you left my soul shattered." Mark knew he sounded overdramatic but he had to bare his soul to her, she held him together in ways he hadn't known he needed. His soul.

"I felt angry but once I calmed down, I cried for days," Lilith has love in her eyes whether she ever admitted it or not. It was there. "It wasn't until Taurtis asked if I wanted you here did everything finally click into place. I belong with you Mark. Only you and I apologize for my harsh words in the tunnels. My anger has always gotten the best of me." Lilith bowed her head slightly to him. A smile threatened to break across his face, his warrior refuses to bow to anyone yet for him she will tilt her head.

"No need for that. *Doamne te iubesc, draga.*" He couldn't believe what he had just heard. Mark walked slowly over to the bed, he was dying to hold her and meet his baby but he didn't want to move so fast that he looked as desperate as he felt.

"I don't know what that means Mark but if you hide something like that again from me, I'll kill you." She smiled as she shifted the bundle, cries of a baby filled the room as he watched her gently rock it and hum an oddly beautiful song. The warning hung in the air between them and he knew she would follow through with what she had said.

"Boy or girl?"

"Boy, would you like to hold him?" Even as she asked, he was already reaching for the bundle and the blanket fell away revealing his son. "No need to support his head he can do it just watch out for his teeth they are sharp."

Mark was amazed as he held the boy. Already he looked to be a few months old. The boy had his eyes and jaw line, his hair was a soft strawberry blonde and already ringlets were trying to form. Yawning the child reveled small rows of teeth and two sharp looking canines. Danny had let him know that custos children grew at an incredible rate but nothing could have prepared him for this small toddler he held in his arms. The boy had the same slight tilt that his mother had and also the same creamy skin as her as well but what really amazed him the most was that the boy had the same ice-cold skin that Jase has. He must be an ice user; he didn't care though. This was his boy. Mark was grinning as joy and pride shot through him.

Lilith laughed as she leaned in and kissed the babe on the head. "I know it's a strange feeling when you first look at them, do you want to know his name?"

Them? "What is his name?"

"This one's name is Jordium Rowan Monroe and this little warrior," Lilith paused as Mark's head snapped around as the other custos stepped from a corner chair he hadn't noticed before. The man walked to Lilith's outstretched hands and placed another small boy into her arms and walked back to the chair. The boy tugged at Lilith's ringlets as she laughed and turned him to face Mark. "This little one is Lilium Jason Monroe. Aren't they adorable?"

Mark thought his heart swelled with pride, not one but two striking little boys. Lilium looked just like his mother. He had her eyes and hair, even her feline like features. He couldn't really see any of him in the boy, guess Jordium took all of his genes. Mark nodded to the boy as Lilium stared him down. "I'm not sure I see as much of me in him as I do Jordium," Mark laughed as he held his boy close, "Jordium looks to have stolen all of the Monroe genes from him."

"Lilith said the same thing of that boy," the other custos smiled as he watched them all together. "I think Lilium has more of you in him than you think. Lilith, child, are you ready yet?"

Ready for what? "Yes, I believe so." Lilith turned and handed Lilium back to the strange custos, "Mark, please hand him Jordium. It's time we learned their titles, I told Senoi to wait until you got here so I haven't heard them yet either." Her eyes, he noted, never left Lilium as he squirmed slightly in the elder's arms.

Ah. He hadn't thought of that. Reluctantly. Mark relinquished the boy to the man and the other custos winked at him as he adjusted the boys in his arms. "This will take just a moment."

The man tapped his head to Jordium's forehead as the room grew silent, he closed his eyes and mumbled something low and soft as he slowly raised his head a soft light appeared between them. The light dimmed and slowly Senoi handed the boy back to him and repeated the act with Lilium. As he handed the boy back to Lilith a wide smile appeared on his face.

"These boys will be powerful and trouble if they aren't raised properly. You will need to watch them and make sure they learn their talents for good."

Lilith slid closer to Mark at the man's statement, he could see she was nervous. "Elder, get on with their titles already and stop the suspense."

Mark fit Jordium in the crook of his arm and pulled Lilith under his shoulder and glared at the man. Senoi laughed as he pointed to Jordium, "Well, let's start with this little warrior, you my dear boy are Jordium the bringer of Ice and Hail. He will need special training to be taught to use his ability well or he could very well start an ice age." Slowly, he pointed at Lilium and if possible his smile widened. "With great irony little warrior, you will be known as Lilium the bringer of Strife. He will be a great trickster so watch him closely and raise him well, he very well start many a war otherwise. They both will be powerful warriors but I have no doubt in my mind that you two will make sure they don't get out of hand. Now, I hate to cut meeting you short my boy but I must get back home." The man was out of the room in a blink of an eye, shutting the door firmly behind him.

He felt Lilith breath out a sigh of relief. Mark couldn't help it as he took her mouth, she had tensed at first but then he felt her relax into his kiss. Her lips were soft as velvet as their lips molded together, rain and ash tangling together as he plunged his tongue in her warm mouth as their tongues danced together. Mark nipped at her lip as he pulled back breathless as he placed his forehead to hers, "That wasn't so bad. I thought they would have worse titles." He breathed out trying to get back on track with what was going on but only wanting to pull her close.

"No, not bad at all though Senoi was right we will have to keep an eye on them. Do you think Jase will help train Jordium to control his ice?" Worry had crept back into her voice as she looked up at him, her lips swollen from their kiss.

"Of course, he will be happy to help. He trains people all the time when it comes to torture so it won't be hard for him to get into the training with him, though I'm not sure who will help with Lilium's when he develops an ability." Mark looked down as Jordium began to cry, "What's wrong Jordie?"

"It's Jordium," Lilith laughed as she corrected him, "He probably needs a diaper change, come on I'll show you."

****

Tabitha sat in her car outside a storage facility; she had been debating making the call but she needed the money for her mother's medical bills. The woman Stephanie had paid her ten thousand dollars just to call her if she saw the man with the jet-black hair again, she said she would pay her even more if she got any information off of the man, *Taurtis his name is Taurtis.* It had taken Stephanie a few hours to text her back and set up a meeting place and said she would be back in town in a few hours.

It was the middle of the day but the thick clouds darkened the sky as rain began to drizzle on her car. There were rows and rows of storage units that looked to just keep going deeper onto the property, each row had lights casting low beams around to help customers see. Moments ago, Tabitha watched a man punch in his code and slip inside the property. His presence nearby eased the worry building inside her, she didn't trust Stephanie. *Who gets this creepy over a man? What the hell do I care what happens?* A light tap sounded on her passenger window made her jump and jerk to the sound. Her heart was pounding as she saw Stephanie tug at the handle, with shaky hands Tabitha unlocked the door.

"You scared the hell out of me girl." Her voice was shaking as the woman climbed into the car.

"Sorry, were you waiting long?"

"No, not to long, got here around one." Glancing at the clock on her dash it read one fifteen.

Stephanie nodded as she opened the backpack she was holding. There were bundles of hundred-dollar bills inside, Tabitha had to stop herself from reaching out and counting them, she couldn't believe it. Stephanie smiled and cleared her throat, "I believe this should cover the rest of your mother's bills but first, what do you have?"

Oh, right. Information. "Well, his name is Taurtis and he has been coming around the café almost every day. He always orders hot tea and a slice of pie."

Stephanie looked frustrated as she slowly zipped the bag, "That's all you got? Seriously?" Her hand had reached for the door to leave when Tabitha reached out and grabbed her wrist.

"Wait! I'm not done I have more."

Slowly the door closed and Stephanie looked back to her, impatience was stamped on her face, "Well then what is it?"

"He has two sisters from what I gathered and one is missing; the other one however is pregnant and living with him somewhere in Houston. He talks a lot about his sisters and seems to hold them on a pedistool. He has a sister complex if you ask me."

"I didn't ask."

"Right, well the sister that's with him is going to pop any day now you see so he has been stressed out lately and visiting the café."

"Did you get a name for the pregnant sister?"

"Lil, he calls her Lil. I don't know if that is her full name or not but it's her nickname from him. Is that enough information for you?" She didn't want to involve Maddison so she had kept out the fact that they were often talking together. Maddison had been helping her with everything going on with her mother's cancer treatments, but even still she really needed the money because she was in debit with all of the doctor's office visits. Stephanie smiled as she reached for the bag, she sat up quickly lashing out her arm and something sharp flew across her throat. Something red sprayed the windows as she looked in wide eyed horror at the other woman's smile. Blood covered the car, not just any blood her blood she realized. It had happened so fast Tabitha hadn't realized what was happening. The sprays stopped and she felt her body get cold. Tabitha's vision blurred as she felt the warmth of her blood trickle out of the wound on her neck. *This is how I die...what about my mom....*

The car door opened and Stephanie stepped out into the now pouring rain. As the door closed the last thing she heard from the woman before the darkness took her was, "Yes that should do."

****

Lilith was laughing as Mark faught to put the diaper on Jordium. The boy was kicking out and rolling around, he was doing pretty much anything to get away from the diaper. "You would think being the oldest of five you would have changed a diaper before."

"I was still a kid and mom never let me help. She always prioritized my training over helping with the others." He lifted the boy's legs and quickly wrapped him in the diaper and proudly lifted him in the air, "Ah hah. Gotcha Jordie."

"Good job." She was so happy as she stood on her tiptoes and kissed Mark swiftly on the cheek. Mark was so good with the boys she observed as he talked with them and played with their fingers and toes.

Mark focused on her with a loving stare, his eyes looked like flowing blue flames. "How long will they stay this size? I heard Danny say that Custos children grow like weeds."

"Hard to say. They are growing even now; in a few days their growth should slow down giving them time to learn and train. Is their growth weird for you?"

"*Draga,* they are a part of you so no it's not weird. I can't wait to watch their progress and they need time for play too, don't forget that." Mark rubbed her arm with one hand as he pecked her lips.

This man...

A soft knock sounded from the door. Mark trailed his hand down her arm as he left to check who it was. Lilith had almost forgotten he hadn't come alone. She began to dress the boys to meet their new uncles, a soft smile was still on her lips as she heard Mark tell them to be calm and quiet when they came in. Bending down over the twins she whispered in her sing song voice, "You boys be good for mama, okay? Your uncles wouldn't know calm if it hit them in the face." The boys sat quietly blinking up at her with bright intelligent eyes that warmed her heart.

Lilith turned around blocking the twins from view, she had a proud smile on her face as she heard the door open fully and one by one the boys filed in. She wasn't all that surprised to see Taurtis stand back a little from the rest, he was probably standing to cover the door. Lilith waved as the men grinned at her and tried to look around her, "Hello boys."

Jon was grinning as he held open his arms, "Give us our niece or nephew Lil. There is no hiding them from us at this point."

"I'm not hiding him," Lilith laughed as she hid Jordium from view and plucked up Lilium, Mark stepped around her and leaned on the dresser with a wide grin. She was pleased he had wanted to mess with his brothers too. Walking over to the wide-eyed men as they assessed her little mini-me. "This is Lilium, Lilium these are your uncles Jon, Jase, Danny, and Taurtis."

"Lil, he looks just like you," Jon said in amazement, "he is adorable."

Danny pushed on Jon's arm as he peered down at Lilium. Jon was holding him with one hand under his butt and the other hand was on his middle. "What's his full name?"

Lilith couldn't help laughing at these giant men who were holding her son like a breakable doll as they cooed over him, "His full name is Lilium Jason Monroe," looking at Taurtis she added, "the bringer of Strife."

"Jason? Did you name him after me?" Jase asked so excitably, she couldn't tell him it was after a Greek hero. Not after seeing him soften like this for the first time.

Smiling she nodded, "Yes after you. It fit him I thought, as he doesn't cry really and is strong."

Jase beamed and froze as she followed his eyes to Mark, he was carrying Jordium over to Jase. With a warm smile Mark placed him in Jase's shocked arms. "How does he feel to you?"

Jordium reached up and touched Jase's neck. His eyes grew wide as he peered down at the baby, a moment passed and Jase's head shot up. "He feels normal."

Mark shook his head. "Try freezing. He will need your help when he gets older learning how to control his ice." Jon and Danny were excited and surprised as they examined their new nephews. She laughed as they passed the boys around and realizing nobody had asked, she added, "His name is Jordium Rowan Monroe, bringer of Ice and Hail."

Taurtis had yet to hold one of them she noticed as she plucked Lilium from Danny and walked over to him. "Want to hold your nephew?" She smiled up at her brother.

Slowly, Taurtis gripped the boy under his armpits and held him up as he looked the boy over. Lilium was eyeing Taurtis curiously as he reached out trying to touch his new uncle. Taurtis smiled slowly at him and brought him closer to his chest, Lilith was going to warn him about Lilium when he bit down hard on Taurtis's hand. She was pretty sure she saw his little fangs grow as he bit down, if it had been anyone but Taurtis they would be bleeding out. Taurtis laughed as the boy gnawed on his hand, "This little one is something else."

"Lilium stop that. Biting family members isn't nice," she signed as he released and looks at her; her heart warmed as he blew a kiss at her. "Sorry Taur he fights everyone at first it seems and I can't get him to understand biting isn't okay."

"He is a cheeky little thing, isn't he?" Taurtis laughed.

"He is. I petty the string of broken hearts he will leave behind in the future." Lilith laughed as her stomach growled, "Let's get something to eat, shall we?"

"Pizza?" Danny asked as he walked over to try and pluck Lilium from Taurtis.

"Um, yeah," Lilith grinned. She had missed them, her eyes found Mark's as he stared lovingly at her. Her man. She had realized she couldn't live without him again. He was her soulmate; she was sure of it as she lightly touched the mark he had left on her throat. Lilith felt herself blush as Mark walked over and pulled her into his chest, he was cradling her to him as he stroked her hair softly. Lifting her head, she kissed him softly before pulling away to look up at him. She was still touching the mark when he smiled down at her, his deep baritone voice enveloped her, "What's going on in that beautiful head of yours *draga?*"

"Yes," Lilith said quietly.

"To what?" Mark asked his voice dripped sex. She could feel his length through her clothes as he pressed into her. Her breasts ached to be touched and her panties grew damp and slick with need, slowly Lilith licked her now dry lips. A wicked smile tugged on the corner of them as she watched Mark's stare fixate on the movement of her tongue. Taking a small nervous breath, she squared her shoulders.

"You never truly asked but with my culture I am required to give you an answer in front of witnesses." She felt Mark's sudden intake of breath as she continued, "So with that being said, I, Lilith of Tragedy, in front of witnesses, and with speaking with the oldest male within my family tree, do so accept your mark of marriage. If you will still have me?" She watched as a bright boyish smile lit Mark's face; Mark lifted and spun her around in a circle while he pulled her close. Her feet had barely touched the ground before he was kissing her with white hot passion. She opened her lips to him as his tongue plunged into her mouth to intertwine with hers. Mark kissed her over and over before pulling back and tilting her chin up at him.

"*Draga*, I will always have you no matter what."

Lilith through her arms around his neck and kissed him deeply as the other men whistled and cheered. Her life was almost complete, now the only thing that would make this better was finding Daina.

Lilith's stomach growled again and Mark laughed, "Let's get some food in you."

"While you do that, I'll build onto the house; let me know when the pizza is done." Taurtis was smiling as he went to leave.

"Why does he need to do that?"

Lilith laughed as she pulled Mark along, "The boys aren't big enough to fly just yet. Give it a few days and they should be good to fly out with us."

"Do you have a map?"

Puzzled Lilith looked over at Jon, he had found the bottles and was feeding Jordium. "Why?"

"We need to put our heads together and try and locate Daina now that we are all here. Someone had to have seen something in Paris we just have to figure out and look for any obvious signs of her."

****

Daina hurt all over. Gregory had left moments ago when his phone rang; his punishments for her silence had only grown increasingly worse with time. Today he had ripped out her finger nails and smashed her toes while demanding she answer his questions about her siblings. She would never give him anything. She may not have the physical strength like the others but she more than made up for it with her mental strength and determination. Gregory messed up. He would have broken her entirely if he had not said he was dying to get her siblings in the same spot as she was in now. The man wanted to sell them for parts when he was done with them. Daina hadn't opened her mouth once during his many torture sessions, in fact she hadn't made a sound as he ripped and stabbed her flesh. Only the sound of a furious thunderstorm could be heard beating at the windows of the old building she had been taken too.

Daina felt a masculine consciousness press on her mental walls trying to get into her head once more, she sucked in a deep breath as pain shot through her. It hurt to breath. It was the same man she felt in the tunnels, as strange as it was, she felt he wasn't there to harm her as she felt his presence try and mesh with hers. Daina could feel his sudden anger coming off of him in waves as he felt what was done to her. Slowly, she opened up her mind to him and he slipped in quickly. *Who are you?*

It was quiet for a moment before she heard a calm masculine voice. *A friend. I have been looking all over for you.*

Glad someone has been looking for me.

She felt his rumbling laugh, *Try everyone. The Flemming coven has had a search party out for over a month now. Do you have any idea where you are? We will come and get you.*

No... but I've heard a lot about that coven from my captor. Why does he want info on them?

Never mind that. What was the last thing you remember seeing before you ended up in that room?

Persistent wasn't her.

Honey, you have no idea.

You heard that? She thought she had blocked that from him.

Yup. Can you trust me to go through your latest memories? I have an idea but I need you to work with me.

Daina's head jerked up as she heard Gregory's echoed footfalls approaching. Panicking she tried to break the chains that bound her, her wrists were slick from her blood but she was unable to get free. *Please, anything. Take anything you need just get me out of this hell.* She felt his total invasion then. Whoever this man was he was more powerful than she first had thought as he quickly got the information he wanted.

Got it. I will be coming for you soon so hold out a few more days, I have to round up your siblings as well. From what I hear they miss you.

Tell them I said, movere asinos.

Got it.

Daina felt him leave as she was now alone with her thoughts and a now smiling Gregory...

****

The last two days had been amazing, her boys were growing like weeds as they ran around the house. Lilith had been amazed at how fast they grew, Custos children always grew at a rapped rate and typically slowed down when they looked like children. A Custos stopped aging in their twenties to mid-thirties; they could die but it was rare to die naturally. Lilith had stopped aging at twenty-four so it wasn't too much a jump to say that the boys would stop around there too. The boys currently looked to be about five and had already showed signs of slowing down as far as aging went for the time being. The pair had stunned Mark that morning when he had woken up to them staring down at him, they had asked for food because their Uncle Danny had burned the toast, he had made for them.

Taurtis was watching the kids today as they stretched their legs and hiked the surrounding woods. Lilith and Mark had been hiking for a few hours and had just stumbled into a clearing with a crystal-clear lake. "Wow this is beautiful draga," Mark mused as he walked to the lakeside. The water was so clear they could see the pebbles and small fish swimming. The ground was soft and flowers were scattered around the surrounding forest. Lilith tugged off her shirt and shorts, she hadn't been wearing anything under the thin fabrics; it was too hot. Mark hadn't yet noticed she was completely naked as she padded up behind him and hugged him close.

"Right! It's beautiful here, would you like to swim?" She asked as she let him go so, she could jump into the warm lake. She had barely breeched the surface when a huge wave hit her. Mark had cannonballed into the lake beside her sending water everywhere. Her head breached the surface once more as she splashed at his cocky grin.

"Was that necessary?" She laughed as he pulled her into his arms.

"Absolutely and do you know what else is?" Mark was leaning in, his lips softly brushed hers as he teased her with gentle kisses. Slowly, he kissed down the side of her neck. Lilith's heart was pounding as the heat between them sparked. Into rolling desire. Lilith arched her back as she wrapped her legs around him, she felt his need for her grow. His cock was rock hard and it twitched against her butt, his head dipped as his arms banded fully around her as he lifted her up. Mark's tongue lashed out and filched her nipples he slowly licked and suckled her naked breast.

Mark could hear her suck in a quick surprised breath as he continued to worship her perfect breasts. Her arms around his head while her hands tunneled into the thick tendrils of his hair. Lilith's moans filled the air as he slowly inserted a finger into her velvety folds, his thumb rubbed her clit in small circles as he worked her. Her hot channel squeezed his fingers as he pumped them in time with his suckling, his cock throbbed as she reached down and began to stroke him.

"Baby...I'm not going to last long if you do that." Mark bit down playfully on her nipple.

"Ah...Mark please?" Lilith purred as more moans escaped her kissable full lips; Mark added another finger stretching her as he rubbed her interfolds and the sensitive area that was there.

"Please what?" Moving his head slightly Mark kissed and suckled all the way up her neck. Flicking her clit, he felt her vagina clamp down hard as she rode his hand into climax. Her sexy scream filled the lake clearing, birds took off from their perches and soared away; no doubt annoyed at the humans in their clearing. *Too bad they weren't done.* Mark didn't let up on her clit as he slowly pulled his fingers out one by one.

"For fucks sake...Mark...fuck me..." Lilith moaned. Mark quickly pulled her up and positioned himself at her entrance. The lady wanted him so he was damn sure going to deliver. With a strangled cry he slammed into her, her vaginal walls clamped down on his sudden intrusion as they slowly milked him. Mark pulled back and slammed into her over and over. Water splashed around them as slowly he built up speed as he pumped into her over and over again. Lilith pressed herself into his chest as she cried out his name; he felt her vicious release as she clamped down hard onto his cock practically strangling his release from him.

Mark fought the erg to cum inside her, she felt like heaven, pulling out his seed shot out of him and into the clear water. Lilith sighed and sagged into him a bit as the water around them calmed down. They were clinging to each other and panting hard as they locked eyes. Lilith pulled back as a shy smile played on her face. "Well, that was unexpected."

Mark laughed as he brushed a kiss to her soft lips, "But welcomed."

Lilith looked sleepy as she slowly swam away in the direction of her clothes. Didn't surprise him that she was tired; they had been playing with the twins before going on this little hike. Mark swam up behind her as he watched her climb out of the lake. His cock threatened to stir as her heart shaped ass swayed as she moved; Mark cleared his throat as she slowly turned to him. "Let's head home it's getting dark and we should get the kiddos to bed."

"Mark..."

"Yes?" Mark watched as she slowly blushed.

"I love you."

A wide grin split across his face, "I love you too. Let's get out of here."

******

Night had fallen around the field house. Everyone seemed to be asleep but Taurtis as he padded barefoot throughout the house, he had been trying to sleep but the nagging feeling of being watched wouldn't go away. His gut was rarely wrong about these things and he wanted to check it out, but not alone, he needed his partner as he softly tapped Lilith's door. A moment passed as he heard a soft rustling of blankets followed by the soft sound of bare feet on the stone ground. Softly as not to wake anyone, her door eased open and Lilith slipped out clad in black sweatpants and a tight dark top. Her hair was tossed in all directions as she searched the hall for any prying ears, Taurtis circled her wrist and they walked to the sitting area. "I feel like we are being watched," he whispered.

"I think so too, I heard rustling in the bushes when you knocked."

"You take the sky and I'll take the ground, cover me?" Taurtis knew the answer but still liked to hear it.

"Of course."

Just like that they broke away and headed for opposite ends of the house, it was a well-practiced move they had made thousands of times back home. They had kept their meeting brief and headed to work as Taurtis slipped silently out the front door and into the lily covered field. The air was hot and humid and, in the distance, he could hear the cicada clinging to the trees. The moon was high and full tonight as it cast a dim light over the clearing, the lighting was perfect for him as he searched for the source of his unease. Nothing looked out of place as the flowers swayed in the soft summer breezy. *Lilies...the funeral flower...they are lovely though.* Turning he began to head back to the house. Taurtis had stopped a few yards from the house when and unfamiliar scents drifted to him. *Pine, cedar, and grass?* They were surrounded by lilies not grass and the trees that surrounded the clearing were oak not pine or cedar.

The hair on his arms raised as slowly he lowered to the ground and, tunneling his hands slightly under the ground, he summoned the earth. As he stood the ground shook as it woke up and thick stone walls sprung on all sides of the house effectively protecting it from attack. Taurtis had had it, something wasn't right.

Scanning the outskirts of the clearing he spotted slight movement in the trees. What looked like a tail twitched bringing attention to a large shadow that was launching from the trees. Smiling, Taurtis braced his feet as the shadow sprinted at him, with a snap of his fingers the ground below shook and the shadow split into two creatures. One was hiding in the others shadow. *Not wild animals. They don't hunt like this.* Taurtis thought as they came at him from both sides.

The ground shook as the earth split and shot out at the creatures knocking them back once more. Now out in the open and not moving Taurtis recognized the creatures. The larger one was sleek and solid black as its deep jungle cry filled the clearing; the massive jaguar circled and tried to repeat the attach as the smaller leopard watched for an opening. *These cats shouldn't be here.* The ground shook as he hurled large rocks at the beasts; since these creatures were here it could mean only one thing.

"Come out assholes or I'll kill your familiars!" Taurtis shouted into the night. "I'll give you to the count of three. One..."

The ground furrowed below the beasts; "Two..." Stone bars flew up and caged them in. "Three..." Picking up a huge chunk of rock he began to press it down on the cages and the leopard started snarling and howling.

"Wait!" Two men came charging out into the clearing, both men were armed to the teeth with guns and knives. The larger man took a step forward and place the gun that was in his hand to the ground, "Test, it was a..." His words were cut off as Lilith dropped from the sky and slammed her heel into the man's skull, an audible snap echoed from the man's nose breaking as he howled in pain.

"Bitch," The other man went to lunge for Lilith but a snarling white wolf cut him off as it planted itself in the middle of the fray. Taurtis watched the man with the broken nose launch himself at Lilith and grab her around the middle, he hurled her towards the stone walls no doubt trying to knock her out. Taurtis smiled as he watched her get thrown through the air. With lightning speed her wings shot out allowing her to balance herself and push off the wall, she tucked her wings away as she slammed into the man.

*****

Lilith had always been quick as she dodged and parred the man's blows. She threw out three quick jabs to the man's kidneys and followed through with an elbow to his sternum. This witch was big and she could easily feel the power coming off him as he threw out the punches and kicks; no doubt he could cause some damage if he actually could keep up and connect a hit. Blood smeared his angry face as he grew more frustrated that his hits weren't hitting her; an explosion from the other side of the wall threatened to distract her and give the man an opening. *Fucking Hercules.*

"Dylan enough!"

The man immediately halted his assault and dropped his fists to his sides. From the trees a man seemed to materialize from the branches and walk into the clearing; he was cloaked in fur and leather. He appeared to be average in height and broad in shoulders with power emitting from him in waves; she could sense the strength he possessed even from where she stood. He was walking over to them with quick powerful strides; his ash blonde hair getting tasseled with the wind. With his broad shoulders the cloak hung on him effortlessly. Now that he was closer, she noticed he wore a white tunic, dark brown leather pants, and a matching pair of boots. *How medieval...* The man stopped in front of her with a wide cocky grin and offered his hand. "Thousands of apologize ma'am for my guards rude welcome."

Lil tell Taurtis to lower this fucking wall! Mark is losing it over here! Danny yelled in her head as another explosion sounded behind her.

Ignoring the mans outstretched hand and glancing to her brother. "Can you lower the wall Taur? Mark is having a conniption over there."

"Fine but I'm not lowering the bars on those cages till we figure this all out." Reluctantly, the walls lowered and Mark surged forward furious only to come to a dead stop next to the white wolf. Shock was plastered on his face as he took in their company.

"Fuck...whatever they did your majesty they didn't mean too." Her eyes widened as she watched Mark and the other brothers bow slightly to the strange man behind her. *King?*

The man flashed a cocky grin as he gripped onto her shoulders from behind. "So, you're telling me this creature didn't mean to drive her foot into Dylan's face and break his nose then proceed to kick his ass?"

Creature?

Lilith's temper flared inside her as she knocked the man's hands away, the wind in the clearing responded and picked up tossing lilies in the air. His eyes grew wide as she glared up at him, "Look you fashionably challenged freak; I am not a creature. I'm a Custos you sonofabitch and I will be shown respect, you sorry excuse for a king." The wind picked up and sliced a thin cut into the man's cheek.

The wind howled along with Taurtis's laughter. "Shit, Lil enough please." Mark shook with worry as he pulled her protectively under his shoulder. "I'm sorry your majesty she doesn't..."

"Don't you dare say I don't know better Mark." Lilith cut him off, "My siblings have been dealing with royalty since this man's great grandfather was probably ruling, so yes I do know better. We have been abused by those same people for too long and I refuse to let it happen here as well." Jerking her chin back towards the king she added, "We are not lesser than the likes of you nor will we ever be."

Lilith felt Mark soften into her, with a sigh he hugged her close and silently watched his king. Mark was choosing to stand with her as she challenged his king, Lilith felt comforted, he was choosing the side of adversity for her.

"I've never been told I'm fashionably challenged, nor that I'm a sorry excuse for a king." The words came out as a statement, not a judgement, as he watched her curiously. "I like this one Mark." Lilith felt the tension drain from him as the king smiled down at her, "You are absolutely right on one thing; I was disrespectful and I do apologize. I was just taken off guard by your skillful use of your wings earlier, let's start from the beginning." He offered his hand out once more and this time she took it, "My name is Ash Wolfpaw and I'm going to need you and your brother to come with me to Denver."

The hell was a Denver? "Why?"

"Movere asinos."

"Do you even know what that means?" She knew she sounded condescending but she couldn't help her surprise; he was the first person to speak their language since they got to this plane.

"Move your asses, from what I gathered from Daina but she was a bit preoccupied when I spoke with her. Well, am I right on the meaning?" Ash's eyes were no longer playful as they locked with hers, she knew he saw her eyes widen. Lilith's heart pumped faster as adrenaline shot through her system, her heart actually hurt for the speed it was beating. Taurtis pushed past her and grabbed the man by the fur.

"You better not be fucking lying or I will skin your wolf and wear her pelts." The threat hung in the air as Dylan and the other man stepped forward; the white wolf growled softly from where she stood.

"Why would I lie? I told her I would bring you two to her as soon as I found you both. She is hurting pretty bad but isn't breaking." The man sounded proud of her sister.

"*Draga,* breath please." Mark whispered into her ear.

I'm not breathing? She hadn't noticed. Ash had spoken with Daina; she wasn't breaking? *What did he mean by that?* Her chest hurt and her vision began to tilt and right itself. Lilith gripped Mark's arm as the world spun and slowly dimmed into the familiar feeling of her visions.

They were in a secluded warehouse at the edge of an unfamiliar town. Hundreds of creatures were pouring out and coming after her and her small party that had gathered to get Daina. An overwhelming need to lead the lost souls surged through her as the winds howled sweeping them away from this earth and onto the next. They would make it inside and a battle would ensue between herself and a vile woman that would try and overtake her mind. A man's laugh filled her mind as she searched for him in the fray of creatures, he had Daina. Pretty Daina, the one that was sweet as candy was now a bloody pulp sagging in an angelic looking man's arms. Her blood dripped off her bruised and nail less fingertips. Her eyes were full of pain and her lips were swollen and bloody. The man looked at her and smiled as he dropped Daina to the floor and drew out a pistol and fired at her; she wasn't sure why but suddenly Mark fell in front of her as blood pooled around him. The gun was aimed at her, where had Mark come from? His blood splashed across her face. Horror filled her as a violent scream torn from her lips.

Her screams filled her ears as she felt strong hands shaking her and calling her name gently. "Lil...Lilith honey, come back to me *draga*. It's not real we have time to fix whatever it is love." Slowly the vision faded and she was back in Mark's strong reassuring arms, throwing her arms around his neck she hugged him close. She felt him tense slightly then relax as he hugged her back and kissed the side of her neck. "What's the matter?"

I can't tell him. She shook her head and let her hair hide her face from view of the others, "Nothing. I love you." Lilith didn't care if the others heard her, she loved this man and would do anything to keep him from falling to the ground in his own blood.

Mark laughed as he stroked her hair gently, "I love you too *draga.*"

"Mama?" She hadn't heard the sound of the front door opening as she looked over and saw Jordium, he looked scared as he took in their new visitors. Lilith immediately let go of Mark and rushed to him, she couldn't stand the scared look on his face as he took a step back. The boy was standing barefoot in the flowers clutching hard on his yellow stuffed bunny, this was his first-time meeting people that weren't family so she wasn't all that surprised to see a small tremor in his hands. His blue eyes widened when they settled on the massive white wolf that stood a few yards away from him.

"Baby you should be in bed," she softly reprimanded him as she kissed the top of his head, "Everything is fine now, okay?"

"But...I heard shouts and Lilium wasn't there." She froze. *Lilium? Damn that boy.* Lilith had quickly realized after their birth she was tethered to their thoughts much like her siblings used to be, relying on that thread, she closed her eyes. Putting out feelers she searched the clearing, the boy had recently discovered he could turn into all kinds of things and usually she would be proud but right now she was worried. He had been so excited when he turned into his Uncle Jon just that morning. Lilith picked up on his thoughts and narrowed the area down to the wolf, no, the bull frog in front the wolf. It was acting oddly as it sat in front of a predator without showing any signs of moving.

"Lilium," she tried to use her best mom voice, "if you don't get away from that wolf you are going to be in big trouble."

"What are you talking about?" Ash spoke up as he looked around in surprise, he was obviously looking for Lilium. *Could he not sense the boy? That's interesting.*

"Watch," Lilith said proudly as she watched the frog slowly grow and change shape, the sound made an odd popping sound as Liliam slowly turned himself back into his normal appearance. Now human he stood barefoot in the tall flowers glaring at the silent guard with blatant disrespect and open hostility, *that's my boy*, unlike his brother he wasn't scared as he glared up at the man, "You tried to hurt my mama..."

How long had he been watching out here?

The man kneeled down to eye level with him and finally spoke, "That was Dylan, you have the wrong guy little man."

Lilium balled his little fists up at his sides before swinging wildly and the man. "Don't call me little. I am Lilium Monroe, warrior class." *Shit.* Mark crossed the distance to Lilium and tipped him over his shoulder before Lilith could get to him. Without missing a step Mark headed back for the house, as he walked Mark tossed, "Let's take this inside," over his shoulder as Lilium glared daggers at the newcomers.

"But dad they..."

Mark cut him off as he sat Lilium down, "Here is a lesson little warrior, if your opponent is bigger and stronger than you are lay low and call your family to help you, okay?"

Frowning Lilith walked in Jordium as the others followed, "Enough mark he gets your point though don't tell him that."

"Why not? It could help."

"Lilium, if your opponent is bigger and stronger aim for their nose and use maximum force and pressure. It should either break their nose and by you time or if you use enough pressure kill your opponent." Lilith said matter of factly, she noticed Dylan pause in the doorway before he shook his head and entered. "For the record Dylan I would never have killed you outright, I didn't know what you wanted. What kind of example would that make for my kids?"

"That's reassuring." Dylan mumbled under his breath.

Painting on a sugary smile she turned and sat of the sofa, "Isn't it though? Now, come here boys let's sit down and hear what that king over there has to say."

"Yes mama," they said in unison as they piled onto the sofa on either side of her. Mark took his place on the edge of the sofa as he gestured to the armchair.

"Please rest your legs my king, we have a few questions. What do you mean you talked to Daina?"

That had been a question she had also wanted to know. It took a moment for Ash to respond, he was watching the children as if debating what to say in front of them, "Well after you left the castle, I got bored and thought what the hell I might as well help find her. It took me a while because of how strong her mental walls are and she is very good at covering her tracks. At first, I couldn't break them so I settled with brushing them so she knew I was there, then when I finally found her in Paris she was hurt and locking down hard on those walls. Hard enough that I was propelled away. It took me a while to get a lock on her again but I was able to speak with her two days ago." Ash kept staring at the twins with open curiosity, it was clear he felt like asking something.

Lilith tightened her arms around them and lifted her chin, "the hell are you staring at Ash?"

Ash laughed. "I was thinking that you have some cute kids and wanted to know how old they were."

"Umm..." Jordium began nervously, "we are only four..."

"I've known your dad for years and I was just surprised he hadn't told me about you guys, so your four years old." Lilith noticed the reprimand in Ash's eyes as he glanced to Mark.

"No..." Jordium mumbled.

"No what?" Ash asked curiously.

"We are four days old..." Lilith wished she had some way to save Ash's shocked look forever and print it out to hang it up.

"What?"

"Sir, we are Custos...sorry we didn't say that." It was Lilith's turn to laugh, these new witches wouldn't understand.

Lilium looked less than thrilled at Ash, "Mama, is he really a king?"

"Yes sweetie, he is your father's king."

The boy tilted his head to the side revealing a mischievous grin, "not much of a king is he mama? He didn't even notice I was outside." Pride swelled inside her as she pulled Lilium closer and kissed the top of his head. "Your right, he didn't notice you. Good job but don't scare me like that again, do you understand?"

Lilium was still smiling as he looked up at her, "Yes mama."

Mark rubbed his temples. "We can explain later."

Ash nodded as he turned to leave. "Well then let's hop to it, that bastard has been torturing Daina this whole time and I would like to have a word with this Gregory fellow."

"Are we coming too mama?" Lilium asked with a wide grin, the boy was a little too excited about fighting. A since of guilt swept through her, she hadn't even thought about who would watch the children.

"Lilium, no we are too weak to do help." Jordium poked at his brother's face while singing, "Too weak, too weak, we are too weak." It was amusing to see the effects of her constant sing song voice with the children and she secretly hoped they never grew out of it.

Lilium sprung off the sofa with Jordium's yellow stuffed rabbit as he swung it wildly by the ears causing his brother to cry. "Cry baby. You are nothing but a cry baby."

The temperature in the room dropped as Jordium grew increasingly more upset. She could see her breath by the time she was grabbing the rabbit from Lilium, "Boys that is enough." She needed to get to Daina like yesterday, "Your dad will be staying with you." She didn't look at Mark though she felt his eyes burning a hole in her. She couldn't let him get hurt, it would kill her if something happened.

The twins had stopped running about and stared at Mark as he calmly reached out to them from where he sat. "You two need to get to bed now, don't worry someone will be here when you wake up, okay?" Nodding they ran back into the direction of their room leaving Lilith alone in a room of sullen faced men. She took a deep calming breath as she finally met Mark's intense stare; he looked upset with her as his voice turned harsh, "What the fuck Lil?"

He never cursed at her before as she sat in shocked silence. Mark didn't seem to care that they weren't alone as he ran a frustrated hand through his hair. "I'll stay home with them? Then what? You plan on running off to fight god knows what without me; news flash for you that will not be happening. I lost you once and I can't take you leaving me behind again, I won't let that happen again so we will just have to figure this shit out."

Was she hearing this right? Mark with all his strength and power, the same Mark who would charge through fire for his family and take down creatures three times his size was scared she would leave him? Lilith hadn't even entertained the idea. "Hercules, you have it all wrong, I just think it best if you stayed to watch over them in case someone finds out they are here. Have you considered that since Gregory has Daina he may want the full set of Custos? That's why I think..."

"Bullshit," he was in her face now as he leaned over her, "don't lie to me *draga*, it has something to do with what you saw, doesn't it? That's all the more reason for why I'm not going to let you run off and fight. It'll drive me insane woman your visions are always of tragedy and I will always be by your side no matter what. When will you get that?" Mark's breathing was ragged and his hands were shaking slightly. This huge man wasn't just scared he was terrified that she would leave him and he didn't care that he was baring his heart in front of everyone. She loves this man.

Biting her lower lip, a small smile threatened to form as she wrapped her arms around Mark's neck and pulled his head into her arms so she could cuddle him to her chest. Lilith couldn't help stroking his hair as he relaxed into her; ignoring everyone's eyes and looking down to look at him she spoke softly hoping to sooth him. "I'm sorry that I made you worry like this but I'll always come back to you. You're my Hercules and after all I'm going to be marrying you. So, there is no need to act this way, though this does shed some light on why Jordium acts the way he does." Lilith joked as Mark looked up at her looking like she insulted him.

"He's like that because you spoil him too much."

She couldn't help but laugh, "Sweetheart, if that were the case Lilium would be just as bad. Poor boy takes after me with his temper."

Mark was shaking his head but at least he was smiling again, "What are we going to do with the boys?"

"May I make a suggestion?" Lilith turned her attention to Ash who stood in the doorway with a wide grin on his face, "Dylan can stay here with the kids."

"But sir..." Ash held up his hand silencing Dylan and turned his attention to Jase.

"Jase, I want you to go back to being my active guard during this assignment and that should solve that problem." Ash was smiling at everyone as Lilith eyed Dylan suspiciously.

215

"Can you handle the twins?" She had to ask they were only children and he didn't look reliable to her.

Dylan sighed heavily. "I'm the oldest of eight, it shouldn't be a problem."

Mark laughed as they looked at the man's distain for leaving Ash's side. "Dylan word of advice with them watch Liliums teeth and Jordium is as sweet as candy until he is bullied so be nice to him and don't let his brother throw tantrums."

"How is that advice?" Dylan looked baffled.

"Guess it's not helpful but at least you know." Mark laughed as he buried his head in her breasts.

"Hey Lil," She turned her head towards Taurtis who was raising his shirt exposing his stomach, "Got something for you." His face was almost boyish as slowly ran his nail over the firm abs and red drops ran down his tanned flesh into the waistband of his pants; carefully Taurtis inserted one finger then another into the wound and felt around. The skin stretched and the wound wept more as he now had his hand inside the wound probing around as Lilith watched curiously. The look of discussed was on many of the faces in the room but she tried to focus on the probing, Taurtis was still learning her technique and she wanted to make sure he could pull it off without getting hurt. Always was about the timing of it. Taurtis's timing had always been a little off making him have to train harder than others to get the patterns down.

"What the hell are you doing?" Ash sounded flabbergasted as he watched Taurtis slowly pull his hand back out.

Lilith couldn't help the girl like squeal that escaped her as she clapped her hands together and detangled herself from Mark, the squeal started the guards as she jumped up. "You didn't!"

With each tug of his hand she saw more and more of her beloved battle axe; she had given up on seeing it again as she believed it to be lost to the elders when they were banished. Lilith had made everything on it from the black obsidian handle clad with a leather grip, to the large magma hardened warhead; that had been the hardest part to make as magma when solid was brittle. Lilith had had to mix brimstone into it and harden and sharpen for weeks to get it right, now there wasn't a sharper or harder blade like it. The axe could stand at five feet long and had wards and enchantments etched into the bloodthirsty weapon. This axe had made many street thugs turn tail and run on more than one occasion and was easily her weapon of choice. Her favorite feature was that the more blood that it soaked up the more energy the wards received.

Taurtis swiped across the wound once more sealing up. "How could I leave our weapons behind? I had time to grab your Sanguinem and my spear; it honestly would have been a shame to let them sit there on their mantles. Besides, what kind of demons would we be without our fangs?"

He tossed the axe to her as she laughed. Catching it was second nature and the familiar weight of it comforted her as she spun the axe on reflex, flexing her mussels with each spin. "We would just be assholes."

She hadn't thought Mark had moved but as she turned, she ran into him, "Sorry about that..." Her words were cut off as Mark silenced her with a fierce claiming kiss. His arms wrapped around her waist as she opened her mouth to him and he swept inside. He tasted like fresh rain water, so clean and all hers. Her mouth molded to his as he kissed her like a starving man. His tongue swiped and dueled hers as her breathing increased and her nails dug into his shoulders. She nearly dropped the axe as she clung tightly to him, feeling his need for her grow. She heard someone clear their throat as she pulled away and smiled up at Mark. His sexy crooked smile melted her heart as his warm baritone voice wrapped around her heart, "If I'd have known that you had made such beautiful weapons, I'd have built you a forge sooner but looks like I will be building you one when we get home."

"Ash?" Lilith called over to the man without taking her eyes off of Mark, she didn't want to miss his expression.

"What?" He sounded confused.

"When this is all over, I know how important it is that we do this with tradition in mind so, would you please marry us when we get Daina back?"

Mark began to vibrate and heat up as his happiness glowed, "Really?"

"If Ash agrees," she laughed.

"Of course, I would agree, I'm not a tyrant. Seriously though this is touching but we really need to get moving."

"Right, sorry." Letting go of Mark she turned to Ash, "So how do we get there?"

"You do nothing." The smile disappeared from the man's face as vines shot up and started to pull her down Lilith started to struggle but stopped when she saw the other men relax and drop into the ground. With a deep breath she gripped the axe tight and relaxed into the vines as they pulled her further into the ground before she heard a pop and looked up. The ground had swallowed her up as she felt her bones and muscles pull and push against her as she sped through the earth.

****

They had to get this right. Mark feared the worst for Daina. She had been gone for so long and not many people live past the first forty-eight hours of abduction, but Ash says that Gregory had been keeping her and torturing her this whole time. Her siblings may not see it but the rest of them defiantly saw the fighter in Daina. She may not fight like the rest of them but it was obvious she was keeping herself alive by any means necessary and that she hadn't broken yet. His boys would also be safe with Dylan, that man wouldn't let anyone look at them wrong which let him switch his focus on the battle ahead. The ground dipped and pulled as he felt the slow pull upward. *Looks like we are here.* The ground above him opened and spit him out with the others. Mark looked around and saw Dustin throw out his palm and signaled to be silent as the group huddled behind a large warehouse.

Lilith was right beside him as he looked around taking in his surroundings. They were in what looked to be a secluded part of the city. There were needles and bottles littering the ground leading to a massive warehouse that reeked of mutts. Last time he had been at a place like this had been when they had hunted for their mother and sister. Dred filled him as the memory was on the brink of his mind, Mark looked at Lilith. His sweet fiery Lilith, she looked at him with total trust as she gave him a small smile. For her he would bring her sister back or he would die trying.

Dustin motioned for him to slide up beside him as he pointed around the corner. Flattening himself like Dustin had, Mark peeked around and his eyes grew wide. Looks like they had found the mutt gathering. There was a few hundred at least blocking the entrance to the run-down warehouse that loomed over everything. They had a few more hours until day light which would put them at a slight disadvantage against the mutt's superior night vision but what they lacked they made up with pure power as he sent up a silent thanks to the goddess for Ash being there with them. Looking back at their party he noticed that Ash, or Taurtis, had managed to bring the familiars with them which would add to the foot soldiers on the ground. The wolf and the jaguar were a huge bonus as he had yet seen them lose a fight. Ash waived them all over to go over the game plan. Taurtis signaled that he and Lilith were going to look around the wall and keep watch. He had drawn out and marked a strategy for attack in the dirt as he pointed and silently told everyone where to go. Mark was to go through the front door with Jace and Dustin, as Jon and Ash were going to go at the sides to try and pick off the mutts at an angle cornering them in the building. Danny, Taurtis, and Lilith were to slip in through the rear of the building and hopefully get Daina out without a problem so they can all jump ship.

The screams reached them long before they realized what had happened. Mark slid back along the wall with Dustin on the other side as they peered over. "Shit." Mark's heart hammered in his chest as he watched both Taurtis and Lilith fighting in unison as they were ingulfed in the fray. The mutts surrounded them like fresh meat in a tank of piranhas. From where he stood, he could only see the top of Taurtis's head as he mowed down the mutts that got in his way.

Worry creased his brow as he disregarded the plan and took off after them into the fray. A giant beast of a mutt dived at him from the left and he had barely had time to dodge as he dropped and spun on his side making a finger pistole and firing off a small explosive off the tip. With a loud bang the bomb hit the mutt sending him flying at his comrades scattering them. Dustin dashed by him using the wind to slice and pummel anyone who rushed in front of him. He was an amazing wind user and Mark was glad he was on their side as Dustin created a mini-tornado and took out a dozen or so mutts. Blood littered the ground as the pair sliced and imploded the enemy. Mark could see Lilith now as they made their way closer.

She was breath taking. She was splattered with blood and shooting through them like an angel of death. Her long crimson hair flowed behind her like crimson streaks on the stormy sky. She was ducking, slicing, and parring blows left and right as she fought like a demon to get to the warehouse doors. Mark fought through the creatures and found himself in the middle of the fray with her. She was smiling as he started firing off full palm size blasts at the crowd. The wind picked up and she rose into the air with that monster of an axe in her hands. The axe glowed a bright menacing red as she suddenly dropped on a giant mutt. The axe split its skull in two with what looked like little effort as it cut right through and into the mutt's neck. Mark had never seen anything like it as the beast dropped and Lilith stood onto of it like the fierce warrior she was. *His warrior*. Mark felt a sharp rake against his back as he jerked around and fired off a blast. Taurtis was a few yards away splattering the surrounding mutts against the pavement. He had a huge grin on his face as he threw a massive silver spear through a few mutts skewering them together as they screamed. Mark had to look away as the hair on the back of his neck began to stand.

He saw her dark hair first before his eyes rested on the plain looking woman before him. The battle raged on around then but time seemed to stop as he came face to face with his mother and sister's killer. Rage filled Mark as he felt a small prick in his head as she tried to weasel in. Mark could hear the others join the fray from the sides but he dared not look away from Stephanie. Through tightly clenched teeth Mark growled, "Long time no see. Looks like you are still a whore for the mutts I see."

A wide menacing grin slowly formed as she took a step closer, "And you? Still a dog to the king." It wasn't a question it was a statement as she lunged at him with a knife.

Mark jumped to the side and kicked off the ground using an explosion that shook the battlefield. Dirt and debris plumed around him as he stood and looked around. The dirt blocked his vision but he felt her creeping closer. Stephanie's laughter drifted to his ears as he tried to look through the dust clouds. Something was wrong with the dust; it shouldn't be this thick with how he let the explosive off. The shadows from the ongoing battle made it hard for him to locate her. Mark turned slowly to the left and suddenly a shadow moved with lightning speed in front of him as, suddenly, a knife was driven into his stomach and Mark dropped as it was twisted and yanked out. Pain raked at him as he grabbed at his stomach. There was too much blood, the bitch had hit an artery there was no mistaking it. Mark felt like an idiot as he remembered that Stephanie had specialized in taking people apart slowly. A shadow fell over him as Stephanie lifted her knife once more. *This is it...*

******

Lilith was near the door. She could see the way in, but something stopped her and made her look back. Mark knelt on the ground with a woman in front of him grinning. He was covered in dirt and grime from the battlefield and didn't look hurt. The woman was lifting a knife to slice into him when Lilith took off past Taurtis and Ash as they glanced her way. She didn't care if they watched as murder filled her veins and her eyes began to glow red.

This had to be the bitch that tried to control Taurtis and now she was after Mark. She shifted her beloved axe so it would fly out behind her. She ran with such speed that had given her the nickname of angel of death as she leapt and pulled the axe in front of her. The battlefield grew silent around her as she brought down the axe. Blood splattered along the ground as Stephanie's head rolled and her body fell; first to its knees then to the ground with a slick thud. Mutts cheered as they ran at her companions taking advantage of the distraction she provided with the bitch's death. The slight reprieve gave her a moment to look Mark over, he was unhurt but his eyes were cloudy as he blinked and refocused on her. He was clutching his stomach like he had been hurt, "Your fine Hercules I promise."

"Shit. She got into my head again." Mark looked around for Stephanie and his eyes rested on her lifeless head that rolled only a few feet away. Her eyes were still open from shock and her mouth was agape but nobody would be hearing from her again. Triumph filled her as Lilith looked at the womans severed head.

"Well don't worry. I got into her head." Lilith reached down and took Mark's hand as she helped him up. "Come on we are almost there."

Mark lifted his hand around her and she felt steam coming off him as he fired a palm sized explosive into the oncoming crowd. Together they fought their way back to the others. As they approached the warehouse doors, they flew open and a man walked out with Daina in his arms. She was covered in bloody wounds and had blisters all over as the man dropped her on the steps. Rain began to fall as Daina slowly opened her eyes and took in the bloody scene around her. The others were still fighting but Lilith and Mark had made it to her. "Gregory," Mark called to the angelic looking man. Mark halted and shook his head. "You... Your Gregory?"

It was the way he asked that had Lilith looking over the other man once more. He had a slight glow about him that was off setting to her. "The one and only," Gregory grinned and tilted his head slightly, "Marcus."

Mark looked surprised, "You know of me?"

"How couldn't I? Stephanie would go on and on about you." The man looked annoyed.

A smile pulled on Mark's lips, "Well I know about you too... Raguel."

Raguel?

The man laughed. Such a boyish laugh, he sounded so innocent. His dark hair was pasted to his head as the rain fell harder. His hair curled at the ends a bit as his handsome voice filled the air, "How did you know?" Gregory, no Raguel, cocked his head to the side curiously.

"I have worked with your brother Vexrial, he showed me many things. Including you." Mark smiled as furry cracked Raguel's perfect innocent mask.

"Why would he tell you anything?" Raguel took a step down and kicked Daina down the steps. "You are nothing more than a blemish on the earth."

"That may be but I traded for the information," Mark was smiling as he chastised the man, "information for a favor. Want to know what the favor was?"

Raguel was turning slightly pale as he reached behind him nervously, "Why the hell should I care? I have my own empire down here and that bitch beside you just killed my second in command. Do you know how hard it's going to be to replace that whore?"

Lilith edged closer to Daina as her sister looked on in utter terror. Her achilles had been cut and it didn't look as if she could move much. Mark kept talking as he distracted the man, "Vex really wants something you see..."

Raguel cut him off with a sneer, "Vex is the angel of greed of course he fucking wants something, like I want something." Lilith looked up and saw Raguel staring at her with a greedy lust. "Custos are so rare to find on this world and here I have three at the same location. Your sister is lovely, isn't she?" The man had to yell over the downpour.

Mark kept going as he stepped closer to Raguel, "Vex wants to know where his murderous little brother is so he can be taken in for judgement." At his words Raguel's head shot up and Lilith smelled the gunpowder, it happened so fast. The man yanked out a gun and took aim at Mark and fired as Lilith jumped into action pushing Mark out of the way. The shot echoed out into the stormy night as the area grew quiet under Mark's furious yells. He was screaming for her even as he jumped over her and rushed for Raguel. Her chest hurt. Lilith had landed on her back spiraled out next to her sister as she looked up at Daina's rain clouds. "So... pretty..."

She thought she heard the sound of wings flapping but she couldn't be sure, her world was getting dark as she felt the warm blood pump out of her. The wound should have hurt but it didn't. Mark collapsed next to her as he applied pressure to the wound, "Come on *draga*. Stay with me. Who will spoil the kids without you? Please baby...baby."

Something warm hit her cheeks as she slowly looked at Mark, his arm was gushing blood from what looked to be a knife wound. He would be needing to clean that, knife wounds got infected quickly. Lilith caught herself rambling on inside her mind as she looked back at the sky and her vision grew blurry. She felt cold. Numb. *So, this is what it's like to die...I was just starting to want to live though...* She tried to lift her hand but it was too heavy. "*Draga* no please...don't take my soul away sweetheart...please."

She felt her pulse slowing as the wind gently caressed her. The wind. Her lifelong companion. She would miss it. She would miss Mark the most, and her boys. *My poor boys...* Mark sounded angry when he spoke again, he was pressing so hard on the wound in her chest trying to stop the bleeding. Silly man it won't stop. "Fuck...don't leave me...Ash!"

She heard the faint sound of footfalls. *Ah...the fighting had stopped...* Ash came into view as he rushed over and halted. "Fuck me. I'll have a medic here in a few minutes, can you hold her?" He looked worried.

It was soft but she felt Daina brush her hand onto hers. Daina. They had gotten her back. Her goal had ended so that meant she had to go? It wasn't fair. Exhaustion hit her as her eyes began to drift shut, "No!" Her eyes drifted back open to Mark's tortured face, "Don't leave me yet Lil. Not yet I know it hurts but we will get you through this." He bent his head and brushed a swift kiss on her forehead.

With all the strength she had in her she looked up at him and tried to smile. It was okay she was fine; it didn't hurt. She loved him. Oh, so much. She had to force the words past nearly immobile lips, "I... love... you." There she had said it.

"I love you too. Fuck!" Lilith felt herself grow cold as everything went black the last thing, she heard was Mark screaming for someone named Vexriel.

12.

Lilith awoke to the sound of Mark's voice. *I'm not dead? How?* She didn't understand she had felt herself float away but here she was surrounded in Mark's scent. She felt comfortable on the plush bed that was below her; her chest hurt and so did her head but other than that she felt fine. *Wait... her chest hurt...*Lilith shot upright in the bed to take in the unfamiliar surroundings of stone walls.

She was alone in what looked to be a castle. The walls were solid stone and everything was in place. She smelled Mark all over this space which confused her all the more. She had to get up.

Lilith's feet brushed the stone floor and her legs nearly buckled. How long had she been out? Slowly she approached the mirror to take a look at her throbbing chest and found a strange seal where the bullet hole should have been. It was small and pearl white but the strange symbol was there, she hadn't been mistaken that was where she was hit when she jumped in the way of Raguel's bullet.

"Don't tell me too not be worried!" Mark's yell drew her attention to the door as it suddenly opened and Mark stepped inside. His eyes immediately went to the empty bed as he looked around and found her standing in front of the mirror wearing nothing but a silk robe that hung open exposing her breasts, it wasn't her robe. Lilith thought it came from a maid of some sort and it was comfortable and cool to her skin. Jon was right behind him as he entered the room behind Mark. All worry and tension drained from him as he looked her over.

She felt her face redden as she gave a shy wave. Lilith had no idea what was going on, "Hello Hercules."

That was it. All it took for Mark to stop staring at her and finally rush to her and pull her carefully close to him, "Don't 'Hello Hercules' me. I've been so fucking worried."

A small smile tugged at the corners of her lips as she kissed the side of his neck. Lilith peaked over his shoulders catching Jon's eyes as he smiled and closed the door silently behind him. Mark was shaking slightly as she rubbed his back. Her man. He was one hell of a fighter and even more of an incredible lover. "What's wrong Hercules?" She had to ask it was odd to see him this way.

"Two weeks..." Mark mumbled into her hair.

"What?" She was even more confused now.

Mark pulled back and looked down at her with so much love, "You were unconscious for two weeks *draga* even after another deal with Vexriel...I thought I had lost you and here you are. Alive and warm in my arms. I couldn't ask for more."

Lilith's heart melted at his words, gently she brushed a kiss to his lips. He kissed her back gently almost reverently as he slowly lifted her into his arms.

******

Mark couldn't believe it. He had her in his arms again. He had been terrified and didn't know what to tell the boys when they had asked to see their mother. He had just been telling Jon he was worried she wouldn't wake up; it had been a heated argument; would be just like Vex to perform a double-sided miracle; but here she was clinging to him as he carried her to the bed and laid her back down. *God, I love this woman.*

"I love you," he whispered into her ear as he curled on the bed around her, "You are my soul *draga* please don't scare me like that again, I had to make a deal with the devil to get you back to me."

"Who was Vexriel?" Lilith asked sleepily as she pulled his arms tighter around her. Mark would never be able to shake the helplessness as he felt her blood pushing past his fingers and her body growing cold.

Mark took a breath, "Vexriel is the angel of greed, honestly he is the only angel that isn't a busy body so we get along well enough for the most part. Why do you ask?"

"It's the last thing I remember before everything went black."

*Before everything went black...*Mark gripped her a little tighter, "I had lost you. You died on those steps holding your sister's hand as you smiled up at me. I lost it. Maverick had to take a look at my throat I had been screaming so badly for Vex." Jace had tried to pull him off of her nothing any of them tried was going to move him from her as he screamed for the greedy angel. He liked to trade so why not trade him for her, she made the world a brighter place. "He came moments after I felt you leave me. He took one look at you and put that seal on your chest and the wound closed." Mark hadn't been able to believe it when she coughed and began to breathe again. Her chest had risen and fell as her breathing increased. "Vexriel always requires an equivalent exchange always for anything he gives back."

Lilith wiggled into him, "What did he take in exchange for bringing me back?"

Mark smiled, "He merged what was left with your life and mine; I don't know how long you custos live for but looks like we will be together for a while." Mark laughed. "He also said that you will owe him a favor one day, that was his exchange." It was a weird exchange for the guy as he usually took things that would benefit him.

Lilith's warm laughter filled the room, "We live until we drop pretty much. The only time I've seen one of us die it was in battle."

Mark's eyes grew wide as he gave a low whistle. Lilith's breathing had started to slow down as exhaustion hit her; she had to still be exhausted. "You know, I'm sure that Jon has just gone and told everyone in the castle that you are awake." He felt her smile against his arm. "Ash will probably be stopping by."

"So, let him stop by. I'm not moving."

Mark laughed again, she made him so happy. "What I was trying to say was that why don't we have Ash marry us while we are here?"

Lilith stiffened as she slowly sat up and looked at him with a slow smile, "Really?"

"If you will still have me," Mark sat up and kissed her gently.

"Always. Marry me Hercules?" She was teasing him but who cares he would be with her forever. His fiery little red headed, he would always choose her.

"Anytime."

Epilogue

Lilith sat around a table with Daina and Taurtis. Daina had changed quite a bit since she had been rescued, she was more withdrawn and more skittish whenever someone snuck up on her. That was to be expected though. The wind was softly blowing as they sat in the field by the castle; Ash really did have one of the most beautiful gardens she had ever seen. White roses and hydrangeas covered the majority of the garden, she and Mark had been married in this same garden two days ago. Lilith was finally able to meet the whole guard when they had attended the ceremony. It was beautiful. The garden had been lit with torches and candles as they stood under the moon and swore their eternal love to one another. Lilium and Jordium had been flown in first class with Dylan when she was unconscious and apparently as a distraction for when she was recovering Jace and Dustin had started the boys on their training. Jordium was so proud of his little snowflakes.

Daina had mostly recovered from her injuries as she sat cross legged in the chair sipping on tea and watching the children play with Mark a distance away. Lilium was running around as a wolf chasing his brother as Jordium launched snowballs back at him. Mark ran behind them making sure they didn't destroy the garden; Ash would kill them. Lilith sat back and enjoyed her tea and soaked in her family's love. Taurtis got up and walked around the table kissing both of them on their temples. He smiled at them as he whispered, "I gotta go."

Surprise pulled at her expression, "We just all got back together, where are you going?"

He laughed as he hugged her, "Just got a call from a friend in the states she needs a little help with something then I'll come right back I promise."

Daina looked over and touched his shoulder. She was always worried about them when they went off somewhere alone, her experience couldn't have helped with it. "Be safe and come back if it gets to dangerous."

"Of course, may the spirits guild me back to you both once more." He waved and jogged over to Mark.

"May the strength of our blood protect you," Daina mumbled back and once again took a sip of her tea. "He got away you know." Lilith knew she was talking about Raguel, the bastard had flown off when everyone was distracted with saving her.

"We will catch him, promise. When we do, we will give him hell for you." She knew she spoke the truth even as the words left her mouth. Nobody messed with her family like that and lived.

Daina looked over and a small smile edged her perfect face. She would have a few scars Maverick had said but even as she looked at her, she could tell that Daina would recover and become stronger from this. Daina patted Lilith's hand as she looked back to the children, "You have a beautiful family Lil. The children are darling and damn you have one hot husband."

"Thank you." She felt her cheeks redden. "We told them a lot about you D."

"Mama!" The boys cried as they ran to her carrying little frogs in their outstretched hands, this felt all too familiar. They were so proud of their frogs as they tripped over their feet to get to her. "Who's is bigger?"

"Well, I don't know why don't we ask your dad for his opinion too. They both look so big." Lilith laughed as she glanced up at Mark. He was smiling at her his eyes filled with warmth and love. Her man. Her forever. They were married under the moon and twined together forever, that worked for her because forever with Mark is exactly where she wanted to be. *God, I love this man.*

231

Be on the Lookout for May Howell's next Book in
the Unearthly series: **Crushed Horns**.

Check out the sneak preview on the next page!

Prologue

Her heart pounded in tune with her footsteps as she raced through the swampy terrain of the bayou. She raced away from the decrepit cabin and her would be captor that lay somewhere behind her. The dark night sky made it hard for her to maneuver silently through the marshy brush as the echoing of twigs sounded with each step. She could feel eyes on her but didn't know where they were hiding and silently stalking her from as she ran blindly through the bayou. It was hard to walk around in the marsh during the day and she was finding it nearly impossible to maneuver in at night. For all she knew she could be running in one big circle.

Maddison had been packing up her beat-up pickup truck around noon when she felt a hard object hit her from behind; next thing she knew she had awoken inside a cabin that was practically in shambles. Relief flooded her when she realized that she was alone when woken up and even more thankful, she had remained that way up until she got free of her restraints. There was a small nail that had taken time to pry out of the floor board and even more time cutting through the thick ropes that had bound her. By the time she was free night had fallen and someone had returned to the cabin, the barest creak of the rotting floorboards had tipped her off that she was no longer alone. The nail snapped the last of her restraints and she slipped out the window in a last-ditch effort to save herself. She hadn't caught sight of her captor yet; not when she was running with her heart pounding and terror icing her veins. Her eyes were searching the darkness for some sign of help.

Help...someone... Something flashed in the distance and she jerked to a stop. Maddison's eyes jerked back in forth searching for the flash of light she could have sworn she saw just moments before.

Off in the distance a flash of light streaked once more in the night. Throwing caution to the wind she ran to the light screaming out for help. Her feet were soaked from the marshy ground and her lungs hurt from the quick burning breaths she took as she ran. "Help! Please!"

The light blinded her as it hit her. Relief surged through Maddison; *I just want to leave town...* "Help...me"

"Maddie? Is that you?" A warm familiar voice floated to her ears.

"Denny?"

CPSIA information can be obtained
at www.ICGtesting.com
Printed in the USA
BVHW081131040321
601713BV00002B/198